EVERY NIGHT
without YOU

CAINE & ADDISON
BOOK TWO

The UNFINISHED LOVE Series

VIOLET DUKE

ISBN-10: 1-941198-72-4
ISBN-13: 978-1-941198-72-8

Printed in the United States of America

10 9 8 7 6 5 4 3 2 1

DEDICATION

For the people who continue to inspire me to believe in the unbelievable, to hope beyond hope, and to love and trust in the face of pain and doubt. You're the reason I'm not just able to look forward to the future, but also find the strength to look back at the past.

And to Malia.
You will forever be loved.

Every Night Without You
(Caine & Addison Story, Book 2 of 2)

Seven years.

Seven damn years of wondering whether the woman was still alive...whether she'd spent the last two thousand five hundred fifty-five days wondering if he was still alive.

Wondering whether *that night* was as burned into her memory as it was his.

Seven years having his heart tethered to Addison—and now she's back. With even more reasons to run than she'd had then.

Only this time, Caine isn't letting the gorgeous little flight risk out of his sight.

Regardless of how noble her reasons may be.

———•———

EVERY NIGHT WITHOUT YOU (BOOK 2 OF 2) takes place seven years after BEFORE THAT NIGHT, and is the conclusion of Caine & Addison's story of love, sacrifice, and the lengths one will run—and chase—when their past threatens their future.

Note: Each of the four couples in the UNFINISHED LOVE series have two books (duets) that take place years apart.

The UNFINISHED LOVE Series

Four brothers.
Each fighting for their second first chance at love.
Years be damned.

CHAPTER 1

IT WAS DAYS LIKE THIS Addison really missed having the minivan to get around.

Now I get why these sunglasses were so cheap.

Sighing, she pocketed the bargain bin aviator shades now heat-deformed simply from sitting atop her head for the last hour, and scolded herself for not knowing better. Of course the universe would go and melt the pair of sunglasses she'd impulse-bought because they'd reminded her of the ones Caine used to wear. There appeared to be a zero tolerance, zero subtlety policy up there in the cosmos when it came to Addison so much as *thinking* about the man—that fun factoid was made painfully obvious from the very first week she'd moved out here.

It was bad enough she'd sustained minor pedestrian whiplash that day from the heart-seizing mirage of a Caine doppelganger across the street from her. The somewhat less minor mortification she experienced by then walking face-first into a wall as a result was just plain mean. Especially when it turned out the wall wasn't a wall at all, but rather, a brick-like bear of a man.

And not just any man. *Nooo.* That'd be too random. The wall-like bear-man ended up being—of course—a cop.

Named Officer *Payne.*

Bonus efficiency and artistry points for the name rhyme and double meaning in one.

In the months since, with similar cosmic love notes arriving whenever she let her guard down, it wasn't any surprise she never risked wearing the old Arizona Law Enforcement Academy t-shirt she'd once borrowed from Caine to sleep in—the comfy, guy-smelling one that had sprouted feet and hopped into her duffel bag the day she and the kids had left his apartment for good.

Knowing her luck, something like a vat of maple syrup would leap at her and ruin the one thing she had of Caine's that accomplished the feat of *almost* putting her back in his arms again.

God, she missed him.

Don't do this. Not today.

With a determined headshake, Addison looked for a

2

temporary reprieve from the broiling summer sun to get her bearings. A cluster of trees nearby offered a sparse bit of shade that barely covered half her body, but still, she exhaled with relief as she dropped the heavy bags of groceries that had lined both her forearms for the past few blocks, making sure to balance the bag with the gallon of milk and other dairy products on top of her feet. Mostly to keep the perishables away from the griddle-like ground, but also partly to cool off the tops of her baked feet now sporting a lovely flip-flops tan.

She closed her eyes for a few blissful seconds, knowing she couldn't stay there for long. Not with tiny streams of liquid running down the backs of her legs creating a puddle at her feet, thanks to the now thawed Ziploc bags of ice she'd loaded her backpack with to keep the two cartons of ice cream she'd bought for the kids cold during the half-hour trek back home.

Frankly, she was a little surprised the universe hadn't already sent good ole Officer Payne over to give her a ticket for public peeing or something equally humiliating. Seemed like a missed opportunity to mess with her there.

But then again, the all-knowing powers probably figured, why bother, seeing as how very little could get her down today.

Because today, we ice cream.

Royal trumpets resounded in her head as she verbicized the dessert with as much ceremony as she

3

imagined there was in a knighting—a fitting opening celebration for the big night she had planned. Just thinking about Kylie and Tanner making their first-ever homemade sundaes, *with* the scooper she'd splurged on that had those slick mechanical thumb crank doodads, was the reminder she needed that today, it wasn't the journey that mattered. It was the destination. Their very own apartment, to be exact. *Finally.*

In the three and a half months since they'd left Creek Hills, she and her two incredible, roll-with-the-punches little travelmates had had their fair share of nomadic adventures. From the college student studio sublet hiding the non-landlord-approved waterbed patched with more duct tape than anything else, to the housesitting stint in the cram-packed bunker-like barn for the doomsday prepper/hoarder married to the happily enabling extreme couponer, they'd seen it all.

It all started with the closet-like private bedroom—one of twelve—in a house just outside the city. Addison spent her days helping a quirky old antique picker rummage through dusty warehouses and abandoned lots for fifty bucks a day while Kylie and Tanner hung out with a couple of their eclectic housemates who were on a mission to invent the next great kitchen gadget.

From there, she moved on to her next job shoving take-out menus under the doors of every light-on-security lodging in a fifty-block radius of the pizza shop who paid her in cash, pizza, and pasta. Her second day working, she overheard some hotel guests raving about the dirt-cheap discounted rate they got, which led to her researching and finding other places with similar deals. And so began the stretch of back-to-back weeks she'd been able to give her little brother and sister an actual summer vacation of sorts where they got to stay in some pretty nice rooms with awesome pools for the kids. Only in three-day midweek stints between weekends spent in cramped budget quarters, yes, but the sweet kids never complained. In fact, they had so much fun during each mini-vacation, Addison readily pardoned the universe for the 'wardrobe malfunction' she later had in one of those very pools.

A freak filtration system accident, the goggly-eyed hotel maintenance guys had called it.

Sure. An accident. Completely unrelated to the mental tennis match she'd been having at the time regarding the pros and cons of *maybe* creating a onetime use email account to send a photo of Kylie and Tanner to Caine so he could see they were safe.

Her having to consequently get *cut out* of her one-piece bathing suit with the big bow in front after it got sucked into the pool filter was a pretty definitive cosmic answer on that topic.

At least the hotel had credited them two free nights for her little peepshow.

Eventually, when their streak of both lucky and

unlucky hotel deals ran out, Addison turned to the bulletin board at a local co-op market. She quickly found them an *extremely* open-concept basement apartment (aka a big unfinished room with curtains for walls and a tiny bathroom also doubling as the 'kitchen') where she and the kids slept on different thirds of a U-shaped sectional couch in exchange for a few hours a day helping the owners build a garden out back.

The elderly couple who owned that last place had actually been a blast to live with, and kind enough to put in a good word for them with a close friend who managed a building that had a vacancy for an affordable furnished unit. So even though Addison had no long-term employment prospects for the time being, or any official I.D. to speak of, or reasons she was willing to discuss concerning why she had two kids living with her at her age, the couple's glowing referral had been enough to secure her a *six-month* rental contract.

Suffice it to say, she'd been a covertly weepy mess after she got the keys this morning.

She did manage to keep it together around the kids during the entire hour it took them to unpack—one benefit of the homeless and nomadic lifestyles—only to slingshot back to getting teary-eyed over every little excited giggle from Kylie and Tanner while she helped them put sheets and pillowcases on the three twin beds that came with the unit...the first actual mattresses they've each ever had all to themselves.

Hence her royal decree for an ice cream hoopla in the kingdom after dinner.

Just a few more blocks to go.

Hefting the grocery bags back up, she hustled the rest of the way, all the while daydreaming about the lasagna and garlic bread she was going to make tonight after her short shift at the women's shelter. She'd never actually baked a meal from scratch before. Cooking was different. That, she'd been doing since elementary school for her siblings—the alternative being starvation while waiting for their mom to remember to feed them or be sober enough to even get any sort of sustenance from the market. But baking? The only place they'd lived in with an oven that hadn't been used to make drugs had been before Kylie was born.

Addison distinctly remembered having nightmares back then of her mom's tweaked-out bed buddies mistaking Tanner, who'd been a newborn at the time, for a ham or turkey and baking him while tripping on a high. Sure, that was undoubtedly the implausible delusions of a paranoid eight-year-old sleep-deprived from singlehandedly raising her baby brother without a manual, but seeing as how she herself had been mistaken for everything from a pet goat to a glowing Martian by those crazy stoners, she hadn't wanted to take any chances. So when everyone was passed out one night, she'd grabbed some tools and broke that

7

oven good and proper.

From now on, at least one baked meal for the kids each week, she decided as she stifled a tiny sniffle over using her apartment key to officially 'come home' for the first time in years.

"I'm back!" She dropped the bags onto the kitchen counter and peered around the empty apartment.

It was quiet. Too quiet.

While most folks would probably think there was nothing to miss about living in a minivan, for Addison, having yards and yards of space separating her from the kids, and walls keeping her from hearing their breathing as they slept or their quiet chuckles as they watched a movie had all taken some getting used to.

"Surprise!"

The curtain hanging from the opening to the den— aka the .5 of their 1.5 BR, 1 BA apartment—was flung open from the inside, to reveal her twin bed, now adorned with jewel-tone pillows and a matching quilt-like throw blanket.

In that moment, Addison finally understood why homeowners would get so choked-up when they saw the final big reveals in those home makeover shows.

"What do you think?" asked Tanner casually, while palming the top of Kylie's head like a basketball to contain her giddy bounce-bounce-*spring* hand-clapping.

Of course, their little sister simply pranced away

from him and continued her imitation of human popcorn with even more vigor. "Do you like it? Do you like it?" she squealed.

Even though Tanner was playing it cool, Addison could see his eyes silently asking the same question.

"It's stunning, you guys," Addison replied finally, voice thick with emotion.

Her siblings beamed back at her, and pulled her further into her makeshift bedroom so she could see their creations up close.

"There's this cute fabric store around the corner that has lots of scrap pieces marked down super cheap because they're too little to sew anything with," explained Kylie proudly. "We spent hours digging through the piles the other morning."

The other morning...meaning the day they'd asked to go to the public library down the street while she'd been apartment hunting. Instead of using the library wi-fi to play video games and watch movies, they'd been sifting through fabric bins to make her a gift.

Tanner, always the world's best kid brother, assured her quickly, "The fabric shop was just a few buildings over from the library so we didn't go far."

Too moved to utter a response, she simply ran her hand over the three brightly-colored pillows—two new standard size pillows they'd picked up from an overstock store that looked massive next to the travel size one she'd used in the van for the past few years.

For some reason, she hadn't been able to part with that little pillow.

Ditto with the dollar store pool floaty raft she used to sleep on.

"Kylie saw this thing on YouTube where a craft lady just cut some fabric a little bigger than the pillows and then snipped all the edges like fringe so she could tie all the pieces together." Tanner shook one of the pillows so she could see the knots all around the edges.

"After we finished those, we did some fringe-tie *quilting!*" Kylie made *ta-da* jazz hands in front of the coordinating throw blanket with dozens and dozens of brightly colored little triangles and squares tied together at the corners using the same technique, only with a colorful array of about a hundred different little triangles and squares knotted together in a cool open-weave design.

"Yeah...Kylie went a little nuts with the whole thing," added Tanner dryly.

Nodding proudly, Kylie beamed over what they both knew was Tanner's teen-speak for a loving compliment.

Addison peered into the kids' bedroom and saw exactly one sticker on Tanner's skateboard, and two stickers on Kylie's headboard—the projects the sneaky pair had said they'd wanted to focus on today while she was out. Clearly, they'd started on finishing up their surprise for her the second she'd left the apartment. She picked up the blanket and hugged it to her chest even as she cast the world's greatest kids a stern look. "This must have cost you two all the allowance money you've saved up. I'm replenishing your funds."

"No!" they replied in unison, glaring at her something fierce.

"It's only fair," argued Kylie. "You always spend all your money on us."

"And besides," added Tanner, "we were thinking if you had a bed like this, it might help you sleep better, so it was for a really good cause. You're always telling us how we should try to support good causes, right?"

Now that was just unfair, using her own words against her.

And dangnabbit, guess she'd done a poor job of hiding her insomnia the past few months.

What she thought was going to then be a gushy, emotional moment instead seemed to be some sort of checkered flag for the kids to then race over to the kitchen and start putting away the groceries at Mach speeds. "Still two more hours until your shift at the shelter," said Tanner, pulling off the no-nonsense parental tone like a pro. "So you can go take a nap and test out the bed until then. We'll take care of getting dinner ready."

She blinked back at him in surprise. Granted, the cooks at Joe's Diner had shown Tanner how to do some prep work and even cook a few dishes, but before today,

11

he'd never made an entire meal alone. *Plus...* "Are you sure you don't want me to at least handle the—" began Addison.

"I'll use the plastic vegetable knives," cut in Tanner before she could finish. "And I'll use the chopping container for the onions. I'll be careful, I promise."

Guess she hadn't been too good about her newfound feelings toward knives either. Though a few months had passed since she'd last seen the knife-wielding not-right-in-the-head man who'd been stalking her, she still couldn't even skin an apple with a paring knife without flashbacks.

"We checked out lasagna recipes online; we totally got this," said Kylie, booting up their trusty tablet computer. "Just call when you're walking back from the shelter and we'll put it in the oven. It'll be perfect timing. So stop worrying," she ordered, looking adorably stern with her hands on her hips. "Now go take a nap until—"

"Oh, crap!" Tanner shot forward to try and catch the gallon of milk on the kitchen island from teetering over the edge, but only succeeded in shoving Addison's keys off the counter as well.

They all froze at the metallic clang of the keys hitting the tiled floor, the survival of the milk jug without spillage barely an afterthought.

Three pairs of eyes stared at the ground in silence.

It was sort of an unspoken pact, to never talk about

the personalized egg-shaped metal keychains Caine had gotten custom-carved for each of them just before they'd left. Not once all summer did it come up in conversation. Not once did any of them take their keychain out from the hiding places they each kept their deeply private belongings.

Until today.

Tanner nodded over to the coin tray by the door to show his was now in use on his keychain also, just as Kylie reached in her new school backpack and pulled hers out as well.

Invisible emotions hung all around them like a dense fog until Tanner finally broke the silence. "We know you miss him, Addison. We do too."

Missing didn't even begin to describe the growing ache in her chest that seemed to echo a little hollower every day. "I'm fine," Addison lied, not sounding remotely believable even to her own ears. "It was for the best. You know it, and I know it. We owed it to Caine *not* to put him in the position of having to lie for us under oath."

The truth of that prompted small, sad nods around the room.

"Are we ever going back?" asked Kylie quietly, voicing the one question neither she nor Tanner had broached since they'd all made the decision to leave Creek Hills.

She didn't, *couldn't* answer her. Because the hope

13

that came with the answer simply made her chest ache even more. "I wish I knew, guys," she replied softly, honestly.

She had no idea when David's case would go to trial. Caine had said it could take anywhere from three months to a year, depending on how David's lawyers handled his defense, especially given David's mental state. And even if he was found guilty, David could—and *would*—file an appeal, which could take another year, maybe even two if the courts were backed up.

Suddenly feeling the lack of sleep over the past four months weighing on her like drying cement, she glanced back at her bed. "Maybe I will try to nap after all."

…Maybe the horrible nightmares and the heartbreaking dreams that plagued her every night wouldn't hold as much power over her during the day for once.

…Maybe she wouldn't wake up with a raw throat from screaming silently into her clenched fists over visions of David attacking her, attacking the kids.

…Maybe she wouldn't wake up broken and bruised on the inside over visions of Caine looking down at his pillow, at the piece of her soul she'd left there…to try and spare his.

Who was she kidding?

Just that easily, as it always did, the prospect of hearing the sound of her fear reverberating in her head, or the sound of her heart splintering just a little bit more made her insomnia return in a rush. "You know what? I actually remembered I told Stacey I'd go in early to the shelter today."

Addison grabbed her keys and quickly headed to the door. With the shelter being just a few blocks away by foot, she never bothered bringing her wallet. Really, aside from a bus pass, some cash, and a single pre-paid gift card that could be used as a credit card for emergencies, the rest of her wallet was empty anyway—just one of the many 'Staying off the Grid' rules she'd researched, which had since become like her bible.

Hallelujah for the internet.

"I'll be home around seven-thirty. Put the chain lock on. Be good. You're each in charge of the other," she said with a smile like she always did.

Then she left before they could see the first tear fall.

CHAPTER 2

ADDISON QUIETLY FINISHED up some front office paperwork while one of the shelter's new self-defense instructors, a giant of a man named Hale, went over a few tips on how best to use items the women might have on them or around them as effective weapons to help escape an attack. Hale had only started teaching with them a few weeks ago, but his class numbers were slowly growing now that he was volunteering multiple times a week at the shelter like she was.

The shelter was actually the primary reason why she'd picked Tucson to head toward after leaving Creek Hills. When she and the kids had left Caine's apartment that morning, she'd had every intention of heading north and hiding out in one of the small towns near Grand Canyon. But, while she'd been crouched under the van detaching the tracking device Caine lo-jacked her van with, a single crumpled newspaper page had zigzagged across the parking lot like tumbleweed.

There hadn't been any eye-catching photos or anything to snag her attention, but for some reason, as she'd picked it up to go toss it in the trash, the words, 'women and children's shelter' had jumped out at her. Most of the article was smeared and even downright illegible, but she'd managed to make out—and fixate on— several key components of the shelter's mission statement, along with a reference to the city of Tucson.

It was like the universe had thrown a symbolic dart at a map for her.

So, after heading several hours in one direction to sell the van for half of what it was worth, she and the kids hopped on a bus heading the opposite way. She'd lost count of how many more buses they'd taken that day, but by the time they'd been within city limits of Tucson, the sun had been setting. She checked them into the first decent motel that would take cash and had free wi-fi, where they'd devoured their first delivery pizza in years. After the kids finally turned in for the night, Addison stayed up to research cash jobs that would allow her to stay in hiding in terms of identification and taxes.

Her options had seemed discouraging at best...until she walked into the shelter from the article the next day and saw dozens and dozens of women and children whose situations were infinitely worse. That was how she ended up asking the shelter director if there was anything she could do to help. And how her first official job in Tucson had been one without pay.

Now, months later, Addison took volunteer shifts every chance she could around the hours of whatever temp job she was holding down at the time, which this week, was one that paid her in cash on a grassroots urban farm along with a bag of fresh crops every other week. The pay was pretty paltry, but it kept her from dipping into her savings too much. And as with every other job she'd held since moving to Tucson, the farm's no-questions-so-long-as-you-do-your-job policy with its employees was what allowed her to continue to stay off the grid without having to lie.

Feeling the overwhelming need to keep the lying to a bare minimum was now the new norm in her life, seeing as how she'd walked away from Caine—from the best thing in her life next to the kids—*specifically* to keep him from having to lie for her.

There was also that whole cosmic balance she was trying to keep.

Looking down at the pre-paid phone she'd bought at the start of the summer, her eyes touched on the numbers that she never allowed her fingers to dial.

It was getting harder and harder with each passing day.

Even more so with each passing night.

Sometimes, long after the kids were crashed out, she'd replay conversations she'd had with Caine just so she could hold onto his voice, let it wrap around her like a security blanket as she did her best to fall asleep. Over the past few months, she'd nearly called him over a hundred times when her insomnia would strike.

Lately, however, this time of day was even tougher to get through.

Right about now, if she were still back at the diner, this would be when Caine would be coming in for his usual three-hour dinner, which he'd spend saying innocently dirty things to her to make her smile, or looking at her with that dark, compelling gaze that had always been a contradiction of intense, soul-deep depths and playful, laughing sparks.

Before she realized she was doing it, she was dialing another number she knew by heart, and heading outside to the small deserted courtyard to make the call in private.

"H'lo?"

"Joe?"

No response...other than the sound of a door closing softly on the other end of the phone line, which muted the boisterous diner sounds she was actually a little homesick for.

"Did I catch you on your way out?" she asked in a library whisper to match the silent stillness of his office.

"We have maybe thirty seconds."

She checked her watch. "I'm sorry, I should've called earlier. I'll call back. I don't want you to hit traffic on the way to your brother's restaurant—"

"Twenty seconds," broke in Joe, now sounding a little hushed as well. "You doing okay? You need anything? I can overnight money if you need. Just say the word."

Addison felt her heart warm up over the brusque concern in his voice. She'd always thought Joe could've starred in one of those old movie classics as the quintessential Hollywood-inspired Navy submarine cooks, complete with the tatted-up Popeye arms and a cigar-clad bark.

Very few folks knew that on the inside, he was just a big, hulk-like softie.

"The kids and I are doing fine. And you know I'd never call you for any other reason than to talk to you."

"I know." he sighed heavily, sounding both utterly disgruntled and reluctantly charmed by that fact. "Okay, time's up. You ready?"

She frowned. "Ready for what?"

A heavy knocking on the door answered her question pretty clearly.

Oh.

No. No, she wasn't ready. Wasn't sure if she'd ever be ready. "Is that Caine?"

"Yup. He's been in pretty rough shape. I'll hang up the phone if you want me to, but I think you ought to talk to him."

Shoving down the painful thought that this might be her last chance to hear Caine's voice again, she replied softly, "Let him in."

When the second round of knocking—far more insistent and impatient than the first—came to a halt, Addison held her breath and waited.

A burst of busy diner noise echoed in the room shortly before she heard the sound of a door shutting again, and heavy department-issued boots taking several steps forward before stopping.

"Is that her?"

Just three words and every bone in her body shook like vibrating tuning forks, reacting, resonating, to the low timbre of Caine's voice.

"Wait!" she called out to Joe, before he could pass the phone over to Caine. She wasn't stalling. Well, not really. But just in case this was the last time she'd get to talk to Joe as well, she wanted him to hear a few things. "I miss you, Joe. And I miss the diner. You hiring me saved me and the kids; I'm thankful for that every day."

"Damn it," came the rough response, ladled with emotion. "Now I owe Shirley ten bucks."

Before she could reply, she heard him cover the phone and grumble: *"Quit glaring at me; you'll get your turn."*

Knowing Caine wouldn't actually physically take the

phone from Joe's bear like paws—not if he ever wanted to have a decent meal in the diner again—she squeeze in quizzically, "Why are you going to owe Shirley ten bucks? And really, when the heck are you going to learn not to let her sucker you into these bets you've never *once* won?"

"I've won a few," argued Joe indignantly.

Addison gave him the gracious gift of not calling him on that fib.

"I'd win even more if she didn't always cheat and use her voodoo magic. Only way to explain how she keeps predicting things…like how my allergies would suddenly hit when you eventually called."

Allergies?

His meaning hit her not long after when she heard him sniffle gruffly. *Aw.* "You were the best boss, Joe. I mean it. And the closest thing to a dad I've ever had. Or ever wanted."

"You're killing me here," he complained in a wobbly gravel. "Feeling's mutual, kid. I was damn near ready to adopt you the day you interviewed for the waitress job." Another cursing snuffle. "Listen, you better drag your butt back here one day when the shit stops hitting the fan. I don't care how old you get, or how far you get, you always have a home here." He paused for a beat before slipping in one final rumbling mumble, "Stay safe. And make sure to make cheeseburgers for the kids the way I taught you— don't just feed 'em that fast food crap."

Lordy, she really missed the big lug.

Never one for long, emotional moments, Joe was already moving the phone away from his mouth when she heard him mutter crossly: *"No, I don't need a friggin' tissue."* Activity shuffled on the other end before she heard his now distant voice snap, "Here, jackass. Don't screw it up. And don't you dare make her cry."

The sound of Joe's office door suddenly banging shut gave her a quick jolt, which was a nice warm-up to the even bigger, frazzle-her-entire-system thunderbolt she got hit with when she heard Caine come on the phone a second later.

"Addison."

He said it softly, the way she imagined she'd say the word 'rain' after a year-long drought.

It was any wonder she was able to string together her profound answer. "Hi Caine."

The deep, ragged exhale on his end effectively wiped out the possibility of her remembering any of the other things she'd pictured herself saying in this very moment.

He suffered no such problem, however. "Are you and the kids coming back?"

She almost smiled then. Caine just wouldn't be Caine if he didn't start with the hard-hitting questions right off the bat.

"Because you shouldn't," he added quietly.

Wow.

She'd always considered herself a tough girl, but that just about gutted her. She hadn't been at all prepared to discover today that the thing she'd thought was the feeling of her heart breaking was just a tiny paper cut in comparison to the wrecking ball that was demolishing most everything inside of her chest now.

"He jumped bail, Addison."

She jerked back and stared at the phone in disbelief, stuck somewhere between a bone-deep relief that there was an explanation for his saying what he did...to an oxygen-stealing terror that the explanation had anything to do with David.

The terror was winning out.

"It happened days after he made bail a few weeks ago. He just vanished during a meeting with his lawyers, and hasn't been seen since." Anger, worry, and a whole host of other emotions dropped his tone down to a coarse-ground gravel. "You and the kids need to keep hiding...like your lives depend on it."

She learned then and there that her nightmares in broad daylight were somehow even scarier, like a menacing shadow she couldn't hope to ever be free from.

"I don't understand how he made bail." It was funny how, in the absence of any early warning response type of system for life itself, a person's auto-response to the unfathomable was often to find a random anchor point to focus their disbelief and frustration on. "I...I thought the judge was going to set bail really high."

And sometimes, that anchor wasn't all that random.

"Did the judge go lighter because I wasn't there as part of the case anymore? Is this my fault for running?"

"*No*, of course not. Don't ever think that. Honey, his bail was set for a million dollars, just like we thought."

To hell with staying calm. "So you're telling me David isn't just a psycho, he's a psycho with a million dollars just lying around?" *Seriously, universe? You didn't already give him enough tools in his stalker arsenal?*

"No, he didn't have to pay the whole amount. He got a bail bond—a promissory contract with the court and paid a bond agent a fee. Probably twenty percent or so of the bail amount."

Two hundred thousand dollars. That was still a ton of money. She'd probably never smell that much in her savings in a single lifetime.

"Truthfully," admitted Caine, "Drew hacked his accounts a while ago to keep track of them. Based on his available funds, we didn't think he'd be able to pay a bondsman. We had no idea David had so much hidden away in cash."

"Jesus, he was even able to outmaneuver *Drew*?" This was getting scarier by the second.

"Cash is hard; we can't track it, and it opens a lot of doors he wouldn't normally have access to. But, Drew was able to dig into David's past and calculate a fair estimate of how much he likely has stashed. The guy wasn't rich or anything; but he saved every cent, and didn't have a lot of expenses. Full scholarship to college so no loans, and a family farmhouse he was living in out in the Midwest for over a decade rent-free. When his folks died, he made a decent amount when he sold that land. And far as we can tell, he's had good-paying jobs in pharmaceutical sales since right out of school. Drew has been doing the math and looks like David's been keeping a portion in cash with every paycheck. Same with the farm land settlement." Agitated worry graveled his tone. "With liquid funds like that and morals like his, he probably got a new identity overnight, which is why we haven't been able to find him."

Addison was beyond frustrated. How was it fair that a stalker could basically buy a new life, while his victim was sentenced to an identity-less existence working for part-time pennies simply so he wouldn't be able to find her? "I can't believe the system just let a man like that walk right out the door." Where was the justice? "What if I'd been in Creek Hills when he had cut and run, Caine? Me and the kids?"

"You don't think I've asked myself that every single damn day?" he burst out in a near roar, sounding tortured, raw. As helpless and furious as a caged animal. "You don't think that even though it *decimated* me to find you all gone that day, I'm actually thankful you disappeared without a trace? You don't think I *know* beyond a shadow of a doubt that if you'd been here instead of wherever you've been hiding off-grid for the past few months, and something had happened to you or the kids, I would've..." He dragged in a battered and broken breath.

Addison finally felt the tears fall. "*Don't.*"

"Don't what?" he asked quietly, sounding tormented in a whole new way. "Don't admit I would've murdered the bastard with my own two hands?"

"*No.* No, Caine. You wouldn't have."

An incredulous grunt grated out of him, hardening his voice even more. "You really think I would've been able to stop myself?"

"Yes," replied Addison without hesitation. "You're a good cop, Caine. But more than that, you're a good man. The kind that holds true to the oaths you take, and gives actual meaning to everything your badge represents. Integrity, honor, trust—those aren't just words to you. You have faith in the things you believe in, so much so that even those around you who don't, can't help but find the hope they need to eventually get there too." Admittedly, she was in that very group. "I may not believe in the system the way you do, but I believe in you. Just like I believe you'll do what you feel in your gut is right if you find David."

"*When* I find him," he rumbled.

"And there it is," she said softly, smiling because she could visualize the fierce expression he was likely wearing after that deadly serious, no-two-ways-about-it assertion.

27

"You can't have conviction like that without believing in yourself the way I do."

He was silent for a long moment, before he finally asked again, "Are you coming back?"

This time, she knew he wouldn't be telling her that she shouldn't.

Which is precisely why she answered, "No."

For both their sakes.

As if expecting that very reply, he said next without missing a beat, "Do you have a pen?"

She pulled one out from her ponytail, and poised it over her hand. "Yes."

He recited a long string of digits slowly, twice, before explaining, "That's the number to an untraceable satellite phone Max, Gabe, and Drew built for me that should withstand everything short of a nuclear crisis. I'll never be without it, and you're the only person with the number to it. If David finds you, you call that number. Promise me. Promise me you'll call the number and let me protect you."

He wasn't using his cop voice—far from it—but still, his words felt as binding as an oath.

And just as powerful.

"I promise."

"This isn't over between us, sweetheart." Again with the conviction, the incredible, hope-inspiring confidence. "When I find him, I'm going to come find you and the kids." His voice roughened. "...So I can bring you all home.

Home to me."

A silent second passed before she heard him gently hang up the phone—saving them both from the hope-killing finality of an uttered goodbye.

She stared down at the phone and wondered if he hadn't hung up, if she would've said a whole different set of parting words, the three words she'd never gotten a chance to say to him yet that had been burning a hole in her heart for months now—

"I didn't mean to eavesdrop," called out a low, familiar southern drawl not ten feet away from her, breaking into her thoughts. "Okay, that's a lie. I was listening in on everything you were saying." He flashed her a lazy, unapologetic grin.

Geez, the man was charming—in an audaciously impertinent sort of way. *Has he been standing there the entire time?*

"You're Hale's brother." She looked at the man who reminded her a little of Caine in build and behavior, but was maybe a few years younger, and just a tad less gruff around the edges. "Alec, right? The other P.I. in Hale's company."

"I'm the *actual* P.I.," he corrected with a frown. "Hale just handles the paperwork, and rams his fists into things when they get in our way. I can't believe he told you he was a P.I." Peeved annoyance thickened his country accent. "He's my brother and my momma says I need to keep loving him and all, but the man wouldn't be able to find a neon-blinking toy in a cereal box with a map and a cheat sheet if my life depended on it."

Despite the heaviness of the past few minutes, Addison found a ghost of a smile trying to creep across her lips over how disgruntled he looked. In that moment, Alec looked a whole lot like Caine whenever his brother Gabe used to come up in conversation.

She took a giant step back then and peered up at the sky in the off chance a bolt of lightning with her name on it was heading their way as a result of the comparison. At Alec's puzzled expression—and no cosmic intervention—she returned her attention to the relative stranger who now knew more about her situation than she'd ever willingly share with anyone.

While she'd originally had every intention of simply walking away from him after his confession that he'd been eavesdropping, the candid and clearly genuine brotherly annoyance showed a real side to him that prompted her to ask curiously, "You're standing there like I shouldn't be upset you were shamelessly listening in on a private call—why is that, exactly?"

"Because I'm as good at hiding people as I am at finding them," he stated plainly, more factually than cockily. "And you may not want it, but sugar, you *need* my help."

CHAPTER 3

PHOENIX, ARIZONA -- PRESENT DAY

CAINE PUNCHED IN a few notes on his patrol car tablet on scene while two other squad cars took away the three men who'd started the bar brawl that had sent over a dozen people to the hospital with injuries, and caused a shitload of damage to the newest sports bar in the area during what had apparently been their very first big NFL Sunday hoopla.

Damn crowd mentality.

Fights had broken out all around the bar because of those three drunken idiots, turning into a massive brawl where half the people couldn't even remember why they'd gotten to the point of throwing blows to begin with. And of the two men who had been foolish enough to take a swing at Caine, one hadn't even realized he was a cop until mid-strike. Poor guy almost dislocated his own shoulder and popped himself in the eye trying to pull back at the last second. Meanwhile, the other had seemed to get an adrenaline boost *because* Caine was a uniformed officer—hulking out and doing this whole running and leaping into the air with a roar bit like the Wolverine, before delivering a Hollywood action scene worthy punch.

That had missed by a mile.

Seriously, that guy's broken hand was between him and the brick wall; Caine hadn't even had to duck. Frankly, he was contemplating not even dignifying the entire thing as an attempted attack on an officer in his report. It was way closer to simple vandalism of the wall, really.

Decisions, decisions.

The sudden sound of an ear-splitting scream cut off his mulling and yanked his attention from his report.

…Over to the sight of a screeching woman running in a pair of platform shoes that had to have been six inches high, designed to look exactly like fur-trimmed hooves with pencil-thin crystal-encrusted stiletto heels that looked like glitzy torture devices.

Honestly, Caine could live to be a hundred and never understand women's fashion.

Collectively as a group, he and a few other nearby officers immediately began shuffling and swaying to the left and the right as the woman neared, getting ready to dart forward to catch her if need be every time she teetered and tottered throughout her entire perilous sprint down the sidewalk toward them.

His buddy Grayson was the one closest to dive and prevent her from falling on her face when she pitched forward while trying to come to a stop.

Clearly, this was the owner of the ice pink luxury Barbie-mobile convertible parked out front of the bar with the white fur seats and blinged-out steering wheel. After getting a good look at the damage to her car, the woman finally dropped the bounty of boutique shopping bags she'd been clutching—not even during the windmilling of her arms during her fall, had a single one of those babies been in any danger of hitting the ground. Kind of impressive, actually.

The brief silence that followed was the calm before the storm.

Or in this case, the shrill, apocalyptic conniption of epic proportions.

"Do you have any idea how much these repairs are going to cost?! More than you all probably make in *a year*! Who's responsible for this?! And who the hell is in charge of this rat hole? I'm calling my lawyers!"

Figured even her phone would be bedazzled.

Some exhausting, long-ass minutes later, when it became obvious her shrieking rants and threats to sue everyone in the bar and their mother was falling on deaf ears, she redirected her hysterics at the remaining officers still taking witness statements.

Somehow, she found a way to even blame *them* for the gigantic dents smashed into the hood of her car, and the shattered windshield with what looked like the leg of a bar stool still sticking out of it. "What good are you guys if you can't even move a stupid fight away from the most valuable car on the street?" she shrieked, at ear-splitting decibels. "How hard would that have been?! For you to, heaven-forbid, do your frickin' jobs?! You have guns don't you? Some useless public servants you are! Can't even stop bad things from happening to the good people paying your salaries!"

Caine sighed. Just a normal day in the office.

Thankfully, a tow truck arrived a short while later, and the furious f-bombs she'd been flinging all over the place finally came to an end.

Not that anyone was around to care. She'd managed to clear the street of every last sympathetic being. By the time her car was hooked up to the tow truck, Caine was the only cop left on site.

Despite her having just been a pretty heinous bitch to a half dozen of his buddies, Caine still didn't want the distraught woman to wait alone for her ride to come. So he walked over to where she was standing, deflated, silently watching the tow truck cart her car away.

Years of experience had taught him not to ask any

unnecessary questions in these situations. A simple 'are you okay' could backfire big time, sometimes turning into the equivalent of kerosene on embers packed full of crazy. The subsequent atomic meltdown that could potentially result was often even worse than the original flare-up.

He proceeded with caution.

The woman was looking more lost than angry as he approached. And silent. Silence was progress in her case. When he saw her guarded expression dim and finally disappear with a fizzled sigh, he pointed at a nearby chair she could sit down in, and then headed for it without a word.

Nine times out of ten, they followed.

She did.

As soon as she sat down, he handed her an unopened travel pack of tissues from the case he kept in his trunk for just this purpose, and a bottle of water from the cooler in his front seat.

She stared at his offerings.

And then burst out into tears.

Yup, just another day in the office.

They didn't talk. They just sat there while she cried and drank her water to replenish the amount pouring out of her eyes and nose.

Right around the time her ride came to get her, she'd calmed down almost entirely. Enough to point out to him, "You have blood on your uniform," before climbing into her friend's car and driving off.

He went ahead and chalked that up as a successful turnaround.

All in all, a pretty fitting end to his week. This past stretch on the day shift had been the most eventful he'd had all month. And to think, they were still days away from Halloween when all the *really* crazy shit happened.

"You've got the patience of an effing saint," remarked the bar owner who, along with a few other employees, came filing out of the bar guardedly, peering around as if expecting to see natural disaster like devastation in the wake of the irate woman's rampage. "Here." He handed Caine a to-go cup of coffee. "I'd offer you something stronger from the bar, but it looks like you're still on duty."

Caine smiled his thanks and took the piping hot cup. "I've got a few more hours left in my shift so coffee works great. I appreciate it."

"I already told your other police colleagues before they left, but I owe y'all a debt of gratitude. If you boys hadn't intervened when you did, I would've ended up with a hell of a lot more damage. So stop by here again when you have a night off, and ask for T.J. at the bar. I'll make sure you guys are taken care of." T.J. gave him another grateful, hearty thump on the back before heading back in to continue the massive clean-up efforts.

Personally, Caine never took any forms of thanks for

doing his job beyond crayon drawings by the kids in the schools he was invited to for presentations, and maybe the occasional doughnut or cup of coffee. The school art pieces, he always took home to put up on his fridge and in his office. The doughnuts, he ate in moderation because he didn't have the time for daily mountain runs and grueling workouts every night like he used to back in the day.

But the coffee…well, the coffee, he would hold onto to be polite until he was back at the station, where he'd toss it without drinking a sip.

Like most former addicts, Caine could remember the exact day he'd had his last drink.

It was the morning Addison and the kids had left seven years ago.

Once a ten-mugs-a-day drinker, he hadn't touched the stuff since—not even in the form of barely caffeinated mocha ice cream or the popular java liquor truffles from his buddy Luke's chocolate shop in Cactus Creek that everyone he knew was obsessed with.

Yep, Addison hadn't just ruined him for all other women, she'd ruined him for all other coffee as well.

Strangely, he didn't miss it as much as he thought he would. Ditto when it came to women.

After failing miserably at being remotely good company during the handful of blind dates some of his friends had pushed on him over the years, all the folks in his inner circle finally accepted that he had no interest in anyone that wasn't Addison.

His heart was a damn stubborn thing. And he was okay with that.

It didn't matter how many years passed, Addison was it for him. He may not have had a lot of time with her back in Creek Hills, but he knew himself well enough to know he'd fallen in love with her, plain and simple. So much so that he found himself hoping that wherever she was, she was finding happiness, even if it wasn't with him.

Of course, his brain wasn't *nearly* as sadistically sappy as his heart.

He'd managed to pulverize a good number of punching bags beyond repair by imagining they were possible new men in Addison's life. He was only human. In his perfectly reasonable and rational mind, the only sort of happiness she was engaging in was the celibate, nothing-more-than-a-peck-on-the-cheek variety like he was.

Christ, he missed her.

Little things reminded him of her every day. Even now. Here he was just driving on back to his regular beat, when a memory hit him of how Addison always used to have little notes jotted down on the back of her hand, a lot like the scribbled words on the back of the dainty hand attached to the raven-haired woman a car length ahead of him in the next lane over.

Over the years, he'd gotten better at not overreacting to things like that.

He'd come a long way in that regard.

Seven years ago, before Addison's stalker had jumped bail, those few scribbled words would've had Caine already running that car's plates to get info on the driver— who, with her jet black hair and badass biker babe make-up, didn't look even *remotely* similar to Addison.

And if the woman in question had briefly met his gaze through her side view mirror and quickly slid her sunglasses back down over her eyes like this woman was doing now, he would've gone batshit crazy and called an APB out on her right then and there.

But it wasn't seven years ago.

And Addison's stalker was *still* friggin' at large.

As a result, Caine had had a long time to develop the kind of rigid self-control necessary to resist looking for Addison every second of every day.

So…when the well-disguised woman that he knew in his gut was *definitely* Addison began weaving her way to the farthest lane away from him to get to a freeway on-ramp, he called on every available bit of restraint he possessed to fight back the urge to follow her.

For all of two seconds.

Then he did the only thing that a man with no reserves of self-control left did when he found himself just a few car lengths away from the love of his life, who was not only out of hiding after seven long years, but hightailing it away from him.

…He chased the hell out of her.

———— ◆ ————

Addison pulled up her parking brake and turned off her car in gobsmacked astonishment.

He'd actually *pulled her over*. Caine Spencer. With his flashing sirens and everything. For no good or remotely plausible reason.

The man had even had the nerve to use that squad car bullhorn speaker when she'd first slowed to a stop on the side of the road. *"Keep your hands where I can see them."*

Seven years since they'd seen each other last and *this* was how he was greeting her.

Unbelievable.

The Caine she used to know would never have done anything like this, not even as a joke.

And judging by the unrelenting clench of his jaw, the edgy steel in his frame, and the intimidating all-cop way he was now walking over to her, he definitely wasn't trying to be funny.

Truth be told, Addison had run this reunion through her head thousands of times over the years—how coming face to face with the man she'd lost her heart to back in Creek Hills would play out.

Not *once* had she imagined anything like this.

Maybe he doesn't know it's you.

She nearly snorted out loud over that. Sure, he was wearing dark tactical sunglasses, but no manmade metal could contain the intensity of his gaze, or hide the way he was pinning her in her seat with his focused stare via her side view mirror.

And even more damning, no amount of distance or time could temper *her* irrepressible reaction to having Caine's eyes on her again.

His eyes know it's me as surely as my body knows it's him.

That's when she finally looked beyond his still-impressive biceps to the metal clipboard and traffic ticket booklet he was carrying. He was really going to do it. He was seriously going to write her a ticket when she'd done absolutely nothing wrong.

She didn't know what he was trying to accomplish with this whole tall, dark, and relentless vibe, complete with the brooding police Jedi mind tricks, but she refused to let it ruffle her.

"Hands on the steering wheel."

Okay, it was starting to ruffle her a tiny bit.

Maybe that's it. Maybe he's just trying to throw you off balance, control the situation.

Well, it wasn't going to work.

It didn't matter how criminally sexy he'd looked strutting over in full uniform with his massive arms

41

reminding her how he'd once held her up against a wall and…

Damn it!

He's treating you like a perp on the side of the road. She tried like heck to hold onto her indignation over that as she placed her hands on the steering wheel and listened to his boots crunch a few steps closer until his muscle-bound frame filled her driver's side window.

Having never in fact been pulled over before, Addison hadn't realized that a six-foot cop standing right outside her car positioned her right at eye level with his—

She yanked her wandering eyes back in its sockets and then turned to stare straight ahead, keeping her focus on her tight grip on the steering wheel as she asked extra-politely, "What seems to be the problem, *officer?*"

From the corner of her eye, she watched him cross his arms over his distractingly broad chest as if saying silently, *"Really? That's how you want to play this?"*

It was the only play she had. Because it was one thing to pretend that she didn't notice how her memories clearly hadn't done justice to how devastatingly gorgeous the man was, or how somehow, he'd managed to become even *more* dangerously compelling now that he was seven years older, harder, and hotter. But it was another thing to attempt to stem the flood of emotions that came rushing back simply from being this close to him again.

"License and registration."

Lordy, was it entirely necessary for him to use that husky, gritty voice on her?

She reached over for her registration, willing herself not to reach back and pull down her tee-shirt, which she could feel sliding up the small of her back a bit. It was just an inch of flesh; no need to get paranoid that his eyes were on that sliver of skin above her waistband.

So saying, she could *feel* his gaze on her back, and couldn't help the resulting tremble in her hands as she handed him her license and registration.

When he reached forward to grab it, her eyes stuck like glue to his strong, calloused hands. His sinewy forearms. Good god, it was like that uniform was custom tailored to mold to the hard, flexing muscles of his laser-cut arms, and broad chest.

She slid her eyes back to the safety of her dashboard.

It was a good thing she still had her sunglasses on.

"Remove your sunglasses, please."

Cripes, the man played dirty.

"You didn't tell me why you pulled me over. What was I going, a whole five miles over the speed limit?"

His lips twitched at one corner. "More like three miles, could even be two."

The ass. *Don't you dare smile, woman.*

"The sunglasses, ma'am."

Ma'am? "I'm guessing this isn't one of those 'I take mine off if you do' scenarios," she asked as she tossed her

43

glasses onto the passenger seat.

In reply, he deliberately pushed his own sunglasses up the bridge of his nose. With another maddening lip twitch.

She tried to recall if they'd ever had an exchange this...*incendiary* seven years ago.

None came to mind.

Shame.

As he continued to study her driver's license, his voice sobered a bit as he observed quietly, "You've only been a few hours from me all this time."

Feeling the blast of emotions ebbing out of him in waves, she decided to answer his non-question, figuring if their roles were reversed, she'd want him to. "All my research on going into hiding indicated it would be best to move to a city that wasn't too small or too big. And since the kids were still minors I couldn't take over state lines without adding to my growing rap sheet. So I went with Tucson."

That's when he began typing something into his tablet computer with the black industrial-looking department-issued case.

Oxygen refilled her lungs when his attention finally shifted away from her, and over to whatever he was reading on his tablet that was making him frown.

The reprieve lasted all of two seconds.

"You're living in a homeless shelter."

Her gaze snapped up to clash with his again. "It's *not* a homeless shelter; it's a transitional housing community for homeless families," she clarified adamantly, well aware that she was about to see him morph into alpha protective mode.

She'd forgotten how that barely-leashed, wholly male reaction to things regarding her living situation did ridiculous things to her insides.

Caine took a step closer, perched his tablet wielding hand on the roof of her car and the other on her side view mirror. She couldn't see his face, but she could hear his measured breathing. His entire frame was a rigid mountain, and she could practically hear him counting silently to keep from spewing like a no-longer-dormant volcano.

Dangnabbit, what was it about the man that could make surly Hulk-like protectiveness seem so insanely cute.

His face reappeared in the window, outlined by the sun. "Are you homeless, Addison?"

"*No.* I'm the director of the housing complex. We officially opened our doors a little over a month ago, but the entire project's been almost a year in the making."

That made the tension in his forearms lessen a bit. The tiny tell held so much relief, she broke standard pulled-over-by-a-cop protocol and reached for something in her purse.

He looked at the business card she handed him. "CORE Family Housing?"

45

"That's short for *Co*habitate-*Re*habitate Family Housing. We help families transition out of the cycle of homelessness."

Instead of returning her business card, Caine pocketed it and asked another non-question, "You're in Phoenix now."

She glanced at the police badge on his uniform. "So are you."

His voice gentled then. "How are Kylie and Tanner?"

The affection in his voice put a slight wobble in hers. "Tanner's in college in California now. Dean's list every term. And Kylie's doing well too. High school, straight A's." Seeing the lines around his mouth soften, she then proceeded to do something that conjured mental images of worms bursting out of cans. "Do you want to stop by and check out the housing complex? I'm sure Kylie would want to see you."

He stilled.

After a beat, he checked his watch for the time and scrubbed a hand over his jawline. The man didn't say a single word, but her ears were ringing and her pulse rate was picking up. *Good God, he must be highly effective in the interrogation room.* She felt compelled to confess something even though she wasn't hiding anything.

"Your beard is thicker," she blurted out. "And your muscles have grown new muscles."

Alright, *maybe* she had been hiding something...like

the fact that she'd been checking him out and cataloging an apparently very detailed list of all the new things about him.

In response to her outburst, he retorted, "You're not wearing a wedding ring."

Was that why he'd ordered her to keep her hands where he could see them?

He stood there in silence, waiting for her to reply.

"Was that a question?" Truthfully, she hadn't meant to say that out loud. But interestingly, the accidental sass made him do the whole looming thing again. And even though a normal person would *and should* be a tad bit terrified right now, for some reason she felt like smiling.

But she managed to hold back.

And instead, did the next best thing.

She zipped her lips and waited him out, using his own classic move on him that she remembered so well.

His lips flattened to a straight line.

Though she couldn't see for sure because he was still wearing those dang cop shades, she'd bet good money that the scowl he had on now wasn't *quite* reaching his eyes.

She missed those dark, intense eyes of his—equal parts stormy and sexy—and wholly mind-melting whenever they used to fix on her. Man oh man, she was sorely tempted to reach up and drag his dark *Terminator* sunglasses right off of him.

But first, she had a standoff to win.

He continued to loom in silence.

47

She continued to wait.

He broke just a second or so before she did. "The name on your license and registration—Addison James..."

Him and his non-questions. "It's real. Obtained legally, years ago."

His entire frame relaxed a fraction at her declaration—lordy, she'd forgotten how intensely sexy a man with a code of honor to live by could be.

His jaw remained clenched tight when she didn't expound any further, however.

"Are you. Married?" he gritted out finally, in a graveled rumble so raw with exposed barbs of unmasked feelings it liquefied her bones, along with the concrete foundation holding up the walls around her heart as well.

She shook her head and somehow managed to push a reply past the emotions clogging her throat, "No, Caine. I'm not married. Never been married."

A new electric jolt of tension seemed to rack him then and she saw his hand grip the top of her car door just a little bit harder. As if bracing...or rather, *restraining* himself.

After a long, charged moment, he nodded briefly and rasped matter-of-factly, "Your housing complex is outside of my beat, but I can still stop by to say hi to Kylie in two hours, at the end of my shift."

And then he was gone.

CHAPTER 4

CAINE WASN'T SURE what he'd been expecting to see at Addison's housing complex. Maybe a modified shelter. Or a group of government-funded duplexes sparsely outfitted and straining at the seams with families squeezed into studio-sized apartments.

But then again, this was Addison.

He should've known that a project she was heading for a cause she herself had experience with would be as extraordinary as the well-thought-out complex before him. He passed rows of efficient apartments and family-oriented communal buildings with everything from a student computer lab to what looked to be a full daycare center. Not to mention a half dozen areas for children to play and families to gather across the property. It was homey, happy.

Hell, *he* wanted to live here.

Finding Addison in the main office talking to two staff members, he hung back in the hall until she was done, taking the opportunity to survey all the changes she'd made to her appearance.

Where once she used to have rich mahogany brown hair always up in a simple ponytail, now it was a glossy obsidian black in layers around her face with silvery chrome highlights and cobalt blue tips streaked throughout.

Her make-up was now equally dramatic to match. Usually, he only saw that much dark cosmetics on women in clubs going for a bad ass biker or rocker chick look, but on Addison, the smudged charcoal liner, and the blend of gunpowder black and metallic gray across her lids, combined with her new witchy ink-black contacts, just made her look darkly ethereal.

"Hank, where are we on the updated list of specialized diets for the residents?" Addison reached over to grab a printout from the printer. "The farm-to-table nutritionist is coming next week to work with Francine and the parents who signed up to learn new menu items to make with the fall crops. Remember, these eleven new families just moved in within the last week so you need to check in with each of them. Don't let them be shy. We need to know allergies, obviously, but also, if someone is watching their carbs or another is really into fish, I want it on that list."

"Will do," replied a young guy in his twenties feverishly taking notes.

"And Francine," she turned and shot an affectionately scolding look at the older Hispanic woman with a large cast on her leg, and an apron splattered with about a dozen different fresh food stains. "I know you're going to fight me on this, but the reality is that your broken foot isn't going to heal right if you don't stay off it."

"I'm doing just fine," argued the woman, even as she continued to wipe some sort of red sauce out of her hair. And shirt. And jeans.

With a sighing headshake, Addison went into a back office and came out with what looked like the love child of a rolling office chair and parts of a coffee kiosk cart. "I know you're 'fine' but it'll make *me* feel less guilty as your boss if you try to do some of the prep work on this new work station Tim built with some old kitchen islands he found at the salvage building materials store. He souped it up so you can roll around the kitchen, and even, *oh* I don't know, carry pots of spaghetti sauce so they don't erupt all over you…" She showed Francine all the various cutting boards that rotated up from beside the arm rests and swiveled down to a flat surface sort of like those old school airplane trays that came out of the arm rest. "What do you think? It'd *really* help my peace of mind, strictly from a liability standpoint."

Francine hobbled to the chair, and fell into the seat

with a relieved, albeit silent, groan. "Well, I don't want you worrying about all that worker's insurance stuff so I guess I'll give it a try."

"Thank you, Franny. I appreciate it."

Throughout the brief exchange, Caine couldn't take his eyes off Addison.

"Still all goodness and light," he muttered to himself. Of course she was. Which is why her staff clearly adored her, and vice versa.

Seeing her soft, happy smile as she peered out the window at all the families communing in the courtyard after Hank and Francine left, Caine had to forcibly root his feet to the ground to keep from going over there and dragging her into his arms.

She was closer than they'd been in seven years, and still not nearly close enough.

As if hearing his thoughts, she spun around.

And positively glowed. *"Caine."*

God, this woman. The way she said his name hadn't changed at all.

She'd always been able to make him feel ten-feet tall every time he saw her eyes dance and lips curve up into a happy grin by the time she got to the end of his name.

"You've built something else here, Addison. Never seen anything like it."

Her face transformed into a radiant smile that nearly put the Arizona rising sun to shame.

Instantly, he lost track of what they'd been talking about.

"Thanks. I'm really proud of everything we've built here."

Right. Okay. The housing complex was the topic of the moment. Not her ability to render him stupid with a smile.

"Like I mentioned earlier, this is a transitional housing facility where we take in between fifty to seventy families, depending on size, for three to nine months at a time as they get back on their feet. We did a soft launch two months ago with some families we'd been working with through the project development phase. And as of this past week, we're now at full capacity."

He followed her gaze as it landed on the big group photo under the CORE: *Co*habitate-*Re*habitate sign on the wall next to her. In the photo was a large cafeteria filled to capacity with families eating and talking…and a teary-eyed Addison watching on from the side door.

"At first, my investors weren't keen on the dining hall idea," she admitted with a quiet smile. "They didn't understand the point of having a supplementary meal plan *and* a kitchen in every unit. I explained to them how invaluable it was to have Joe's Diner take care of some of the kids' meals, and how equally important it was for us to cook and eat together as a family. So far, the combination has been going great. The residents eat most of their meals in the cafeteria when they first move in, and then each month, they're responsible for more of their own meals until they transition out fully." Her shoulders rose and fell proudly. "And from what I've heard, every single family has broken bread with another family at least once, most now fairly regularly."

"I get it now—the name you chose." He watched her light up over that. "You're building a true communal community here, not just a housing complex."

"That's the foundation we built everything on. Whether it's cooking, or pitching in with landscaping or babysitting, to more teaching and mentoring roles with any of the residents wanting to learn a new craft or trade, everyone plays a part to help their neighbors, and work together." Her tone firmed with conviction. "We're strict. No drinking or drugs. Everyone does their part on site. No one pan handles. Pets are welcome only if they are well cared for and up to date with all their shots and vet checks—luckily, we have a local vet who helps with that. Everyone is responsible for upkeep in their areas. Kids all go to school. Able adults go to work. If you're not willing to be a part of the community, you won't pass go. And if there are ever any issues of violence—zero tolerance—one strike and my armed security guards escort you out."

Caine whistled low under his breath.

Sweet lord, the woman had always been fierce. But now, she was a hurricane-like *force* to be reckoned with.

Running his eyes over her head-to-toe then, he observed aloud, "I can see now why you added a whole *six* inches to your height on your driver's license." In full business-badass and lioness-protecting-the-pride mode, she stood head and shoulders over mere mortal women.

Taking his observation as a literal one, she pointed down at her boots and shrugged. "The four-inch heels completes the new look. I just fudged the perfectly acceptable two extra inches that lots of folks do to get myself in the six-foot range, which, as you know, puts me in a totally different bracket as far as DMV searches go." Tugging on her drastically different jet-black hair with its streaks of silver and neon blue tips, she added, "Had it on good authority that it's better to embrace a bold new identity folks won't question and live out loud in plain sight rather than try to shrink away in the shadows and hide. So I tried a bad-girl persona on for size to see if I could pull it off. Took a few adjustments, but eventually, I landed on this blend of tatted-up leather-loving biker babe who doesn't take crap from anyone, and dressed-for-the-club-24-7 lace-loving rocker chick, with a little bit of a woman-of-mystery vibe thrown in there for fun."

That description was right on the money. And despite her looking so different from the Addison he remembered, he had to smile at the new look she'd chosen to put together. It was the perfect, unapproachably sexy disguise...that still couldn't hide her inherent sweetness.

"So basically you've been hiding in plain sight." Smart.

"Yep. And as a bonus, I've found that no one asks the woman with spiky dominatrix stilettos and brass-knuckle jewelry many probing questions about where she grew up, or whether a kid Kylie's age could really be her daughter, or why she's running a transitional housing complex for homeless families."

She frowned then. "I actually still have no idea how you knew who I was—"

"Of course I knew." He gazed at her still-familiar features, carefully hidden though they were under all that dark eye make-up and wine-colored gloss that was making her lips damn distracting. "You've changed, but not in ways that make you unrecognizable to me."

"Good," she said softly. "Because being unrecognizable to *you* was never the goal. I only changed to stay off the radar of sick, psycho stalkers. Old and new."

Knowing she'd felt the need to change at all for that reason was a punch to the gut.

"Is he…" she began. "Is David still on the loose?"

Correction. *That* question was the mother of all gut punches. His eyes narrowed. "How can you even ask me that? Of course he's still out there. I've been hunting him this entire time. I would've come to find you and the kids if I'd caught him. You know that."

She nodded. Slowly.

He didn't like the shadow of doubt in her eyes. Not one friggin' bit. "Did you think I forgot about you? Or gave up? Because I never did, not once, Addison."

"I-I...wasn't sure. I would've understood completely if you had. Seven years is a long time. No one would expect you not to move on after—"

"I didn't," he broke in before she filled her head with those kind of thoughts. Which begged the questions that burned his throat to vocalize. "Did you forget? Or give up?"

Shit. That wasn't fair of him to ask. She was right; seven years was a long time. "Never mind. You obviously don't need to answer that."

"I didn't," she replied softly. "Forget. Or give up."

The muscles in his jaw unlocked, and he finally took in some much-needed oxygen.

...Only to feel the air halt in his lungs when she added, "But, I have recently started to try and think of you as a part of a past I can't go back to."

If not for the pain he could practically see hemorrhaging out of her as she said it, her words would've slayed him. "Why the change?" He had to know.

She took in her own deep breath. Then another. Until finally: "I can't *begin* to imagine what it's been like for you all this time, Caine. All I know is what it's been like for me." Fresh anguish filled her gaze. "The past seven years have been...slowly breaking my heart. In ways I didn't even realize because the ache in my chest had become my new normal. The wondering, the *waiting* never stopped."

Her voice now barely above a whisper, she painted him a heartbreaking picture he couldn't unsee. "Every time the phone rang, or a knock came at the door, I'd find myself holding my breath and hoping, wishing, *praying* that it'd be you. And when it wasn't, I'd feel my heart split at the seams just a little bit more, find myself needing to hold onto you in my dreams just a little bit tighter so I didn't break completely. Only…every night, the dream would turn into the same nightmares I haven't been able to escape since I first saw how crazy David really is." A tortured black cloud shadowed over her then, making her look every bit as haunted as she sounded. "Soon, it became a vicious cycle—me wanting to sleep so I could have you near, but knowing that it'd end with me screaming myself awake and running to the kids' room to make sure they were safe."

Every quiet confession stabbed him deeper than the last. The very idea that she'd gone through that type of hurt and torment every day since she'd left robbed him of the ability to reply. To rage against the bastard who'd put them in this neverending hell.

When a tear slipped down her cheek, the rage took a backseat. Never should this woman be crying over him. "You should've stopped waiting, baby. Sooner than just 'recently.' If I'd known you were going through that, I would've…"

Chased her to the ends of the earth to put a stop to it himself.

But *first*, he'd have screwed police protocol and taken the sniper shot he'd had of David several years ago when he'd had the chance. With the Spencer Securities custom rifle his brother Gabe and sister Lia had used their unique expertise to build for him, he damn sure wouldn't have missed. He would've—

"You would've what?" she asked quietly, stopping him from thinking the unthinkable.

Bringing himself back to the woman he loved so much it hurt, he answered truthfully, "I would've found a way to contact you…and told you to do exactly what you decided to do finally."

Put us in the past.

Thankfully, she didn't ask him to say the silent statement aloud.

"It was a good decision, Addison."

She lifted a shoulder as if unconvinced. "Jury's still out. Probably because even though I'd 'decided' this all when the CORE housing project officially chose this site here in Phoenix last year, I couldn't bring myself to following through until much, much later." Heartbroken eyes met his. "I'd spent so long waiting for you, I didn't know how to stop. Didn't really want to give it all up." A small, sad smile touched her lips. "So, I started slow. Toughened up by giving myself manageable goals—like *not* pausing to conjure your image before answering the phone whenever it rang."

Jesus. He felt like beating the shit out of *himself* for being party to her having to 'toughen up' like that, to her having to scab over the cuts in her heart their messed-up situation had caused.

"It took a while," she admitted. "But I got to a point where I wasn't wondering about you and waiting for you *every* single day anymore."

Her eyes widened in surprise when she looked down and found his hand gripping hers. But she didn't let go.

"Surprisingly, I missed it a little bit. That daily fantasy I'd have imagining how you'd show up at my door—what you'd say, what you'd do." Her lips quirked up into a crooked little smile. "Figures you'd manage to catch me off guard. In all the thousands of scenarios I'd played in my head like a movie scene, not once did I picture you outside my *car* door. *After* pulling me over, no less."

He knew it was coming, could feel her slipping away.

Damn the universe for yanking her away from him just when he finally got her back.

"Caine, this limbo we're in is never going to end. As long as David's still out there, you're always going to be looking for him, and I'm always going to be waiting for you. That's not healthy for either of us."

It killed him to say it, but he did anyway. "You're right."

Though he could see she'd been visibly preparing herself for him to agree, she still flinched.

He searched deep for the strength. Surprised the hell out of himself when he found it. "You're right, we need a clean break. You deserve the chance to be happy, to make a life for yourself here, a *future* without one eye on a tragic past. You shouldn't have to wait or wonder over any man, sweetheart."

Rubbing his thumb over her racing pulse point at her wrist, he added so she wouldn't have any doubt, "I know I can't take away those years you spent wondering, but I can swear to you, honey, that I thought about you every single day, too. If David hadn't somehow managed to evade us every time we got close enough to apprehend him, I promise I would've found you."

Her lids slid closed for a moment as her hand squeezed his.

When they opened again, she had that same indomitable strength he'd always been so amazed by. "So where do we go from here?" she asked, finally. "Is this one of those 'we'll still stay friends' situations?"

He had an utterly volatile, *visceral* reaction to the notion of relegating their relationship to friends and nothing more.

While his brain—and heart—struggled to agree to her suggestion, he noticed a small crinkle at the corner of her eyes as her gaze dropped down to his uniform.

He stepped back a bit and peered down at himself. "Is my fly down? Or did I spill mustard on me during lunch?"

"No. You look great, like always." Her smile made another shy appearance. "Just…in my mind, I'd figured you'd be a detective or something by now. Maybe even police chief. But seeing you in uniform again, honestly, I can't imagine you doing anything else."

"I like being a beat cop," he said simply.

"I remember. You were really good at it, too. Bet you still are."

The frank approval in her expression meant a lot. Over the years, a lot of the buddies he'd gone to the police academy with had become detectives, constantly encouraging him to transition as well. But for Caine, being a cop had always been about more than just catching criminals; it was about protecting communities, right out there on the frontline.

He saw her eyes move from his uniform to his beard then. And just like earlier on the side of the road, her gaze warmed with something a touch more than mere curiosity.

Dragging his hand over his scruffy jawline, he tried to remember the last time he'd remembered to shave. He couldn't.

What he *was* able to remember, however, was how his five o'clock shadow used to pink the petal soft skin by her collarbone, more than anywhere else on her body.

The reminder had a very predictable, and soon to be very *obvious* effect on him.

Something in his expression must have given him away.

Abruptly, her eyes dilated and her breathing picked up speed. He found himself wondering if he put his lips to her neck right now, right over her tattoo, if he'd feel her heartbeat pounding away like his was.

She retreated a step, and then—in the spirit of this 'friendship' he still hadn't agreed to officially—asked politely, "Want some coffee while you wait for Kylie? I can brew some up pretty quick."

Lordy, the word 'coffee' was triggering memories of her special brew that were downright dirty in his current mindset. *Not cool getting this turned on by her offering you coffee, dude. At this rate, you're going to look like you're packing a second night stick.*

"That's okay," he eventually replied. "Water's fine."

She blinked in disbelief. "Are you sure? I still remember how to make it the way you used to like."

Seriously, was she trying to kill him?

Before he could politely decline again—*maybe*—a loud, low voice called out from just outside the office, *"Hi, honey. I'm home."*

And just like that every male atom in his body stormed his senses, as if some primal, possessive alert had just been triggered.

He was man enough to admit that when it came to Addison, he had more caveman tendencies than was probably kosher in modern society. And close to zero control over it.

"Alec?" Addison called back. "Why are you and Kylie home so late?"

Not. Helping.

Hearing her reference another man in any sentence with the word 'home' made him just a little more unhinged.

She moved toward the door, but Caine didn't, *couldn't* let her past him.

Then when a man built like a damn NFL lineman came up to the doorway, he couldn't help the growl that erupted. "Who the *hell* is Alec?"

Yep. Zero control.

CHAPTER 5

ADDISON KNEW she shouldn't be ready to turn boneless over his alpha tone. And yet here she was, in nearly a puddle of swoon while his gaze held her prisoner the entire time.

Somehow though, she managed to keep her female dignity in tact by not rushing to answer the rumbling demand.

Not an easy feat seeing as how her emotions had been rocketing around her insides since he'd pulled her over earlier today. The last few hours, she'd been a nervous, discombobulated wreck waiting for him to arrive on site.

And boy had he made an entrance.

In full police gear, of course.

Looking more renegade cowboy than cop, per usual.

With eyes only for her…just like she remembered.

"And here I thought you were exaggerating," commented Alec in supreme amusement as he leaned against the doorway, arms crossed lazily, looking as insolent as can be. "The guy really does sound like he's growling when he talks. A few of my buddies had the same problem—they said switching from tighty-whiteys to boxers helps."

Caine's eyes snapped over to him and narrowed sharply.

Oy. This wasn't going to be good.

"Don't think anything's going to help him with that giant stick up his ass though."

She sighed and put herself between the two men, feeling a little like she was seeing a lion and a tiger sizing each other up. It'd be a close fight, but Caine would undoubtedly win…if Alec didn't irritate him to death first.

"Caine, this is Alec, my business partner. I wouldn't have been able to stay off the grid for so long if not for him," she buffered to play peacemaker.

Thankfully, that tidbit helped. A micro-fraction.

"Since he's a P.I. by trade," she continued, "he's been my on-the-lam expert ever since I met him at a women's shelter I was volunteering at when I first moved to Tucson."

At the time, she'd never have thought the man would become like the tiresome, but irreplaceable big brother she never had. His impact on her life over the last seven years was second only to that of Stacey, the women's shelter director. Stacey had singlehandedly helped change the entire course of her life in hiding by imparting survival wisdom beyond what Alec had been able to teach her, practically from the very first day they'd met.

"The reason I stopped in today was because there are two things I need your assistance with," Addison ventured, after Stacey finished reading through the police reports about David.

"Can't promise anything, but let's hear it."

"The first is a job. Unfortunately, my past work experience needs to stay in the past. So it needs to be a job that doesn't require references. I'll do anything—clean toilets with a toothbrush, stuff envelopes until my fingers bleed. Anything at all…as long as I can get paid under the table."

The statuesque woman that could've been her old boss Joe's female twin looked her up and down then before asking curiously, "What's the second thing you need?"

Praying with all her might that she wasn't wrong about the woman, she confessed quietly, "I need help registering an incoming high school freshmen in school without forwarded transcripts…and too deep a look at his guardian's information. I have all his other necessary documents though—health records, even his birth certificate."

After a surprised double take, Stacey looked over at Tanner and Kylie playing with a few of the younger kids in the rec room. "Just an incoming high school freshman?"

"Yes."

Slowly, she smiled in understanding. "Because your sister is young enough that she could maybe pass for your daughter."

No sense beating around the bush. "From what I've seen over the years, when I respond to folks' questions with a passing comment on how tough raising a baby during middle school can be, they don't ask a whole lot of follow-ups." Addison shrugged. "To be fair, I have been raising my sister since she was born."

Stacey raised an impressed eyebrow. "You're smart. Smart is good. And tough. Tough is even better in your situation." She scribbled down an address. "This is a friend who needs some help painting her house. In exchange, I can get her to offer you room and board for a week. Get settled in and then come back to see me on Monday. I don't get involved with things under the table. But I do know a few folks who can help your work situation."

It was like having to turn down food when you were starving. "I...." Addison wasn't sure how much she should reveal about Caine and why she needed to stay untraceable. "It has to be under the table. It just does."

"That's not your only option. We have finance and tax specialists who advise us on ways where the women under our protection can still work legally, while staying in hiding." Stacey's expression turned grim. *"That's what we recommend for the women here with spouses who miss them in the 'we'd-love-her-back-dead-or-alive' variety."*

Addison snapped her mouth shut. Sure, having a crazed stalker was bad, but nothing like that. She couldn't imagine being terrorized by your own spouse.

"I'm sure you've done your homework," continued Stacey. *"If you don't want to be found, you need to stay untrackable, meaning no ID, no bank account, no government forms, nothing traceable. Which makes getting a job, a home, a credit card, a car all really difficult. But, it is possible to survive. As long as you're willing to—"*

"Anything," Addison cut in. *"I'll do anything to keep my brother and sister fed and safe with a roof over their heads. Anything to give them as good a childhood as I possibly can."*

Stacey sighed. *"And this is where I pull the reins in. Like I said, you're a smart girl; smart is good. And tough. But in this case, tough isn't better."*

Startled, Addison just stared at her.

"You need to set boundaries, Addison. Or you'll find yourself halfway over a line you don't want to cross...with no way back."

She thought about that for a moment—if there was

anything she wouldn't do for the kids.

There wasn't.

"That right there is where your toughness is a detriment," said Stacey softly. "You may think you'll be okay doing anything for the ones you love. But when that 'anything' reaches lines a normal person should never have to cross...let's just say that there are some decisions people shouldn't ever have to make, some choices they shouldn't ever have to live with."

Addison studied the heartbreakingly violent scars crisscrossing up and down Stacey's arms, now seeing the impressive steel in her spine with new appreciation. "Do you need any help here at the shelter? Not for pay. But a volunteer position? A couple times a week, maybe?"

"You want to volunteer instead of get paid?" Intrigued amusement colored the older woman's voice. "So not such a smart girl, after all." She nodded approvingly. "Being smart is overrated. Doing good is just as important as doing well."

She paused then, as if making sure that last statement sunk in, before declaring, "You're hired." One final look. "Just remember what I said about boundaries."

Boundaries.

Looks like it was Stacey's advice again for the win.

If Addison wanted to attempt any sort of 'just friends' relationship with Caine, *boundaries* were exactly what she needed to set for herself. Specifically, boundaries that would help her ignore all of Caine's alpha protective and possessive tendencies—which, if possible, seemed to be even stronger now than it'd been seven years ago.

Ditto on her irrepressible reaction to said tendencies, if the last few minutes were any indication.

Alec interrupted her slightly derailed introspection with a simpering smile she didn't trust for a second. "Kylie is just putting some stuff away in her room. We got everything off our shopping list. But, I didn't remember until we were halfway home that you're running low on body lotion; I'll be sure to stop by the store again later."

Geez, he'd worded that just so. Sometimes, having a friend as invasively observant as Alec right next door wasn't all it was cracked up to be.

Addison could practically see Caine grinding down on his molars

"Alec, cut it out. Behave."

She turned to Caine. "And *you*, stop with all your posturing and rumbling."

Caine's gaze shot back to hers, and immediately went from intense to contemplative.

Then just plain hungry.

She stepped back and managed to release a sound from her throat that resembled a verbal question mark.

"Didn't think it was possible," he commented gruffly, practically eating her up with his eyes before leaning in and making sure his next words were for her ears only. "You're an even bigger temptation now than you were before."

If not for the fact that he looked genuinely surprised, she would've thought he was boggling her brain on purpose.

Be strong. Remember. Boundaries. "Thought you said I didn't change that much."

"You didn't. And yet here I am, more tempted than I've ever been to throw you over my shoulder and drag you off to my stone age cave...so I can tempt you right back," he replied, voice now barely louder than a whisper.

Her breathing quit altogether.

"Well, damn." Alec shook his head. "Not sure what the guy just said to you, but I'm pretty sure he just shot my chances at stealing you from him straight to hell."

That effectively shattered the moment, and made her roll her eyes. "Ignore him, Caine. Now he's just making up stuff to mess with you."

Caine quirked a surprised brow. "No. He isn't."

She turned to Alec to get some back-up, and was shocked to find him shrugging.

His subsequent retort stunned her even further. "Can't blame a guy for falling for you, babycakes." Though he said it in his normal playful Southern drawl, there was a sobering truth to his words. "At least now, I know to throw in the towel."

Trying—and failing—to wrap her brain around what he was saying, she walked over to him, remarkably, without any resistance from Caine. "Alec, you never... I swear, *I* never..." She took a good, hard look at her best friend who she'd never once thought of in that way. "I didn't know," she finally managed.

He gave her a hey-don't-sweat-it smile. "I know you didn't. If I'd really thought I'd stood a chance, I assure you, I would've made a little more effort to clue you in more." He gave her a wicked little grin. "But don't worry. I console myself with the knowledge that if you *had* known, you would never have let me help you in the shower the first few days after you broke your arm a couple years back."

Aaand, their status quo was back.

"Quit trying to make that sound dirtier than it was." So saying, truth be told, Addison was having a hard time even remembering that shower scenario beyond a few fuzzy details. You'd think a guy helping her lather up would've made more of an impact on her memory banks.

"Man, way to kick a guy when he's down," he lamented dramatically, looking miffed, but not unsurprised. "You forgot all about that until now didn't you?"

Now she felt bad. Mostly because she was positive that if it were Caine that had helped her in the shower, there was no way on earth she'd ever be able to forget something like that.

A blast of heat cloaked her back a moment later

73

when Caine slid in behind her fully.

Alec waved jovially as Caine proceeded to then unceremoniously close the office door in his face. "So I guess I'll just wait out here while you two work some stuff out," Alec called out from the hallway, chuckling when the deadbolt clicked shut not long after.

Caine tugged on her elbow to turn her around.

Surprisingly, it wasn't jealousy greeting her when she looked up at him, but rather, a raw sadness. And concern. "You broke your arm? What happened?"

Criminy, why was he always saying exactly the thing that could make her legs—and resistance of any sort— weaken and wane. She didn't stop him when he lifted both of her wrists up as if he could x-ray her bones with his eyes alone.

"It was just a minor break. Tanner was trying to teach me and Kylie how to skateboard one summer. Kylie picked it up great, while I pitched forward and somersaulted in the air, onto my butt."

A look she couldn't describe crossed his features.

"Caine, I swear, it wasn't a big deal."

His expression shuttered even more.

"What's wrong?"

"Nothing," he replied, gently squeezing both forearms before letting her go.

"Was it what Alec said?" she ventured. "Because truly, nothing happened." Why she felt compelled to hammer that point across, she wasn't sure.

"That guy is ten different kinds of annoying, but no, it's not that."

"Then what?"

"I don't know which arm you broke," he said quietly, running his eyes over both. "I hate that I don't know. That I wasn't there."

"Caine, I was fine. More embarrassed than anything else."

"But it was a moment I missed."

"I don't think me falling on my butt counts as a moment," she reasoned lightly, wanting so badly to erase that lonely look from his eyes.

"Not the falling part. The skateboarding. It was a family moment. One of countless others I missed out on over the years."

Her heart constricted. And the ache that followed overwhelmed her in its intensity. Largely because it was echoing the pain she was hearing in his voice.

Yeah, she hated that he missed out on those, too.

Though she'd never once admitted it out loud, during Tanner's high school graduation ceremony, Addison had purposely sat next to an open chair.

Just in case.

Knowing Caine would've moved mountains to be able to be at Tanner's graduation if he could've, Addison reached for his hand in an attempt to try to comfort him.

It was like picking up a live wire.

Directly synced with every nerve ending in her body.

A long, charged silence passed between them before finally, he grated out in a low, strained rasp, "Tell me to go, Addison."

Stay.

The single word slipped out of her heart and past her lips before she could stop it.

His eyes flared.

In the end, it was *Alec* who kept her boundaries intact. By unlocking the door with his key, and then pretty much poking Caine with a stick. "It occurred to me while I was standing out there that I didn't get to properly introduce myself. How rude of me. Caine Spencer, right? I'm Alec. Alec *James*. Good to finally meet you."

Oh lord.

One... Two... Three...

Boom.

The very second Alec's last name fully registered, Caine looked ready to throw him out the window...while simultaneously looking like he'd been kicked in the gut.

"I didn't lie to you earlier," Addison explained, quickly. "I've never been married."

His voice was *all*-cop now. "Then how *did* you get your last name changed...to this asshole's one? You said it was done legally."

She sighed. "You're not going to like it."

His jaw flexed. "Tell me anyway."

"The actual legal change part was totally above board," she reassured him brightly. "Since common law name use was in effect for a few years by that point."

"Rewind back to the part I'm not going to like."

"Okay, in order to *start* the process of me getting to use that name without filling out official name change paperwork that would've made it possible for David to track me down, I had to get one photo ID first with that name on it. And the cleanest, easiest way to do it, according to Alec, was to get a college photo ID."

"You went to college?" Caine's eyes immediately softened around the edges. "Just like you always wanted."

Jesus Christ. The man had impeccable aim when it came to arrows at her heart.

"Can we get to the part where I'm a genius?" said Alec, taking over narrating the story, even though Caine looked to be trying to ignore his very presence altogether. "The thing with college ID office windows—especially back then, exponentially so if you go during the busiest time possible—is that if you find one run by student workers, they're not expecting to handle a ton of official identification documents because these IDs are typically just for campus gym and library use. All they really care about is that the correct student ID number matches up to the photo ID connected to the right student file—to determine that the person in question has access to the campus amenities."

Admittedly, Alec's plan *had* been brilliant. And almost frighteningly simple. "Alec got us a pair of matching fake rings and we told the student worker my name was now Milan James, but I just hadn't had a chance to go in to take a new driver's license photo yet."

"The student worker didn't even care," added Alec. "There was such a long line, the kid just rushed to type in what Addison wrote on the half-sheet application form— Addison Milan James—and printed out the ID a minute later." He rocked back on his heels proudly, "After that, it was just a matter of telling folks her middle name was Milan."

"And that I was his *cousin* on the James side," she clarified emphatically. It kind of felt good to get all this off her chest. "From there, we got more photo ID's from gyms and shopping clubs, along with utility bills, a library card, the whole nine yards, sometimes with a middle initial M, but usually not. Within a month, I had a dozen forms of ID with my new last name."

Caine nodded. "Creative." He gave her a puzzled frown. "Why did you think I wouldn't like that story?"

Flabbergasted, she blinked up at him. "Be-because I broke the rules."

"Not really. It's not like you forged any documents for the student worker or anything. And the law does say you can use whatever name you want—all you did was find a way to circumvent a paper trail between your common law name and real one. Sounds like you managed to stay inside the lines, for the most part."

When she continued to stare at him in astonishment, he groused, "Addison, are you under the impression that I'm some sort of boy scout or something?

Alec raised his hand and piped in unhelpfully, "I know that's how *I've* always thought of you."

Caine tipped her chin up and pierced her with his dark gaze. "I'm definitely *not* a boy scout. *Especially* when it comes to you, Addison."

That forceful fun fact reminded her of another time he'd been compelled to be the furthest thing from a boy scout for her. When he'd been ready to lie under oath in court for her.

Nicely played, universe.

But before their full-circle moment could rain some reality down on their reunion, an adorable Tasmanian devil like energy came zipping into the room and practically tackle-hugged Caine where he stood.

"Caine!! Ohmigosh, we've missed you so much!"

CHAPTER 6

ADDISON FELT her heart do a somersault when she saw the awed, proud paternal affection filter across Caine's expression as he ruffled Kylie's hair. "You're all grown-up."

The follow-up ultra-male throat-clearing, foggy-eyed-for-a-nanosecond way he got choked up just made Addison melt even more. "Dang it Kylie, couldn't you have turned out a little less beautiful?" he complained immediately. Turning to Addison, he sounded distraught. "Tell me you don't let her go out at night yet."

Geez, at this rate, her ovaries were going to faint. "Caine, she's fifteen."

Seemingly even *more* grumpy over the truth in that alone, he insisted, "Well, then her curfew should be an hour after sunset, no later. Unless it's with adult supervision."

Kylie giggled. "You sound just like Uncle Alec."

Caine looked thoroughly insulted over the comparison.

Which seemed to entertain Alec to no end.

Caine swung his glance over to him. "Have you been making yourself useful and keeping the boys away from her?"

Alec simply gave him a look that said, *"Duh."*

Oy, the pair were like two overbearing peas in a pod.

To be fair, they did have good reason to be overprotective. More often than not, Kylie had smitten teen boys staring at her all day long. Not that she ever noticed. No, Addison's modern day hippie gypsy sister usually spent her days like a sweet, dancing-to-music-only-she-can-hear Alice in Wonderland meets Ariel finding mermaid magic in every little slip-n-slide journey she took in the world.

With her hair usually in a loose, garland-like braid over one shoulder, and her outfits consisting mostly of gauzy, flowing floral tops paired with secondhand denim capris and patched hobo bags she made herself, Kylie had an effortless, earthy beauty that probably would've resorted Caine to threatening all of Kylie's male friends with a loaded shotgun by now had he been in their lives all this time.

Kylie quickly tucked her bag behind the desk and came around to link her arm with Caine's. "Did Addison give you the grand tour yet? If not, can I? Walking around and seeing all the families spend time together around the property is one of my absolute favorite things to do."

Just like that, he was putty in Kylie's hands, just like he'd been back when she'd been in grade school and the incredible man had gone—in his squad car—to every McDonalds in the area, ordering the Hello Kitty Happy Meal until he had the complete set of toys to surprise her with.

To this day, Kylie still had the little Hello Kitty figurines on her dresser.

"I'd be honored if you'd give me a tour, princess."

"Oh my gosh, no one's called me that in years." Her radiant smile fell apart then, turning down at the corners, likely at the realization of what she was saying, and who she was saying it to.

Addison squeezed her hand in sympathy. "Hey, why don't you start with a tour of the gardens?" she suggested, knowing that would help cheer her up like nothing could.

Sure enough, Kylie perked up. "You have to see it, Caine. We have *three* produce gardens that all the residents help maintain—the big family crop garden at the center of the property, a hydroponic one on the walls that Tanner helped engineer over by the pool, and one with a partial greenhouse back by the doggie play area that Franny watches over like a hawk to make the most amazing menus for us every month."

On the way to the gardens, Kylie detoured them through the courtyard to show him the little co-op kiosks in the small farmer's market type set-up they had there, run by the residents every other afternoon with everything from snacks to handmade crafts. From there, they hit the biggest garden first, filled with families tending to the crops.

Caine looked around in redoubled admiration. "I didn't realize your lot kept going so far beyond the buildings." He shook his head in wonder. "Addison, this is incredible. You've practically built a small gated town here."

Addison crouched down to pet a nearby autumn lettuce cluster while Kylie ran off to pick a sweet cherry tomato off the vine for Caine to taste. "You should actually get partial credit for these gardens, you know. Since it was that Venus Fly Trap you gave Tanner back in Creek Hills that started his interest in plants, which led to our business proposal for this complex having the urban gardening focus that secured us some really big grants and investors."

She smiled, thinking of the nomadic adventures that little plant had accompanied them on. "It's still alive, in fact. I know those things live like a hundred years without its owner doing much, but still. I think it inspires him. He has it with him in his dorm room at USD where, by the way, he got a full scholarship to get his degree in botany, specializing in sustainable horticulture."

Caine was back to looking choked up. "I always told that kid he was smart."

"That you did. And he never forgot it."

"Does he visit sometimes?"

"He tries to return to Arizona once a month or so. You guys should hang out. I mean, regardless of what's going on between you and me, that shouldn't stop you and Tanner from—"

She cut herself off when she saw Caine looking *defiantly* opposed to the words tumbling out of her mouth.

"Addison, I agree we can't keep going on the way we have been all these years. But you're *not* getting rid of me. Don't talk like you and I aren't going to still—"

Kylie's return with three perfectly ripe cherry tomatoes for them cliffhangered wherever he was going with his impassioned speech.

And it was driving Addison crazy not to know what the end of that sentence was.

"So where do you want to go next on the tour?" asked Kylie with a smile, totally oblivious to the situation.

Caine didn't miss a beat. "Where do you guys live?"

"In the same building we were in earlier." Kylie pointed back the way they came while munching on her tomato. "The lower three floors have the main office, staff and community kitchens, dining hall, computer center, daycare, a few rooms for night school and other classes the parents sign up for, and different areas for the kids to study and hang out in. We live up on the fifth floor, across from Uncle Alec. The other management staff who need to be on site like the maintenance super and main groundskeeper live in the other apartments on the floor too."

Always the officer, Caine studied the building and nodded at the row of identical windows a floor below the apartments. "So what's on the fourth floor?"

"Commercial office spaces," answered Addison, feeling suddenly shy about the part of the housing complex she'd had to fight the hardest to get funding for. "We encourage folks to be self-employed if that's their passion and strength. So if they work from home, but need more space or specific equipment, whether they're bakers or artists or carpenters, we have commercial spaces they can share."

As he surveyed the row of office windows—all clearly occupied—the tension in the air between them dissipated completely. Caine gazed at her in awe. "Sweetheart, what you've built here—the sustainable living, the communal classes, the be-your-own-boss initiative—you're changing these families' lives. Giving them a real shot to get out of the homeless cycle."

Addison had long passed the stage in her life where she felt the need for validation over a job well done. But Caine wasn't just offering praise. He was seeing her vision.

Alec reappeared out of nowhere and tugged on Kylie's braid. "C'mon, Kyles. Let's give Addison and Caine some alone time. The kids want us to play kickball with them and be team captains again." Not bothering to wait for a reply, he started jogging over to the big grassy area by the pool where a group of kids were waiting and waving

Kylie over. "Hopefully, you don't bounce any more pitches that knock little kids on my team over like last time."

That made Kylie dash after him in an indignant huff. "I didn't knock that kid over! You had him lean in over the plate to get the walk, you big cheat!"

A friendly shoving race between the pair commenced as they sprinted to the field.

"I'm sure he's good people. Especially since he's got your approval and all. But that guy is a serious danger to my admittedly single-minded sanity where you're involved," confessed Caine, not sounding homicidal or even jealous, really. More...envious. "He's gotten to be a part of all your lives in more ways than I ever did."

———◆———

SAYING IT OUT LOUD hurt like hell.

And seeing Alec giving Kylie a laughing noogie with a camaraderie second only to the kinship Caine had seen her have with Tanner just rubbed salt in the wound.

Seven years ago, when he'd offered to become foster dad to both Kylie and Tanner, he'd been wholly prepared to be as involved in their lives as his own parents had been in his. So truth be told, when Addison left, Caine didn't just lose the woman he'd known in his gut he was meant to be with, but the two kids he'd wanted to become a permanent part of his life as well.

"Was he good with Tanner, too?"

She pondered that for a sec before answering, "I think in the beginning, Tanner didn't *want* to like Alec. Because he wasn't you."

Caine thought an announcement like that would make him feel better, but it didn't. "You could've called me. I would've talked to him, encouraged him to give the annoying guy a chance."

She smiled. "I know you would've. And Tanner did, too. Which is why he did eventually grow to become close with Alec." Her gaze held his unwaveringly as she added, "But you were never far from his thoughts. In fact, he even wrote his college application essay about you—the man who taught him about the person he wanted to become. I kept a copy to show you one day."

Hells bells, that news immediately prompted his brain to issue a storm watch for his eyes. Heavy precipitation imminent. Possible flood warning upon arrival of that essay.

"For both Tanner and Kylie, yes, they hit it off with Alec because he's fun and cool and super caring in his own way, but with you back in Creek Hills, it was like they'd...*imprinted* on you or something."

Where had he heard that before? "Isn't that a werewolf thing?"

Addison's brows hopped up in surprise. "I'm impressed."

87

He'd have to remember to take Millie out for some ice cream for insisting he watch her favorite vampire movie with her on TV.

"I still remember how easily they'd bonded with you. From the very beginning, they'd felt safe with you, looked up to you. With you, it was always a two-way street for them—a given that you'd be as much a part of their lives as they were in yours."

Huh, maybe there was something to this imprinting thing.

"Alec, on the other hand, is more like their big brother. More fraternal than paternal. Definitely a one-way street kind of guy in the life-sharing department." She held his gaze meaningfully. "So Alec may have hung out with them for longer than you got to, but you were right there with them all along in more ways than you realize."

Hearing that helped like nothing else could. Those kids had left permanent footprints in his life, of that he had no doubt. "I thought about them all the time, too."

"Did you—" Shaking her head abruptly, she pursed her lips to stem whatever she'd been about to ask and quickly looked away. "Never mind."

"Don't do that."

Slowly, she turned back to face him.

He cupped her cheek gently. "Don't hide your thoughts from me."

At that, she just gave him an incredulous head tilt.

"You say that like I was any good at it before; you always read me better than anyone ever could. Like an open book."

He grinned. "My favorite book." As more memories came flooding back, his voice roughened to a coarser grit. "It's right up there with the bedtime storybook Kylie left me." The copy of *Sideways Stories from Wayside School* by Louis Sachar had been one of the first things he'd unpacked when he'd moved to Phoenix, and it was still the only book he kept on the shelf in his living room, next to his family photos.

At the flash of pain in Addison's eyes, he instantly regretted his words. He hadn't even meant to bring up any of the gifts they'd each left for him. It just came out.

Possibly because he wanted, no, *needed* to talk about the gift she'd selected to leave behind as his parting memory of her.

...Too soon.

"What were you going to say just now?" he asked, changing the subject for both their sakes.

She hesitated again, but then finally whispered shakily, "D-did you hate me for leaving?"

Shock held him mute for a second, before he answered, probably more forcefully than he needed to, "How could you possibly think that? Baby, you gave up everything, started over with nothing, and survived against odds most people wouldn't be able to even fathom, just so

I wouldn't have to perjure myself in court."

"Because I knew it would've been more than just lying on the stand for you. It would've been breaking an oath that's at the very foundation of what you believe in, of who you are."

God, this woman. "I repeat; how could you possibly think I'd hate you for what you did for me?"

Her lower lip wobbled. "But...but I disappeared on you after—"

Still too soon. He lifted her chin. "After a night we won't talk about right now," he finished, his words weighted with emotion.

When she looked ready to argue with him about it, he gently cut her off at the pass. "To answer your earlier question about us: Yes. We should try just being friends. I can't promise I'm going to be good at it. In fact, I'm probably going to stink at it pretty bad. But I'll do my best."

The need to kiss those now softly smiling lips of hers felt like a compulsion he just knew he wasn't strong enough to combat.

So he stepped back, mentally cataloging all the reasons why he needed to keep walking right off the housing complex. He'd planned for this, purposely bringing his patrol car so he'd *need* to leave to return it back to the station. "Call me if you need anything, you hear?"

"You too," she replied softly.

Well, hell. That just brought a whole new meaning to his innocent parting statement.

And apparently, she thought so too. Wide-eyed, she was now blushing something fierce, and biting her lower lip like she wanted to call the words back…or say something more. He shook his head slowly. "Still as cute as you are tempting." Running his eyes over her face one more time, he commanded his feet to start walking as he added, "Somehow, I knew that'd never change."

With that, he finally managed to turn and leave.

She's happy. That's all that mattered.

That's why he was going to keep his distance—or at least try his damndest to.

And why she was *never* going to see the inside of his bedroom.

Seeing as how he rarely slept, Caine hadn't bothered with a bed when he'd moved back to Phoenix. Instead, he'd turned the master into his own command central, filling it with whiteboards with charts and surveillance photos and triangulated maps, file cabinets full of intel Drew had hacked, and basically every bit of recon and research he'd ever collected before and after each of the dozen times they'd just *barely* missed apprehending David.

Seemed like whenever Caine would get close, somehow the son of a bitch would be a step ahead. Sometimes by few days, others, mere hours. Then immediately after, they'd hit a drought where the trail ran cold for months on end with no evidence of David even being on the planet.

Aside from the annual notes, that is.

IF I CAN'T HAVE HER, NEITHER CAN YOU

Caine flicked on the lights of his apartment and headed to the boxes of evidence in his bedroom where he kept the note he'd received the day David had jumped bail.

And every year since.

Seven years, seven notes. Though it was the same note each year, Caine had separate file boxes for each, as every one of the deliveries had been a deliberate message in itself, showcasing the fact that David had had both specific knowledge of Caine's plans for the day, and direct, *untraceable* access to make the drop.

The first letter had been waiting for him when he'd returned home after first learning David had disappeared after posting bail. It had been slid under his apartment door, on a secured lot, where not a single camera managed to catch David on property.

The second had been placed on his seat at a bar he'd been hanging out at with his buddies while he'd been at the restroom.

The third arrived by messenger at a school he was volunteering at that day, which he'd only just agreed to go to an hour prior.

The fourth was left on his parent's porch, on literally the only day he'd been there visiting in months.

The fifth appeared under the windshield wiper on his squad car *after* he'd transferred back to Phoenix PD, the week he'd had a different car since his had been getting serviced.

The sixth came taped to the inside of a pizza order that was delivered to a friend's house shortly after he arrived.

And the most recent? He'd found it in his *locker* at the precinct, on a floor where only cops and guests registered with a photo ID have access.

Maybe that's why Caine had been so on edge over Addison (and evidently, Alec) thinking he was some sort of boy scout.

Because *maybe* he'd be standing here in his bedroom right now with an actual bed, and the woman he wanted to spend the rest of his life—instead of surrounded by seven years of intel—if only his badge and code of honor didn't keep him from simply bringing the bastard back across the border in a body bag.

CHAPTER 7

"YOU WANT ME to do *what* now?"

"The job is perfect for you," Caine reasoned innocently as he helped his friend Georgia set the table while her two kids washed up for lunch. "A sewing class at Addison's housing complex would be a hit. And you *are* one of the best seamstresses I know."

"*One* of?" She shot him a look of sheer offense. "I'm the *only* seamstress you know.

"Okay, fine. *The* best," he amended, hiding a grin.

At the sound of stampeding feet coming down the staircase, he hollered out over his shoulder, "Did you two use soap?"

A chorus of pouting, "*aw man*'s," echoed through the hallway before two overly dramatic pairs of feet clomped back upstairs at a sloth's pace.

"But we had soap all over our hands when we washed the car," argued Kevin.

"And *you* didn't wash your hands before you grabbed that corn cob," grumbled Millie.

Georgia chuckled. "They have you there."

"Okay, I'll make you guys a deal," Caine offered. "If you two are cool with going outside and licking your mom's tire rims right now, you don't need to wash your hands before lunch. Since that'll basically be the same thing."

Silence.

When he heard the siblings start daring the other to do it, Caine shook his head and chased the kids back up to their bathroom so they could all wash up together.

Studying their reflections in the mirror, he couldn't help but see their late dad Rick in their features. Kevin was practically Rick's mini-me, while his big sis was more an even blend of Rick and Georgia. They'd made a picture-perfect family.

That's why for a while, Caine had thought that pure shame had been Rick's rationale for his very public suicide after damning evidence proving he was a dirty cop had come to light. But after analyzing all the corruption he'd been involved in, he was convinced now that Rick had shot himself to protect the family he'd loved so much. Because a dead man couldn't be a threat, and a dead man's family couldn't be leverage.

None of his fellow officers saw it that way, but for

Caine, that's how he was choosing to remember his old friend's last decision on earth. And probably why he was still able to think of Rick as a good man who'd made some really bad mistakes—unlike the rest of his precinct, most of whom had refused to even go to his funeral.

"Lunch is ready!" hollered Georgia.

They ran back to the small dining table, now overflowing with fried chicken, mac and cheese, cole slaw, corn on the cob, dirty beans, and red-skinned garlic mashed potatoes with country gravy thick enough to scoop with a fork. His favorite.

Georgia always made sure to have some favorite of his on the table for these weekly Saturday lunches at her place. But today, so soon after seeing Addison and Kylie again after all these years, he was finding it harder than usual *not* to think about all the Saturday lunches he'd missed with Addison and the kids. How many Sunday morning breakfasts, holiday dinners with friends, and cookouts with family—

"Oh, I know that look." Georgia shook her head as she excused the kids to go watch TV while she cleared the table.

Meanwhile, Caine was arriving at the very belated realization that nearly an hour had passed while he'd been deep in thought. And he'd hardly touched his food. "What're you talking about? What look?"

"That's your Addison look. All sad puppy eyes like

you lost your favorite bone."

Did he really have an 'Addison' look?

"What's the matter? Trouble in paradise? Figured you'd be all flying unicorns pooping rainbows now that she's back."

Millie and Kevin cackled, parroting and morphing the colorful description until it devolved to some pretty creative insults to each other. They put their dishes in the sink and ran off to the living room, chanting, 'thunder farts,' all the way.

Caine began loading the dishwasher. "Things aren't that simple."

"I thought you'd gotten over her." Tone no longer teasing, she tilted her head in sympathy. "Seemed like you were getting ready to get back out there. I mean you haven't scowled at the prospect of a blind date set-up lately. And it's been at least a few years since you've flinched when a woman—me included—kisses you on the cheek."

"Shit." He spun around. "I'm sorry, Georgie. I didn't even realize I used to do that."

"No worries. I know all about holding a torch for the love of your life, believe me."

He sighed. Rick had been her high school sweetheart, her soulmate; she'd been absolutely inconsolable when she lost him. "God, we're a sad pair, aren't we?"

"You way more than me."

Smiling, he kissed her cheek. Making sure not to do anything that could remotely be construed as a flinch. "Thank you for lunch." Backing away, he slipped in nonchalantly, "So let me know what nights are good for you regarding those sewing classes. If we time it right, I can pick up the kids from your sitter, and drive them over to hang out at the complex until you're done. They've got great playgrounds, and a ton of kids Kevin and Millie's ages."

"Now this is just *sad*. You're totally using me as an excuse to go visit your girlfriend."

He snagged a plump strawberry from the leftover pie and corrected, "A cover, not an excuse. Big difference."

She frowned. "You think that guy, David, would start stalking her again if he found out she was here?"

Just the sound of the sick bastard's name made his stomach turn. "Remember how I traced him back to his fancy Mexican villa near Rocky Point last year? Frickin' just missed him by a few hours that time." His hands fisted in frustration at the reminder. Part of the reason why it'd been so hard to catch David over the years was because he always seemed to be in two places at once. And well-funded enough to escape without a trace at the last second. "I went through the stuff he left behind at the villa and found old photos of Addison. *Multiple* copies of them."

She shuddered. "Creepy."

"And judging by the lifestyle he's living—well beyond what he could afford even with all the money he'd gone on the run with—and what the locals have said about his daily activities, I'm positive he's getting bankrolled by some folks pretty high up in the drug trades out there."

"Didn't you say he used to be in pharmaceutical sales? You think he's working in distribution or something out there?"

"Worse. Back in Creek Hills, the investigators' report showed that most of the date rape drugs in David's possession—the ketamine in particular—had been homemade, with some pretty customized alterations. So I searched back through his first priors when he was in college, and had Drew dig up as much info as he could. Apparently, David studied pharmaceutical science during his undergrad, and from what Drew could find, a lot of David's old credit card receipts showed him buying more and more advanced chemicals and equipment through the years."

"Jesus," murmured Georgia. "You're thinking he's helping *make* designer date rape drugs. Holy shit, Caine. If that's true, then he's bound to have some powerful connections with a ton of resources on both sides of the border."

Exactly.

In a way, Caine had a way easier time talking to Georgia about all this than he did his brothers or his friends outside the force. She'd been a cop's wife her entire adult life. She knew as well as he did how much evil there was in the world.

"So really, I'm your hired muscle to protect her, is that it?" she deadpanned, trying and succeeding in lightening the mood.

He chuckled over the hilarity of a girly, Southern belle like Georgia acting as bodyguard to Addison with her tough new disguise and insane propensity to do things like confront a madman with a knife to try and save a friend.

"So does that mean you'll do it? You'll teach the class?" he volleyed back, surprised she was giving in this easily.

"Maybe. What's the job pay?"

Damn. He hadn't actually discussed the idea with Addison—all a part of that 'no-crossing-paths' plan he'd been sticking to for the past two weeks. Two *miserable as hell* weeks that landed him here, attempting to find a loophole in his own mandate regarding his keeping his distance from Addison unless absolutely necessary.

It only sounded stupid if you said it out loud.

Georgia tsked, reading his expression with candidly opportunistic amusement. "You didn't even clear this with her did you?"

Suddenly, his eyes snagged on one of the chic homemade aprons Georgia sold at craft fairs. "I'm actually going to talk through the details with her daughter Kylie.

She's always making her own clothes, and I figured she'd be the best person to set this all up." *Holy crap, this idea might actually have some legs to stand on.*

"I know you're not expecting me to work for free."

He shot her his best thousand-dollar smile. It was a little rusty, and it certainly didn't make women giggle and toss their hair like Gabe's million-dollar grin did, but at least it showed him to be respectable *and* respectful in his cajoling, which was more than what he could say about Max's two-buck-brow-quirk.

"Those Spencer brother facial spasms aren't going to work on me."

Damn. He forgot who he was talking to there for a sec.

"Well," he switched gears, "think about how good you'll feel helping some down-on-their-luck folks learn new skills that could help them when they eventually get back on their feet."

"Ha! You're mistaking me for you. Or your little goodie-two-shoes paragon. Remember, I stopped believing in people when ninety-nine percent of my husband's precinct decided to ignore their code to look after a fallen cop's family."

He couldn't exactly blame her for being bitter.

Sadly, the code his brothers on the force stood by when it came to taking care of the widows and children of their fellow police officers hadn't extended to Georgia and her kids quite as comprehensively, or warmly, as it did for the families of officers who hadn't died a crooked cop.

Some held grudges, but most just didn't want to be reminded that there had been a traitor amongst them—a traitor who subsequently blew his brains out right in front of all his horrified colleagues after he got caught.

That's actually why Caine had transferred to Creek Hills PD seven and a half years ago to begin with. Truthfully, he'd still be there right now if not for the fact that Georgia, who he'd always thought of as a sister, had begun a downward spiral to severe depression following Rick's suicide.

The day six-year-old Millie had called Caine in a panic three years back because Georgia had passed out after drinking a bunch of pain pills with a whole lot of alcohol, was the day he'd put in his transfer request to return to Phoenix to help out however he could.

Thankfully, she was better now, and the kids were no longer terrified they'd be losing a second parent, but still, he continued to go over at least once a week to check in to make sure things *stayed* okay.

"Georgia, you can't expect officers who put their blood, sweat, and tears into cases that Rick singlehandedly sabotaged to forget how many really bad criminals walked because of him. How many innocent victims and informants got hurt as a result."

Georgia's voice lost some of its hostility. "Rick

messed up some of your biggest cases too, and yet you still followed the code. You still made sure to always be there for us. Hell, you were the *only* one who cared when I tried to follow Rick down the rabbit hole."

Not liking the shadows that crept into her eyes at the mention of her suicide attempt, he did a smiling conversational one-eighty and laid it on thick. "Why wouldn't I be here for you guys? Really, I know that *technically* I met Rick first, and there was the whole cop thing, but I'm pretty sure I used to introduce Rick as the super lucky husband of my super good friend Georgia, *not* the other way around. You totally would've gotten custody of me in any sort of divorce settlement scenario, and that's not just because Rick only made microwave mashed potatoes out of a box."

Georgia chuckled. "Wow. You're just fibbing your ass off now. You *really* want me to do this, don't you?" She tapped her finger against her chin, pretending as if she didn't already have a list of demands. "Okay, I'll agree to teach one night a week until Christmas if you take the kids trick or treating this year, and chaperone Kevin's inhumanely boring field trip to the textile factory that Millie went to the other year, *and* agree to take the kids toy shopping on Black Friday."

"Done, done, and *hell* no." Black Friday sales were the devil's playground.

"That's a deal-breaker."

It took a few more unsuccessful counteroffers until it hit him. A proposal that would be win-win for them both. "Did I mention that Addison has a friend you might be interested in? This P.I. named Alec."

"Are you seriously trying to set me up with one of her friends?" Her brows shot up. "Ohhh, let me guess, he's prettier than you isn't he? And it's just eating you up." She reached over and grabbed his phone. "Fess up, how many surveillance photos did you manage to take of him?"

He scowled. "Just one."

Georgia burst out laughing when she landed on the photo in question. "Nice. I love the way you captured him flipping you the bird in such a flattering light." She zoomed in. "Damn. He's gorgeous. Why hasn't Addison jumped on this? I mean, he *sort of* looks like you, but a younger, way less grouchy model."

He gave her a you-are-now-dead-to-me glare.

"Aw, is someone butt-hurt about not being the hottest guy in Addison's life anymore?"

Calling on all his years of brotherly torment as a kid, he pretended she was made out of transparent glass and her voice was the howling of the wind.

She rolled her eyes. "Fine, you big baby. I'll teach the sewing class."

Caine blinked blankly at her like she was a rare female minion, twinkie-shaped and speaking in minionese.

Shoulders shaking with you're-such-a-moron

laughter, she crossed her arms and made her final offer. "*In addition,* whenever I see that Alec guy at the housing complex, I'll be sure to impugn his masculinity and build verbal monuments to your obvious superiority over his feeble, substandard form."

He knew there was a reason why they were friends. "So you think I need to wear my bulletproof vest when I take the kids to the toy store on Black Friday?"

CHAPTER 8

As it turned out, the sewing class idea was a huge hit. From kids and teens wanting to Frankenstein outfits out of their hand-me-downs and thrift store finds, to their parents and grandparents wanting to be able to sew apparel to sell at swap meets or apply for work-from-home tailoring jobs, the number of students who'd signed up for the class had exceeded their expectations by a landslide.

In fact, there ended up being over twice as many students as there were donated sewing machines, which was why the previously agreed upon one-hour class was now a two-hour class, and how he'd come to have a weekly pre-supper snack date with Kevin and Millie in the dining hall while Georgia finished up.

"So which one is your girlfriend, Uncle Caine?" Millie peered around the cafeteria, already about half full with families filing in for the early dinner rush.

"Oh, oh! I know," exclaimed Kevin, before Caine could correct Millie—again—about Addison being a friend and not the 'girl he wants to canoodle' as Georgia's been describing her oh-so-helpfully. "She's the cool one with the black and silver hair, and tattoos all over the place."

Millie shot her eyes over to the one woman across the room matching that description.

The same woman Caine had been having a hard time keeping his eyes off as well.

"Pretty tattoos." Millie nodded her approval.

A very accurate description. Pretty. In truth, all the artistic tattoos Addison had chosen were actually a tiny bit on the feminine side to fit her tough chick disguise. But, the overall look she achieved was stunning nonetheless. A combination of enigmatically sexy and still somehow sweet when paired with her fallen angel looks.

Telling himself he was looking at her ink and not the soft, tempting skin his fingers were itching to touch, he ran his eyes over each tattoo. Starting from the dainty leaves and flowers across her right collarbone touching the base of her throat, to the swirl of vines curling over and down both shoulders—currently bared, he noted disgruntledly, by that leather and lace tank top she was wearing—to the gorgeously detailed lotus mandala patterns on the insides of both wrists.

Last, but certainly not least, his eyes traced the

intricate one-eyed masquerade mask shadowing her cleavage behind the thin straps crisscrossing in a sexy spiderweb across the vee of the otherwise modest top. Seeing the design only halfway visible above the fabric instantly seized him with a deep, dark jealousy for whoever touched her skin beyond that point with their tattoo needle. The mere thought that it had been a man had him seriously fighting the urge to go over there right now and replace any memory of any other man's hands on her skin with his own.

As if hearing his thoughts from across the room, she blushed, and sank her teeth into her lower lip, which was stained a far too tempting lush, plum red today.

God, those lips.

That mouth of hers was a lethal weapon his memories definitely hadn't done justice over the years. Perpetually curved up at the corners as if always at the ready for a shy, quiet smile, with a full lower lip she was constantly biting...like she was *still* doing right now.

"Dude, you're drooling."

Caine tore his eyes away from Addison and looked up to find a thoroughly amused Alec standing next to Georgia and the kids, both of whom were now eating apples that had materialized out of thin air.

"Uncle Alec ate all your fries while you were staring at your girlfriend," Kevin announced, between crunchy bites.

"He bet us he could do it without you even

knowing," added Millie, peering up at Alec like he was some sort of wizard. Or zombie-whisperer.

Alec flashed two wide rows of perfect teeth at him.

Geez, it's like the guy *majored* in how to annoy the shit out of him.

"And since I won the bet," informed Alec, "I now get to pick where I'm taking Georgia and the kids out to dinner tonight. Which means you're going to have to fill in for me to help Addison put all the sewing machines, desks, and bolts of fabric away." Alec gave him a smug 'didn't-see-that-coming-didya' brow waggle.

Wait. *What?*

Georgia leaned over and stage-whispered, "I think that makes it Alec-1, Caine-0." Stepping back, she regarded Alec with nodding approval. "Masterful. Now, Caine is going to owe you one. *And* you got to eat all his fries. I have *so* much to learn from you."

Caine was no longer sure whether to punch him or be impressed by him.

And he said so out loud.

Addison came over with a sympathetic smile, "Yeah...Alec has that effect on people."

Bowing proudly like he'd just been crowned ass-of-the-year, he linked his arm through Georgia's and made a grand pageant-worthy exit processional, complete with a whole elbow-elbow-wrist-wrist Miss America wave as he passed rows of residents who looked thoroughly used to this bats in the belfry behavior.

Kevin and Millie gleefully joined in with two-handed waves at the chuckling spectators while Georgia alternated between gaping at Alec and glaring daggers at Caine.

Caine tugged at his collar. "She's going to kill me, isn't she?"

Addison nodded solemnly. "I'd get my affairs in order if I were you."

After the foursome disappeared around the corner, Addison shuffled her steel-toe stilettos and gave him an awkward smile. "You don't actually have to stay. I can break down the sewing classroom on my own."

Did her stubborn independence used to turn him on before? Because it sure as hell did now. Reaching up to slide a stray metallic silver and blue lock of hair out of her face, he murmured in a deep, rumbling rasp, "I want to stay."

The instant burst of shy heat in her eyes had him exhaling roughly, and admitting gruffly, "Because frankly, I'm not sure how much longer I can keep away from you, sweetheart."

———◆———

HIS WORDS hit her square in the chest. Then took her on a dangerous rush where pure, unfiltered *hope* filled her veins like a drug.

For the first time in her life, Addison understood why her mom used to OD on this feeling as much as she did heroin, why she used to chase it the same way she used to chase a high.

In her mom's case, the men offering her the hope of a future worth dreaming about did so irresponsibly, with no real intention of following through.

Caine would follow-through.

Or kill himself trying.

Lately, she'd been thinking about that constantly.

She'd overheard Georgia and Alec talking the other week about how Caine didn't do much else besides working and tracking David down. *And* how David was apparently involved with folks in the illegal drug trades in Mexico now.

With David's background in pharmaceutics—and lack of any morality issues when it came to drugging innocent people—the news wasn't all that groundbreaking.

But the newly realized fear that David was now connected to dangerous people who could hurt Caine? That scared her more than all of her nightmares of David over the years combined.

Before she managed to shake herself out of her thoughts, they'd already walked over to the closed meeting space they used for Georgia's class. In total silence.

He stopped with his hand on the doorknob and studied her for a bit, with those deep, stormy eyes of his that always saw too much, read her too well. Then, he quietly pushed open the door to the darkened room and walked in.

But he made no move to flick on the light switch.

Instead, he simply stood there, just inside the doorway, holding the door open for her silently, waiting for her to decide if she wanted to go into the pitch-blackness with him.

She knew the choice to step over that threshold, into the unknown, was symbolic of so much more than what he was asking in that moment…a fact she was certain hadn't escaped him.

He didn't back down. But he didn't push, either.

"Alec thinks there's no way you and I can be friends," she whispered, in a feeble attempt to keep them away from a ledge they'd be tempted to jump off of, where there would be no coming back from. "*This* is sort of an experiment he's conducting to prove his hypothesis."

"Did I mention I hated that 'just friends' idea from the start?"

Yeah. Her too.

"You want to know what I was thinking about when you suggested it?" he continued, reaching up to put his forearm against the door jamb, crowding the opening with his broad, six-foot frame.

She shouldn't. No good could possibly come from being allowed inside Caine Spencer's head. *"Yes."*

The gravelly rumble of his voice turned hypnotic. "I

was remembering how those soft, sexy sounds you'd make when I'd kiss you on your neck—right where that new tattoo is—would test me, nearly break me of my control every time."

When his eyes began tracing intently over the lines of her tattoo, the air in her lungs thinned, and slipped past her lips before she could stop it.

His jaw tightened, and his forearms flexed. Once. *Twice.* Before his voice dropped a full octave lower. "A test. Every. Single. Time."

Oh God, she wasn't going to make it.

He took a step back.

She followed him in.

The moment the door clicked shut behind her, he leaned in, very nearly caging her against the wall as he reached for the light switch.

Her mind short-circuited.

That's when her ever-so-helpful mouth decided to fill in without any oversight from her brain whatsoever. "That tattoo on my neck isn't real," she blurted out.

Caine stilled.

She did too. In a don't-make-any-sudden-movements sort of way.

The light switch remained off.

In the ten seconds it took her frantic eyes to adjust to the continued darkness, she felt him sift his fingers through her hair and bare the side of neck in question.

"This tattoo isn't real?" His lips hovered a few millimeters away from her ear.

"A tattoo artist who used to work in Hollywood makes them. They're like those kiddie sticker tattoos you transfer on with water, but more durable. They're the most realistic ones I could afford to buy in bulk, and they last all day, but they make your skin feel different." She was just babbling now, but couldn't seem to stop. "That's why I only chose to put them places where I knew no one was going to touch me." *Jesus, woman, stop talking!*

She finally did. But only because Caine was sliding the back of a single calloused finger against her neck, right over her racing pulse point.

"So no one touches you here?"

It sounded like a question, but it felt like a test.

"Only you," she replied honestly.

A rough male hiss split the air. His forehead came down to rest against hers. "You said you chose places— plural. Are your other tattoos fake, too?

"All but two of them," she confessed, actually really glad to finally get that off her chest. "The real ones are little. You can't see them."

Even though it was too dark for her to confirm, she could *feel* his eyes blaze in response. "Still throwing down dares, sweets?" His voice was deep, smoky. Nearly unrecognizable.

"Wh— *No!* I meant you aren't *able* to see them,

not that you *can't* see them." *Ohmigod.* "I mean you *can't*, of course." Her cheeks felt like roasted red peppers. "Be-because they're not in places you can see with my clothes on."

He groaned.

Oy, if she wasn't so traumatized over the verbal train wreck that had just spilled out of her mouth, she'd be groaning too. She didn't even want to imagine where in the world he thought she'd tattooed herself.

All around them, time seemed to have ceased altogether, as if she'd traveled them so far off-course that the future as a whole didn't know how the heck to proceed.

"New subject." Coarse and clipped, it was more a final decision than a suggestion.

Oh, bless the kind, kind man.

Dramatic pause button on the world now deactivated, sounds and noises returned. The darkness in the room was lifted, too. Thanks to Caine finally reaching over and flicking the light switch on in the room.

He backed away from her then—albeit reluctantly— eyes scorching her head to toe, as if trying to x-ray the locations of her real tattoos.

But he said not a word.

After every inch of her skin felt thoroughly seared and tingly, he turned and started picking up sewing machines, taking them to the storage closet while she unglued her feet and began stacking the extra chairs.

115

"Tell me something," he said, breaking the silence a few minutes later. "That day I pulled you over. Why did you try and run from me?"

Really, in so many ways, the man hadn't changed at all. But right then, she saw how much he had. He was...grittier. Deliciously harder. That much more devastating when his expression would soften for just the briefest moment when he'd look at her.

"I know you knew it was me. So why'd you run?"

What was it about the man that always made her want to reveal every secret she possessed? "I ran because the second I saw you in your squad car, looking even more ruggedly beautiful than you were in my memories, all I wanted to do was stop the car and go to you." She drew in a shaky breath as she confessed, "I'd always wondered what I'd do if I saw you one day. If I'd be able to play it cool. Or if I'd be all spy-like and keep on the ruse to maintain my cover. When I saw you again that day, I had my answer."

She shook her head, still in disbelief. "I seriously feared a full-blown jellyfish moment if I didn't change lanes and get the heck out of there."

"A jellyfish moment?"

She nodded solemnly. "Yep. Me. Wrapped around you. Like a jellyfish in heat."

His mouth quirked up into the tiniest motion possible that could still be considered a smile. "Good god,

I've missed you, woman." He exhaled gruffly. "We're going to need to figure this out."

" *This?*"

"You. Me. Because even though I know I can't have them right now, I want them…*all* your jellyfish moments."

Her breathing seized and went on strike, not willing to go back to work again in her lungs until he said more words like that.

"Keeping away from you all these years almost killed me. Attempting it for a second time in my life is going to be next to impossible."

She'd never seen him look so conflicted. "But…you're going to try? To stay away from me?"

"If by try, you mean fail, then sure."

Geez, the man had his own brand of poetry that never failed to get her knees weak.

When he continued to look at her like she was just out of reach, she had to ask, "You have proof, don't you? You *know* that all of this with David isn't over yet."

"The same way you do, sweetheart."

That, she understood. It had never gone away. The feeling of never being quite safe. Free.

"That number I gave you, the one to contact me. Do you still remember it?"

Again with the mind-reading. "Yes." It was locked in the same memory compartment she kept her social security number. She'd held onto it mainly to keep holding onto *him*. She hadn't been fanciful enough to believe—

"I still keep that phone with me 24-7," he informed her gruffly.

Oh good lord. Another jellyfish moment.

But she held firm to her boundaries. Barely. Partly because of the worry she continued to see in his eyes.

They got back to the task at hand, working in an unhurried, surprisingly easy silence, their gazes colliding every so often as the minutes ticked away. Somehow, the entire experience of just being here with him was almost…therapeutic.

By the time she was locking up the restored meeting room, she felt strangely like she had the one time a minister had found her outside of a church back when she was in high school.

She'd been staring at the historic building, wondering if its powers of salvation would extend to someone like her mother when the old man came up to stand beside her. Neither of them spoke; they just gazed up at the church in silence.

She didn't get any new answers per se, but she thanked the minister all the same.

That night, she packed her first 'go-bag,' and helped Tanner and Kylie pack one as well.

Even now, over a decade later, she still remembered exactly what they'd all packed.

"Two essential items, for every sentimental one,"

she'd told them.

She thought about all those items as Caine walked her up to her apartment. When they reached her door, she told him, out of the blue, "About a month after we moved in here, I unpacked my go-bag...for the first time *ever*."

His eyes ran over her face like a gentle caress. "I hate that you had to wait seven long years, but I'm glad it was here, sweetheart."

She pushed open her door and recognized the irony of their reversed situation—this time with her at the threshold and him on the other side.

When she turned to face him, one foot already inside, he shook his head. "Don't invite me in. Not just yet. Because it'll take a better man than I'm capable of being right now not to follow."

Her heart slammed against her ribcage.

They both looked down to watch his fingers twine with hers. His voice was as rough as she'd ever heard it when he brought up his own out-of-the-blue topic. "Did you always have a bed? Every night for the past seven years? That's the first thing I'd wonder every night when it'd get dark out. If you had a bed to sleep on."

There he went again *raiding* her heart with that crazy wonderful poetry of his.

"Yes. Always."

He nodded, then slowly stepped back from the doorway. "You going to be okay? Do you need anything?"

You.

His reaction was swift. She may as well have uttered the word aloud for the pain and hunger that now surrounded him like a storm of lightning and thunder.

"Stop reading my mind," she whispered.

"No."

The softly growled word was the only warning she got before his arms snaked around her waist and pulled her to him. "There hasn't been a single night since you left that I haven't thought about the way you felt in my arms the first time I'd slept longer than a few hours in years."

She gasped.

His eyes flared. "That right there—*that's* why I'm never going to stop reading your thoughts, baby. No matter how well Alec taught you to hide, knowing that even now, after all this time, you still can't hide all your feelings from me completely? *That's* the one thing that'll help me sleep tonight. It still won't be for longer than an hour or two, but at least in that short time, I'll have something to hold onto again."

Tidal waves of emotion slammed into her, one after another, crashing through every last barrier she'd built around herself, stripping away every protective layer she'd hid behind for the last seven years. Until all that was left was her.

A low, harsh sound broke free from Caine.

Feelings and thoughts, fears and hopes—she bared

it all to him.

For so long, she'd kept everything from everyone, herself included. Now, disarmed and defenseless, anyone with eyes could plainly see the one unmistakably distinguishable part of her that she'd had to work the hardest to hide.

Her heart. Which was still irrevocably tethered to the man standing before her.

"Go inside, Addison. Right now. While I'm still able to let you."

Every cell in her body rebelled against the command.

"Please, honey. Don't do that. Don't flash that look at me. That stubborn rebel-in-stilettos sass will have you under me in your bed in two seconds flat."

He groaned at whatever her eyes were telling him next.

To be fair, he started it with that panty-melting threat.

"Baby, you're killing me."

Right back at you.

He pushed open the door the rest of the way for her, one hand holding the top of the frame as if physically stopping himself from doing anything else.

For a while, the internal battles they each faced with themselves kept them both cemented where they stood.

But eventually, the growing torment and tension racking his entire frame made her back up a single step and clear the doorway.

"Lock the deadbolt."

These overprotective demands just shouldn't be this sexy.

She shut the door and laid her palm against it.

Knowing he was still out there, she confessed quietly to the wooden barricade between them, "That memory stayed with me, too. Even now, the only way I'm able to eventually fall asleep is to imagine your arms around me. Holding me. Keeping me safe."

Loving me.

It was a full minute before she finally heard his heavy tactical boots walk away.

CHAPTER 9

CAINE MANAGED to go nearly an entire week before calling her.

"Hello?"

Considering that he'd wanted to break down her door and push her back up against it the last time they'd talked, changing his default setting of gruff and abrupt after hearing her soft, throaty voice again just *wasn't* possible.

"Do you have a fancy dress you can wear?"

A startled *'oh'* came from Addison's end of the phone line, and he swore he could hear her biting on her lip before she replied, "Sort of. I needed one for an award banquet a few years back so I found a long dressy one at a thrift store that Kylie helped me snazzy up." A smile filtered into her tone then. "Why? Are you taking me dancing?"

"Do you want me to?" he asked immediately, a hundred percent seriously. "I could. Take you dancing, if you want."

Addison chuckled gamely. "I don't know. I might be bad at it. I've actually never been."

He frowned. "What about in high school?"

She gave an audible shrug. "I never went to prom or homecoming or anything like that because I was always watching the kids. My junior and senior year, we were pretty much living in a big crack house so I never let them stay there without me, day or night."

Dammit, he wanted to throw that criminal mother of hers in jail. "Well what about that award banquet you got the fancy dress for? Wasn't there dancing there?"

"Toward the end, but I didn't stay that long. Plus, my feet were a little sore from the strappy heels I'd borrowed to wear with the dress."

He didn't like the thought of her in any sort of pain, even shoe-related one. "Why didn't you just wear your leather boots? The black ones look pretty comfortable." Seriously, women and shoes—he'd never understand.

She laughed incredulously. "My dress was a pale pink. I would've clashed a tiny bit."

"Then I'll get you new non-clashing shoes that don't hurt. But not one of those ankle-breakers with the spike heels or anything." *Did leather boots come in pale pink?* He'd have to ask Lia. Maybe he could paint a pair. "Can't you just wear rubber flip-flops?" Zero chance of falling, and he'd definitely seen pink ones of those.

"Caine, is this slightly odd conversation going somewhere? Are *we* going somewhere?"

Oh, right. "I've got tickets to this thing for tomorrow night. I know it's last minute, but if you and Kylie want to come, the food's supposed to be pretty good." *Inviting Kylie made it casual, right? A 'just friends' sort of thing?* Cripes, even thinking the term 'just friends' when it came to Addison gave him an ulcer. "You don't even need to dress up if you don't want to. You two can wear whatever, really."

"No, no, it'll be fun to wear the dress again. The only thing is, Kylie can't come. She has a study date tomorrow night."

"A *what?*" Talk about getting an ulcer. "What's the kid's name?" he demanded, searching his pockets in vain for his notebook. "Hang on, let me get a napkin to write on."

"I'm not letting you do a background check on a teenage kid, Caine." She was smiling, he could hear it. "He's a nice boy from Kylie's school who's been nothing but respectful all semester. She's just going to be having dinner with his family followed by some studying. On site. They have a big test they're quizzing each other. Tonight and tomorrow night."

He made a mental note to ask Alec about all the boys

125

Kylie's age at the complex. Drew had midterms, but he could be on standby if needed. "Is there going to be adult supervision?"

"Yes. And I've known his parents a while. They were actually one of our pilot families that I met with during construction, who moved into the complex before we officially opened. They'd all been seriously injured in a car accident where the other driver had been broke and uninsured. With both parents unable to work for a while, and all their hospital, surgical, and rehab bills piling up, they lost their home within a year and were never able to get ahead of their debt enough to recover. And now they're on track to becoming our first success story. They're good people, Caine. Humble, hard-working, and very sweet. Just like their three boys."

Well that made disliking the kid a lot harder. But not impossible. "Did you tell him he has to come by to pick her up? He can't punk out on being a gentleman just because they live in the same complex."

"He actually offered. He's coming by in a little bit to walk her over to his building." Her voice was back to sounding terribly entertained.

What in the world was so funny?

"What time will he be there?" His shift at the station didn't start for another hour...if he left now, he could be at the complex within—

"You are *not* coming by here to flash your gun at the

kid."

Huh, he could see now why Addison wasn't a fan of his reading her mind all the time.

"Besides, I already had a firm chat with him the other day."

Caine was sure she had. Addison was nothing if not fiercely protective of her siblings. But still. Sometimes teenage guys needed visual aids to help scare the stupid out of them. "Does Kylie keep the pepper spray I gave her on her keychain like I told her?"

"You mean the contraband item that would get her suspended from school if the administration figured out what it was? Yes, I believe she never leaves home without it. But you can tell your boy Alec that Kylie and I both thought the novelty taser he gave her would be a bit overkill to bring."

Caine scowled, hating that he hadn't thought of that first.

Addison's amusement turned into outright chuckles. "You are *unbelievably* cute when you're in protective papa bear mode, you know that right?"

Cute? Now he wanted to skip his shift altogether in favor of going over to supply her with a dozen other adjectives she could call him.

"If you're done making yourself crazy, do you want to tell me more about this event you're taking me to? Am I going to know anybody?"

Hell, he almost forgot the reason for his phone call to begin with.

"It's one place I *know* even David wouldn't be crazy enough to crash. And yeah, you'll know a few people."

———◆———

"A BLACK-TIE police fundraiser." Addison grinned. Yep, not even David would dare lock himself in a ballroom full of cops. "Caine, this is…" *Officially her first night out where she wouldn't have to look over her shoulder.* "This is beautiful. Thank you for inviting me."

Caine grabbed her a beer from the bar. "Alec mentioned you rarely go out. Aside from work meetings and occasional store runs."

Of course he did. The tattletale. "I just figure better to be safe than sorry."

"And my blood pressure thanks you for that."

She chuckled. "Glad my homebody ways please you."

His smoldering dark eyes ran over her, head to toe, as he murmured for her ears only, "Sweetheart, *everything* about you pleases me."

Oy, she'd walked right into that one.

"Except this."

She blinked up at him in surprise.

"I hate that you're afraid to go out. And that it's

because of a psycho that I haven't been able to bring to custody yet."

"Caine, it's no big deal, really. I'm not missing much." She took a sip of her beer to avoid his all-seeing gaze, realizing belatedly that it was her favorite brand. *The man really was an expert at recon.*

"You're a crappy liar, babe." A slow smile crinkled the corners of his eyes. "And there are a few folks here who want to help me prove it."

He nodded over to a small cluster of folks coming toward them.

Puzzled, she turned.

And nearly dissolved into a puddle of tears on the spot.

Joe, Shirley, Aunt Bernadette, and even Marco.

Caine had brought her all her favorite people, her family back in Creek Hills who she hadn't been able to contact all these years. To protect them as well as herself and the kids.

"How is your mascara not running?" complained Bernadette from a fast-approaching motorized senior scooter, packing what looked to be about ten mouthwatering Ziploc bags of Joe's famous giant muffins in the front basket. "You're crying as hard as I am and your eye make-up is still perfect." Joe and Marco hopped out of the way to avoid getting their toes run over as she screeched to a stop ahead of the others to get to Addison first. "What are you waiting for, missy? Come here and give me a hug."

Tears turned to laughter as she ran forward to do just that. Lordy, she'd missed the ole battle axe, in all her fabulous glory. "You look amazing, Bernadette."

"That's still *Aunt* Bernadette to you. I don't care how grown you get." She leaned back. "Now let me get a good look at you." Nodding her approval, she fluffed her own short, stylish hairdo. "We almost match. I tell you, ever since I had my stylist accentuate my natural silver and add these blue highlights, I can't keep the randy men at the senior center away. Is it the same for you too, dear?"

"Aunt Bernadette!" Addison's new tears were full of mirth.

"I bet you get all the bad boys. Ooh, maybe *I* should get some tattoos, too."

"Aaand that's my cue to go grab another beer." Caine leaned down to kiss Bernadette on the cheek. "Here I thought you were just a sweet little grandma when we first met."

"That's what *all* my gentleman callers say."

Caine barked out a laugh and finished greeting the others while Addison did her best not to get all weepy again when Joe came up to her next. "You've gotten too skinny. Are you eating enough?" He frowned at Bernadette. "Stop with the inappropriate comments and hand over one of the muffins. I need to start feeding the girl again to put some meat back on her bones."

Geez, waterproof or not, her mascara was never going to last. Addison threw her arms up and squeezed the stuffing out of the big, grumpy teddy bear.

"Guess I can just send the muffins home with you," rumbled Joe, voice now a tiny bit wobbly. "Packed some of Kylie's favorite mini chocolate strawberry poppy ones, too."

Shirley stepped forward to show her a big beach tote with what had to be another ten muffin-filled Ziploc bags, before pushing past Joe to deliver a rib-bruising hug. "Crazy man's been baking all day. I had to call in one of the other chefs to do the actual kitchen orders to cover."

"Only 'cause I told you too," argued Joe. "*You* wanted to shut my whole diner down for the day."

And they were off.

Shirley crossed her arms and grumped, "If the other workers had found out we were getting to see Addison today without them, they would've thrown a fit." Her cheeks turned a rosy color of miffed and mulish. "And since my pure heart doesn't always do well with secrets, I just thought it'd be better if *maybe* we made everyone we know stay home."

Joe rolled his eyes and gave Addison a droll look. "See, this is why I never told her about you living in the van, baby girl."

Shirley gasped in outrage. *"I would've taken that*

131

secret to my grave!"

His face softened then. "I know that. I just meant you would've probably bawled and blubbered every time you saw her and the kids or something."

"Think you've got us confused there, buddy," she huffed back, mumbling something that sounded a whole lot like, *"big crying baby."*

Honest to God, the two bickered with each other more than they did their actual siblings. It was a borderline exhausting, crazy codependent friendship both of their spouses actually relied on to keep their home lives that much more pleasant.

And Addison had missed it all so dang much.

"I still can't believe you didn't tell me." Shirley sounded more hurt now than anything else. "I would've helped."

Joe exchanged a look with Bernadette. "That's exactly *why* neither of us told anyone, Shirls. Because standing by and *not* helping was a constant struggle."

Bernadette nodded. "He's right. It was hard not to worry myself silly. Every time we had a freak cold front or lordy, that time the kids came down with the flu." She wrung her hands and frowned. "Luckily for me, my oldest daughter had figured it out too, so I had someone to talk to."

Addison looked at her in shock. "Heather knew too?"

"She knew before I did. Remember how she works as a clerk for the Sheriff's station a few towns over? Well, she dug into your background a little more after I hired you and learned all about that good-for-nothing mother of yours." Bernadette reached over to squeeze her hand. "You did good, sweetie. I know it was hard, and lonely, but just know you were never truly alone. We would've swooped in to help if ever you'd needed it."

Even though those days were long behind her, it *did* mean a lot to know now that she'd had their support then. That someone would've been there to help the kids if she'd failed.

She turned to Joe. "Caine said you knew early on, too. How?"

"I have a small surveillance camera out back."

How had she never noticed that?

"It only activates if the motion sensors are triggered."

Addison sighed. "And thanks to Kylie's small bladder, it probably caught us going back into the diner almost every night."

"Yup. Truthfully, for the first few weeks, I kept expecting you to give up and come ask for help. Talked to Claudia about letting you and the kids stay in our spare room and everything. But you never did quit. Every day, you came back to work stronger and happier than the day before. The kids, too." He nodded over at the bar, where

Caine was talking to a bunch of officers…with his alpha-protective gaze fixed on her the entire time. "Caine was pissed as hell when he found out I hadn't forced you to accept help from the beginning. But I didn't want to spook you and have you take off altogether. At least this way, you had someone watching your back, even though you never needed it."

He put a big Popeye sailor paw on her shoulder and told her firmly, "You did right by those kids. Don't let anyone else tell you different. You fixed what your mama broke, gave them a childhood, built them a good, strong home—who cares that it was in a van, or on the run. Those kids grew up whole because of you."

Addison hadn't been expecting that at all. Suddenly, it felt like there was too much oxygen in the air. And she was definitely feeling some eye allergies coming on.

"Well, crap," grumbled Shirley, as she reached into her purse for a twenty-dollar bill, which she handed over to Joe. "I can't believe I broke first," she sniffled, dabbing at her leaky tears. "How are *you* so insightful about all of this? When you're about as deep as a puddle when it comes to making sense of simple things like why your wife is pissed at you?"

Joe shrugged. "Because I didn't grow up whole." A mask of deeply rooted pain clouded over him as he told them all brusquely, "My folks were angry drunks who made my kid years hell. They used to send me to bed with a beating the nights I didn't catch enough mice for the local farmers to bring home more than spare change. Then when I'd be too sore the next morning for my paper route, they'd burn cigarettes into my legs until I'd get up, and then tell me I wouldn't get another meal until I found a way to make up that lost money."

Shirley and Addison cried out in unison, horrified.

"When they wanted me to start stealing, that's when I ran away. I lived on the streets from middle school. Got my GED and worked a few jobs before eventually enlisting. Never did see my folks again." He shot Addison a meaningful look. "I would've given anything to have a sister like you back then. I was rooting for you from the start. Helped in the best ways I could."

Suddenly, a memory hit her. "You purposely spilled that cooler of fish on the sofa in your office didn't you?"

"The old thing wasn't big enough for both Kylie and Tanner to sleep on. So I stunk it up bad enough that you wouldn't suspect nothing when I got a bigger one."

Fresh tears welled in her eyes. "Wish I'd thanked you. There were some days in the summers the van stayed boiling hot long into the night. That couch was a lifesaver for the kids."

"Thanks were never needed, baby girl. It was a privilege to watch you raise those kids right. Healed some of my own scars, I think." Red-rimmed eyes met hers. "I was damn proud of you then, and words ain't even been invented yet on how proud I am of you now."

"Aw, crap," muttered Marco who'd been uncharacteristically silent the entire time. "Now *I'm* ready to pay up twenty bucks."

Addison's tab was running pretty high at that point, too.

Being more of a doer than a talker, Bernadette practically knocked Marco and Shirley over with her scooter as she launched a bulldozer hug at Joe and smattered his cheeks with loud-smacking kisses until he was wearing more of her lipstick than she was.

From there, the tears quickly dried up, and merriment ensued. Grandkid photos were exchanged, along with seven years' worth of stories that filled cracks in her heart she hadn't even known were there until they were patched up.

It had to be a good hour later when Addison finally felt Caine come up behind her.

She spun around and just tucked herself against him, clinging jellyfish tight when his arms wrapped around her. "Don't let go. Not just yet."

"Not sure I could even if you asked me to, sweetheart."

———◆———

CAINE MEANT that literally.

Being able to hold Addison like this—in public—was kicking up some serious possessive tendencies. He wasn't anywhere near ready to let her out of his arms. "Are those pink shoes you're wearing hurting your feet?"

Addison smiled up at him in surprise. "No. They're good."

"Then could I have this dance?"

She did a surprised double-take as if only just now realizing they were standing on a dance floor. "I-I wasn't kidding before. I don't know how to dance."

The reminder of how she'd missed out on every opportunity to learn in high school just made him hold her tighter. "We'll do it junior high style and just sway side to side." He studied her shy expression as she looked around at the dancing couples around them. "But we don't have to, if you're not comfortable."

"Oh, just dance with the man," interjected Joe, who was cutting across the dance floor like a jaywalker. "He's the one who arranged for this dance floor at the last minute. The event organizers had to rush to reconfigure the entire ballroom to make it fit and everything."

"Dammit, I told you that in confidence."

Joe was unrepentant. "At this rate, you two will be my age before you get together. So dance with the poor putz. Before I get too old to walk you down the aisle." With that, he veered off to the buffet line.

Addison took a step back, but didn't let go. "You

did all this for me?"

"He also got you *this*," chimed in Shirley, appearing out of nowhere, carrying the casual gift he'd intended to give Addison later. Away from all their nosy spectators.

Pleasure, pure and simple, tugged the corners of her lips up as she surveyed the unique little corsage he'd had to get from a florist outside the city since no one nearby could fill such an unusual order. "Cactus flowers and succulents?"

"Kylie may have mentioned those are your favorites."

Lush lower lip trapped between her teeth, she slipped the corsage on her wrist and stared at it for a moment. "Can I tell you a secret?"

"Sure."

"I was a little jealous of Tanner's Venus Flytrap and Kylie's purple hydrangea."

Not having had the chance to get Addison flowers back in Creek Hills was one of the things he'd regretted a lot, too.

Her fingertips pressed against his lips before he could apologize. "Don't. This was better. Now my first dance and my first flowers are together in one memory." She replaced her fingers with the briefest brush of her lips before resting her head against his chest.

He spent the next minute or so trying to tamp back the rush of blood in his ears enough to hear the music they were supposed to be dancing to.

"Caine?" she asked when a new song started up and they kept right on dancing.

"Yeah?"

"I don't think we're doing this friends thing correctly."

He drew her in closer. "I think you may be right about that."

An obnoxious tap on his shoulder put a quick end to that line of discussion.

Just when it was getting interesting.

And dangerous.

"My turn to dance with the belle of the ball," called out Marco, commandeering Addison's hand and twirling her toward him.

Laughing, she gave him a hug and studied him both curiously. "Why aren't you in your police uniform, too?"

"A lot's happened after you left, sugar. Caine got his brothers to hire me after I left the force. Been doing security work for them ever since. We're basically besties now. Total BBFs—best bros forever."

Her lips twitched to the side in amusement. "You two are *very* much alike. Throw in my friend Alec and you three could be musketeers."

Caine shot her a horrified look at any scenario grouping him with Alec and Marco.

Admittedly, the former Creek Hills cop now working for Spencer Securities was one of their most requested private security detail now, for some of their biggest functions and clients. Caine definitely respected him. But the guy liked pushing his buttons almost as much as Alec did.

"I don't care that you're in a committed relationship, dude. You peek down the front of her dress one more time, and I'll be replacing the fuzzy dice in your car with your balls."

Marco grinned at her. "See? Best buds."

Addison's shoulders shook with laughter. "He was just looking at my tattoo, Caine."

Caine continued to glower.

When Marco just waved and waltzed her away, Alec came up and offered him a beer. "Do you like need a hug or something, too?"

"Shut up."

"Was it entirely necessary to threaten the man's testicles? It's not like he's even batting for the same team as you."

That made Caine finally turn to face him. "Shit, you're good. I can count on one hand the number of folks who know Marco's gay. He hasn't even come out to his family yet."

Alec shrugged, in a rare showing of modesty. "I've been keeping tabs on all of you for years. Back to my question. The fact that he's into dudes doesn't lessen the crazy jealous thing even a little?"

They turned to see Addison laugh with delight over something Marco said.

Caine scowled. "If you were in my shoes, would *you* be any less jealous?"

Alec replied matter-of-factly, "I wouldn't have invited the laughing hyena to begin with."

Huh, maybe they *were* more alike than he thought.

"Would you poach her from me?"

"In a heartbeat. I'd step right over your body before your blood had a chance to get cold."

Caine wouldn't put it past him. "You really are a jackass." Despite everything, he found himself smiling. "So, no Georgia tonight?"

"She didn't want to come. In fact, she looked pretty upset about the entire thing."

Right. A night in a room full of cops from Rick's precinct wouldn't be high on her list of fun date outings.

Caine swiped a fancied-up pig-in-a-blanket hors d'oeuvre from Alec's plate. "So did you think about my proposal?"

"It's going to take a lot more than one black-tie dinner to get me to join your little Scooby squad, but I'm down for comparing notes and working together to protect Addison."

"Good. Then you can start by telling me about the guy who tailed my SUV almost the whole way over here tonight."

CHAPTER 10

A WEEK LATER, with the partial license plate Caine had managed to get of the man tailing Addison the night of the of the fundraiser, Drew was eventually able to track down the driver.

Turns out, it was an old P.I. acquaintance that Alec had known back in the day. Definitely not hired by David, according to Alec.

When Caine asked then who *had* hired him, Alec responded simply that he'd need to have another 'semi-friendly chat' with his buddy and then twenty-four hours to verify the intel.

In the spirit of plausible deniability, Caine didn't ask any follow-up questions.

As Caine was discovering more and more, while he did everything by the book, Alec ignored the book altogether. But he got results, there was no denying that. And truth be told, Caine was starting to actually respect, hell, even like the guy.

That is, when he wasn't being so damn *irritating*.

"So..." sing-songed Alec, in his now *daily* call to Caine. "Tonight's the big night, huh?"

Honestly, it was a testament to his self-control that he hadn't assaulted the man with a weapon yet. "Would you *shut up* about that. I'm sorry I ever mentioned it."

He really was. Ever since he'd made the *giant* mistake of telling Alec what he'd been doing the past couple of nights, the man had been like a dog with an annoying new squeaky toy.

"Just saying, man," replied Alec, thoroughly amused, "You've been out of the dating game a while. There are rules about this sort of—"

Caine hung up on him.

And to think, this all started simply because he'd been sticking to his plan about keeping his distance from Addison. Well...*sort of.*

He picked up his phone and started dialing.

"Hello?"

God, her voice alone could get him from zero to sixty in a no time at all. "Hey sweets, you have plans tonight?"

"Nope, another lazy night home for me." Addison's voice held a soft smile he wished like hell he could see.

143

"Me too. You want to have takeout dinner over the phone again?"

It wasn't as weird as it sounded.

As he'd explained to Alec, it'd all happened by accident, the night following the fundraiser. He'd called while she'd been eating, and they'd ended up talking—or video-chatting, rather—through her entire meal.

His next night off of work? Coincidentally, same thing. Then, it became a thing. Now, two more video chat dinners later and here they were again.

"I was thinking Chinese take-out tonight. Max and Gabe are stopping by a little after midnight with some new equipment I wanted to check out so I figured I'd order extra for them since they'll be coming directly from the airport."

"Chinese sounds good. Hey, if the guys aren't meeting you until that much later, do you want to come over and Netflix a movie or something? Kylie and a bunch of kids on the property are having a reading marathon challenge in the teen lounge downstairs until midnight—supervised, of course—so I could even bring the takeout and movie to you if you want."

Way too dangerous. For a number of reasons.

"My place is a mess," he hedged half-truthfully, looking at his formerly meticulous master bedroom, which now looked like a bomb had detonated in it, thanks to Hurricane Alec going through his files the other day. "Why don't we watch the movie by video chat too? Your pick.

We'll load it at the same time, and eat while we watch it."

Her amused voice grew intrigued. "You're serious. You want us to watch a movie from our own apartments?"

No. I want to take you to bed and do everything I wanted to do to you that last night before you left...plus all the thousands more I've imagined since.

"It'll be fun. This way, you can stay in your PJ's and stay comfy all night."

"Actually, that does sound kind of great. Okay, I'm in. What time are we doing this?"

"Around seven?"

"I'll call you back when I get settled in."

Of course, just when he was congratulating himself on another successful distance-keeping night planned with Addison, a text from Alec came rolling in:

> Remember, fifth date rules. If this turns into phone sex, practice safe phoning. No glove, no love. Left some protection for your phone the other day.

Well, that explained the random box of plastic wrap that had been on top of his TV.

The ass.

———◆———

AT A FEW MINUTES TO SEVEN, Addison finished removing the last of her make-up and scooped her hair up into her bedtime ponytail.

She dialed Caine's number and then propped her phone on her nightstand when he answered. "Hey. I've got the movie all loaded up and ready to go. Let me just go get my food from the kitchen. Be right back."

Chinese takeout box of noodles in hand, she settled back into bed. Wearing her comfiest yoga pants and tank for an in-bed movie night with Caine was already climbing the charts as one of her greatest nights in recent memory.

"I decided to order some Chinese too—"

She stopped and did a double take when she found Caine seemingly in suspended animation on her phone screen. He was staring intently at her, looking as peaceful as he did pained.

"What's wrong?" she asked, more concerned than alarmed.

"You took off all your fake tattoos."

She blinked, startled. It hadn't even occurred to her to keep them on.

With tomorrow being her day off, she'd planned to spend the day at home relaxing. If there were any site emergencies to deal with, she could always just throw on one of her jogging sweatshirts with the zippered high collar and thumb hole sleeves to cover all traces of her missing tattoos, which she usually did more and more when the weather got cooler. Partly to save money, but mostly because having a bunch of artwork stuck onto her skin wasn't the most comfortable thing in the world.

That said, until now, she'd always left her tattoos on during her video chat dinners with Caine. But tonight, she hadn't even thought twice before removing them.

She wasn't sure what to make of that.

The rough, uneven breath he expelled on screen redirected her thoughts back to his reaction to seeing her au naturel for the first time in seven years.

"Sweetheart, as sexy as you are with your make-up and tattoos, without it…" Another low, gruff sound echoed out of his chest.

She couldn't help herself. "Without it…what?"

"Without it, you're so damn pretty you make me forget all the reasons why I need to stay away from you."

It was a gritty, near reverent remark that had her insides doing triple axles.

Addison discovered in that moment that he was absolutely right. The distance between them *was* rather imperative. Because if he were actually there in the room with her, she'd want to do something she really probably shouldn't.

"I know I'm probably going to regret asking." His voice had dropped a husky octave lower. "But what thoughts are going through that busy brain of yours?"

She hesitated, chewing on her lip in debate, before eventually answering, "I'm thinking I want to show you something."

"Show me." Not a request. But not a demand, either.

Suddenly as shy as she'd been when she'd first met him, she attempted to change the subject completely. "How about we watch the movie first, and then—"

"Show me." A little more demanding this time. And packed with a current of electricity she could practically feel sparking through the phone line.

Slowly, she dragged her blanket off to the side. And pulled her yoga sweatpants up her leg. Just enough to reveal the outside of her ankle.

"You're showing me one of your real tattoos?"

The deeply masculine pleasure in his voice had her wanting to show him a whole lot more.

"I could…take a photo of it for you with my phone."

"No. Just hold your phone closer to your ankle."

Why did that make this so much sexier than a screenshot?

Having a hard time keeping her hand steady, she braced her wrist against a pillow and let him look his fill.

"It's a basket of apples," she supplied helpfully.

"With three decorated Easter eggs in the bunch," he finished with a warm smile she could clearly hear.

She propped the phone back up in front of her so she could dive back under her blanket. Not that it would help all that much. Caine had an uncanny ability to make her feel stark naked.

And *not* in a bad way.

"Why not an Easter egg basket?"

Only a handful of folks had seen her without her boots on over the years, and thus, the tattoo. And they'd all asked her the same thing. Well, all but Alec, that is. As was the case with the matching Easter egg keychains she and the kids carried, he'd never once asked about her real tattoos. For everyone else who did, she'd always give a vague answer prevaricating the meaning of the apple-picking basket a bit by saying it had to do with their love of urban gardening, while balancing it with a partial truth about the three eggs amongst all the apples in the basket representing their embracing their unique differences.

"After about a year of ordering all the fake tattoos from that artist I told you about, one day, she told me since I was such a good customer, she'd do a real one for me on the house, if I wanted." Lifting her gaze back up to his, she chuckled lightly. "Took me at least a year to get up the nerve to agree, and then another year to figure out what I wanted her to design for me."

Peeling back the blanket again, she ran her index finger over the colorful, intricate details of the dainty tattoo, which, in its entirety, was no larger than the size of a credit card. "I'd known from the beginning that I wanted to do the three Easter eggs."

Caine's eyes crinkled at the corners affectionately.

And she felt her heart fill up every open cavity of

149

space in her chest.

There was something so...amazingly intimate about knowing that Caine—more than anyone else in the entire world—understood exactly why those three hand-drawn eggs were so special to her. "But the apple basket was more of a game day decision." She smiled, remembering the morning she'd finally decided on this particular design. "On the wall of my friend's tattoo parlor, there was a photo of a tattoo she'd recently done that I couldn't take my eyes off of. It was this gorgeous tree that had lost most of its leaves, with a single red apple laying at its roots. I remember finding the meaning of the tattoo as beautiful as the artwork...but, obviously, not applicable to me and the kids."

The reminder of why that was had her tucking her leg back under the blanket, and needing a moment to regroup.

Caine's deep voice through the speaker was like a balm on her soul. "Of course it's not applicable. You and the kids are the furthest thing from the apple that didn't fall far from the tree."

She gazed at his fiercely adamant features, loving that he saw it that way, too. "When that saying first echoed in my head after seeing the tree tattoo, I remember instantly thinking that Kylie, Tanner, and I didn't just fall far from our roots, we'd fallen from the branches as a whole different *fruit*...heck, not even fruits at all in the context of that metaphor..."

"You fell from the tree as Easter eggs."

His words rang so proud and sure, so *absolute*, she felt her emotions catch in her throat.

"One day, I want to see that tattoo in person." His eyes locked on hers. "Along with the second real tattoo you mentioned."

Her hand automatically shot to the blade of her hip.

His blazing hot gaze followed. "How many people have seen that second tattoo, honey?"

Well, that was a loaded question.

Knowing exactly what her answer would be confirming, she stalled, half-hoping he'd let the subject drop.

He didn't.

Eventually, she replied, barely louder than a whisper. "Aside from the tattoo artist...none."

His eyes flared. And a look she couldn't begin to describe crossed his features a charged moment later. It wasn't merely possessive, it was *primal*. Only a thousand times more intense.

"We better start our movie, sweetheart. Because if we don't, I'm going to sit here thinking about that tattoo for maybe another five more seconds before I break and head over to your apartment and claim the right to be the first man to see it."

She flicked her TV on.

But she'd been *sorely* tempted not to...for a torturous four and a half seconds.

It took her far longer than that to get her brain un-fuzzed enough to realize she'd turned the movie on in Spanish by accident.

———◆———

"SO," CAINE ASKED, after they both finished eating, "of the new make-up, clothes, the whole nine yards, is there any part that's more transformation than disguise now?"

Addison pursed her lips in thought. "The colored tips in my hair, I adore, but I'm not a huge fan of the silver streaks—they sort of make me feel like an X-Men character." She smiled and wiggled her toes under the blanket. "I've grown to love my stiletto boots, especially the steel-toe nut-kicker ones. Can't imagine myself going back to sandals or heels after that."

Her eyes drifted over to her closet. "Beyond that, the outfits and things are a little much for me. Except..." She blushed.

He was totally going to regret asking, he was sure of it. "Except what?"

"There *is* this black leather and lace bustier I wear sometimes. It's not slutty or edgy or anything. Well, maybe a little edgy, but more pretty than anything else because it has this scallop edge detail that falls right over my bra-line, not that it can be worn with a bra, but—"

"*Jesus Christ*, stop. I get the picture." Did he ever. It was all he could do not to imagine Addison in her favorite thigh-high stiletto boots and a sex-kitten leather and lace bustier, with nothing except for that blush adorning the rest of her.

She looked startled for a second, but then her eyes started to dance, just the tiniest bit.

"You're enjoying torturing me." Despite the fact that he was now hard as a rock, he let loose a small smile. He'd forgotten how fun it was to flirt with Addison.

"No," she denied quickly. "Well...not exactly. I think I just like knowing that I still have some effect on you."

He was thunderstruck. "Did you think it'd *wear off* or something?"

"I don't know. Maybe."

"Sweetheart, I assure you, it didn't. You affect me just as much as you did back in Creek Hills."

After a slight pause, she admitted softly, "Same here."

He was damn pleased to hear it. That said, the quiet confession did require him to shift the angle of his phone so she couldn't see how *much* of an effect those words had had on him.

She snuggled some more under her covers. "Caine?" she murmured muzzily.

"Yeah, baby?" When she sounded like that, it was

hard to keep his replies platonic.

"I've missed this. Missed you."

Ah, hell. "Same here, sweets."

"Can I ask you something?"

"I'll do my best to answer."

"Do you have *any* idea what's going on in the movie?"

He grinned. "Not even a little bit."

She smiled back, looking nearly drunk. "Mmm, me neither…"

"We could rewind it back to the—"

The sound of her deep breathing coming through the speakers stopped him.

She was asleep.

Blinking back a slow smile, he shoved a couch pillow under his head, suddenly feeling like a nap himself. It was only midnight, a full three hours before he normally passed out from exhaustion for his standard hour or two of sleep. But he was feeling damned relaxed right now.

Maybe he'd try to just close his eyes for a second—

The next thing he knew, it was after one in the morning.

…And his two annoying brothers were tilting their heads and chorusing, *'awww'* quietly from the hallway.

He ignored them and rolled over on the sofa to check on Addison. She was still in a deep sleep on the video screen. He muted his phone and pointed at his master bedroom. "Just drop the equipment off. I'll look over everything tomorrow."

Twin looks of shock gaped back at him. "You mean you're not going to make us give you a full descriptive rundown of every single thing we brought until the butt crack of dawn?"

Shit, he wasn't that bad was he? "I figured you two were beat after traveling all day. But if you'd rather take care of it now—"

"Oh, we're totally leaving. No takebacks," called out Gabe as he hustled across the apartment to drop off the boxes he'd lugged in.

"You were sleeping," commented Max, no longer teasing at all.

"Yeah."

"That's new."

"It's Addison. She makes me...I don't know, calm, maybe? Relaxed?"

"I think the word you're looking for is happy, big brother." He smiled. "And it looks good on you."

Caine reflected on Max's comment long after the guys left. Laying back against the sofa, he tried to remember the last time he'd felt like this.

His brothers were right. Normally, he'd probably be going through that box of equipment with a fine tooth comb right about now. He'd be wired, *unsettled*—working or doing a dozen other things other than sleep.

But all it took was one glance at Addison's closed eyes and pillow-mussed hair clouding around her for his limbs to start relaxing, his eyes to begin feeling heavier.

Just like that, he was out like a light again shortly after.

It wasn't until a little before dawn that his internal clock woke him up once more, for good this time. The nap hadn't lasted more than an hour or so, but still, he felt more rested than he had in *years*.

Typically, he'd be itching to go for a run or work out right about now. But the sight of Addison still sleeping on the screen beside him kept him where he was. He wasn't tired, but he was comfortable.

Content.

…And officially clueless as to what to do with his time. Lounging around on the sofa wasn't something he ever did. The only thing he did know was that he didn't want to leave Addison's side. So he shrugged and turned the TV on to restart the movie that neither of them had watched last night.

Luckily, it turned out to be a fairly entertaining flick. Even better, Addison began slow-blinking awake during the end credits, saving him from having to think of something else to do with his time next.

Muting the TV, he turned and watched those gorgeous eyes of her widen in confusion at first, then surprise…and finally wonder. "I slept."

Her expression looked even more astonished when she peered into the phone and saw what he was doing. "I slept, and you hung out on your couch past dawn watching a movie." A teasing smile hit her lips. "Guess miracles *do* exist."

He chuckled. "Guess they do. How about we try it again tonight and see if it's only a onetime miracle?"

The slow, sweet smile that reached all the way up to her expressive eyes had him instantly flipping over onto his stomach—carefully—to tamp down his reaction to her smiling at him from bed first thing in the morning.

"Okay," she agreed, pleased. "Same time tonight? This time you pick the movie?"

Yeah…they were pretty awful at this 'just friends' arrangement.

CHAPTER 11

ADDISON WAS STILL smiling about their impromptu video chat movie night come Monday.

"Oh my god," chuckled Kylie, breaking into her thoughts as she came in to sync her phone to the office desktop to upload new garden photos. "You totally have googly eyes right now."

Addison felt her whole face flush. "I do not."

"Do too. That's your Caine look. It comes with dancing hearts all around your head." Kylie proceeded to then float over to the closest chair and position herself like a yoga deity in classic *nosy-gabbing-girl* pose—elbows on knees, chin perched atop folded hands. "I gave you the whole weekend to process. Time is officially up. Date details, please."

"It wasn't a date," Addison replied automatically.

But then pursed her lips, decidedly opposed to the taste of that technical truth.

Kylie gave her a quiet look. "Caine's holding back because of the psycho douche canoe isn't he?"

"*Kylie!* Language."

"Are you kidding? That was G-rated in comparison to what I call the snot waffle jackhole in my head."

Addison didn't doubt it. Where David was concerned, her normally calm little sister could go pretty postal. *Snot waffle jackhole?* That one was actually really good.

"It's just so not fair that you guys can't spend more time together." Kylie chewed on her lower lip thoughtfully. "What if I make myself scarce this weekend? That way you two can have the place all to yourselves to ha—"

Addison shot her a horrified look.

"*Hang out!* I was going to say hang out!" Kylie jumped out of her chair, looking just a tiny bit seasick. "I know you and I are close and all, but trust me, we're *not* going to be those sisters who share sex stories."

Oh, thank God.

Their silent agreement sealed, stamped, and approved, Kylie dropped back into her seat...and then leaned over to clarify, "Of course, we can still totally talk about kissing and gush over that super intense way he looks at you and stuff."

Addison really did have the most perfect little sister

in the world.

Ten minutes later, while Kylie was mooning over a few alpha-romantic Caine recaps, a knock sounded on her office door. "Addison, you have a visitor—"

"Oh my goodness, look how beautiful you two have become!"

Addison stilled.

Just as a new look of distress washed over Kylie's expression. A real one, this time.

"Like I said, you have a visitor," repeated her front receptionist, adding in a whisper for Addison's ears only, "A kinda pushy one, if you ask me."

Yes, Lara Milan had always been pushy when it came to things she wanted…but generally apathetic over things she didn't care as much for.

Like her children.

"Mom," said Addison, which earned a sharp flinch from Kylie. "What're you doing here?"

While Addison went over to the woman who had abandoned her and her siblings over nine years ago, Kylie stayed rooted to her chair, either unable or unwilling to stand. Maybe both.

As much as Addison wanted to rush Kylie out of the room, get her the hell away from the biggest ghost from their past, she couldn't. She had to let Kylie react and respond the way she was going to.

It took a minute, but eventually, Kylie did react. And

respond. In a big way. With her chin up, and shoulders back, she walked right past their mother and left the office without a word.

You go, girl.

Addison's mental applause halted when she saw the older woman's smile falter, however. It was unnerving. Still one of the most beautiful women in any room, their mother looked lightyears better than the last time they'd seen her because above all else, she looked…sober.

Which was probably why Addison was seeing the woman exhibit something akin to emotion over Kylie's pointed exit.

Blinking and brushing her hands down over her skirt as if to gather her composure, she turned to face Addison. "I guess I'll just have to catch up with Kylie another time. Oh, but look at you. You're so grown up now!"

Funny how that happens with kids and age…

Addison did her best to keep her feelings in check, her voice modulated. "You didn't answer me. What are you doing here, mother?"

"You've ignored my letters and emails. I was sure you'd hang up on me if I called. So I thought it best just to stop by."

The woman gave her more credit than she probably deserved. Honestly, Addison wasn't sure she'd have been able to hang up if she'd heard her voice.

"This place is just amazing, Addison. I am so proud

of all you've accomplished."

Interesting. Now that she was finally hearing the words she'd longed to hear for over half her life, Addison discovered they had no effect on her.

In a nutshell, she didn't give a flying fig what the woman thought of her. So instead of acknowledging the too-little-too-late compliment, she went with a brisk and detached: "That still doesn't explain the *reason* for your visit."

The man she'd disliked almost from the minute she'd met him walked in to join his wife then. "If you'd bothered to read the emails we sent you, you wouldn't have to ask," he said tersely, giving her his token look of disapproval.

Always working his mark. That was Sonny. He used to do this exact thing before, too, calling on his years of experience conning folks to manipulate Addison into feeling like everything was always her fault.

Yeah…not going to work anymore, asshole.

"I'm going to be generous and wait exactly ten more seconds for you to answer my question before I contact my very big security guards to escort you off my property."

God, that had felt good.

Sonny's mouth twisted into an ugly grimace for a split second before he swiftly schooled his expression with a smile. "Okay, business-only, it is. That's probably for the best because this doesn't involve you at all."

"And yet here you are in my office still not answering

my question." She picked up the phone on her desk to begin dialing.

"Kylie and Tanner have an inheritance," blurted out Lara.

Yes, the woman was officially Lara now. Not mother and certainly not 'mom' anymore.

With every passing minute, Addison continued to gain strength. "An inheritance from whom?'

"Their father." Sonny looked down his nose at her. "So like I said, this doesn't concern *you* at all."

While Addison had never cared that Kylie and Tanner were her half-siblings, she *had* cared that she never knew who her father was...because Lara hadn't known which of the many random guys she'd been having drunken hook-ups with had knocked her up.

Of course Sonny would shoot that well-aimed dagger at her chest.

"Okay then." Addison pointed to the door. "You can leave the probate lawyer's info at the reception desk and see yourself out. I have work to do."

"But..." Lara shot a panicked look at her husband. "We need you to talk to the kids for us. Tanner hasn't returned our calls or emails either. And clearly, Kylie..."

"Is your golden ticket," interrupted Alec as he strode into the office, a look of disgust marring his normally charming-cowboy features.

He gave Addison's face a quick once-over. "You

okay, babe?"

She smiled, both grateful for the assist, and even more emboldened knowing that the answer to that question was a resounding yes even *without* his assistance.

"I'm fine. Lara and Sonny were just here telling me why I 'needed' to talk to Kylie and Tanner about this mysterious inheritance."

A person would've had to be deaf not to hear those air quotes.

Another ugly scowl crossed Sonny's face.

But, this time, it wasn't directed her way. Sonny turned an angry glare at Alec. "*You.* I knew you'd lied to us."

For the first time since the pair arrived, Addison felt her composure take a hit.

"Alec, do you know him?"

The guilty expression on Alec's face was a clear answer.

"Of course he knows us," Sonny spat out. "We paid him to find you around seven years ago, but he came back to us and spun a lie about not being able to find you."

"You didn't pay me; I returned your money."

"After lying your sorry ass off about finding them! "

"Oh, that's rich." Alec was *pissed*. More furious than she'd ever seen him. "So tell me, Sonny," he sneered, contempt coating his every word, "what exactly did you tell Kylie and Tanner's dad when you broke the news that you had no clue where his children were? The *truth*?" He snorted. "No. You lied. You made up a story about the kids running away from home so he wouldn't throw your asses in jail for child neglect."

He shot them both another caustic look. "That's right, I know all about it. The P.I. you've had tailing Addison here in Phoenix the past few months has been just a fountain of information."

Addison went from shell-shocked to floored. "Someone's been tailing me for *months*? And you didn't tell me?"

Alec pulled her away from the couple and explained quietly, "He only found you a few days before the police fundraiser. Before that, he, like the other few P.I.'s Sonny's hired in the past, was chasing down all the dead-end trails I've created over the years to keep you hidden. But we didn't know for sure that it was your mom and Sonny who had hired him until yesterday."

"*We.* As in…?"

"Me and Caine."

She nodded, digesting that. "So why didn't you tell me about any of this?"

"Because we thought he might've been hired by David. So instead of confronting him right away, we've been tailing *him* for the past week and—"

Addison put her hand on his arm. "That part I get. I meant before, Alec. Sonny said he hired you seven years

165

ago. Was that before or after you offered to help me at the shelter?"

"Before," Alec admitted solemnly. "The reason why I was in Tucson to begin with was because I'd tracked you there after you went on the run."

"So you and Hale teaching self-defense workshops and advising women at the shelter, that was all part of some...cover story?"

"*No.* We genuinely wanted to help. You're what led us there, yes, but we stayed to help those women. Well, *initially.*" Alec gave her a crooked smile and a shrug, "I also stayed because I thought you were one of the most incredible women I'd ever met...and I knew I'd never be able to live with myself if something happened to you. Something I could've helped prevent."

A few feet away, an impatient Sonny snorted and rolled his eyes. "Sure, you're a regular Prince Charming. You've been lying to her the entire time you've known her."

Alec pivoted swiftly and got right up in Sonny's face. "Again, that's real rich considering why *you're* here today."

Addison narrowed her eyes at Lara. "Okay, *what* is going on? The whole truth. Why exactly did you come here today?"

"They're here to con you."

"Actually," cut in Sonny with a glare, "we have an offer that could help you."

Alrighty then, so definitely a con.

Lara finally spoke up. "The thing is, Kylie and Tanner's dad started looking for them a while ago, after he came into some money from some rich granddad who his father had had a big falling out with. That's when we hired Alec. But when Alec came back and said he couldn't find you, I sort of...lied to their father and told him they didn't want to see him. At least not at the time. I told him they were holding a grudge since he'd left them when they were little and that I'd contact him if they changed their minds. He backed off after that. But then he died late last year, and these lawyers of his told us there's a maximum time period for his heirs to claim their inheritance. And the deadline is coming up real quick."

Addison was lost. "What's the big deal? The kids just need to go meet with these lawyer folks, right? You don't need me to talk to them about that."

Alec filled in the blanks for her. "They need you to convince the kids to go along with the lie she told their dad. So she doesn't get her ass thrown in jail for child neglect."

Lara actually had the grace to look ashamed. "You all will go along with that story, right? For me?"

"What on earth makes you think we *owe* you anything? You abandoned us. Treated us like we were worthless our entire lives."

"Like I said," chimed in Sonny. "We're here to come to an agreement to help you as well. The way I see it, after the kids get their inheritance, some media journalist

167

somewhere is going to be interested in them, seeing as how the guy's granddaddy was somebody in this town. As Kylie's legal guardian, Lara could request that all the info be sealed or whatever it is lawyers do to keep it all under wraps. And we could also be sure to decline any interviews." He gave her a smug grin. "Figured, for someone who's been hiding for as long as you have, you might *appreciate* us for going that extra mile."

Alec grabbed him by the collar. "You *son of a bitch*."

"No! Alec, don't." She knew Sonny wouldn't hesitate to file an assault charge.

"Addison, they obviously know about David. And this sack of shit is willing to put you and the kids in danger just to get their cut. You *know* that's what this is all about. Since Kylie's a minor, Lara will be named the executor of her inheritance. This is all about money."

"Yeah, that sounds about right." Addison had no illusions about the situation. "But you know as well as I do that for a pay cut like that, Sonny would carry out the threat he just laid out without even blinking."

She turned to Lara. "Your husband is threatening to lead a crazed stalker straight to my doorstep. One that wants to rape me, torture me, maybe even kill me." She didn't let the tears in Lara's eyes fool her. Sympathy, guilt, shame—that wasn't the same thing as a mother's love. "You did us wrong then. Just like you're doing us wrong now. For what it's worth, I really do hope that your portion of Kylie's money will help you live with yourself."

And with that, Addison reached over to hit the button for security.

Lara and Sonny hadn't broken her before. They wouldn't break her now. "Alec, let Sonny go. He and Lara will be leaving in about a minute."

Then to Sonny, she said simply, "My lawyer will draft something up detailing this agreement we just discussed in writing. You sign it, then I'll talk to the kids. You breach it, and I'll have you both thrown in jail. Period. There will of course be a provision in it that I never see either of your two faces ever again."

Security arrived seconds later.

But Addison was long gone.

Up in her apartment, with the door shut, and the still quaking floor under her hands and knees, all her superhuman bravado dissipated. Without it, she was just a mortal woman whose mother had never loved her, whose past was continuing to haunt her.

Alec let himself in and sat down on the ground beside her. "Those two aren't worth your tears, babe. Not then, and even more so now."

She hadn't even realized she was crying.

"I think... I think a small part of me kept holding onto hope. That she'd change. That she'd want to be my mother for once in her life."

"Yeah. Seems to be a power even the worst parents in the world wield. Trust me, Hale and I have been there." He bumped his shoulder into hers comfortingly. "So even though that woman definitely doesn't deserve it, you go on and grieve for as long as you need. Don't know why, but it helps."

Strangely, getting the green light for a good cry did help. And eventually, the heart-numbing pain did start to ebb away.

…Largely in part to Alec continually looking down the hall at Kylie's closed bedroom door in total befuddlement.

When the instrumental sounds of *Summer* by Vivaldi boomed through the apartment for the third time in a row, finally, he broke. "Okay, is there a *reason* she's listening to classical music on repeat? At rock concert decibels?"

He looked so completely stumped, Addison felt the beginnings of an amused smile work its way through the dark clouds. "Whenever Kylie is working through things emotionally, she blasts Vivaldi's *Four Seasons* in her room."

"Interesting musical choice."

The smile broke through. "You know Kylie." So saying, she went over to the kitchen to prepare for her unique little sister's emergence from her room. "We've never officially talked about this musical therapy of hers, but I do my part to assist. Say she's playing *Winter*, for example. That one, I know to get out the Oreos and Nutella and be ready for a possible long talk, usually with tissues. On the other hand, *Autumn* means she wants her space. But, I make sure the pantry is ready to be raided because more often than not, she starts baking for a few hours."

"So her blasting *Summer* after seeing her deadbeat mom for the first time in almost a decade means..."

"That I need to give her an *extra*-wide berth, while keeping the pints of root beer floats coming. With an extra shot of hot fudge."

His lips twitched as he surveyed the float essentials on the counter. "Root beer from a bottle, triple chocolate ice cream, a loopy straw, and a cocktail umbrella. Didn't take Kylie for such a big drinker."

"Oh, she can knock back a few of these. The sugar hangover the next day isn't pretty, but it's part of the process. The good thing is that Kylie just isn't wired to stay upset for too long. When she finally plays *Spring*, it means the worst is over and I can close the bar down."

Alec looked back down the hall with new affection. "That girl is so wonderfully weird."

"I always say."

"You know that's all your doing, right? Everything she knows about being great, she learned from you."

An exaggeration, but a sweet one.

His voice sobered. "So when are you going to tell her about the inheritance and everything else that just happened?"

"I meant what I told Sonny. I'll call my lawyer first thing in the morning to get something drafted and have them e-deliver it over to Sonny and Lara for their signature. Once I have that, I'll video call Tanner so I can talk to them both at the same time."

Kylie came out of her room then and beelined it straight to the kitchen. Addison promptly handed her the decked out root beer float.

She took it with a grateful head tilt.

"How long before you threw them out of the office?" Just the slightest wobble, but mostly a fierce calm.

"Not that long. They want me to talk to you and Tanner about something, but I need to get some paperwork signed first. You think you're going to be at *Spring* by tomorrow?"

Kylie gusted out a heavy sigh. "No promises. But I'll do my best."

With that thoughtfully solemn declaration, she finally took a long first sip of her float. And immediately let loose a small smile. "You added caramel to this."

"Thought you could use the extra kick. Pace yourself though, that's Franny's top shelf caramel, which, as we both know, is about 100-proof sugar."

Chuckling, Kylie gave her a forehead-clunking hug before heading back to her room.

A minute later, the welcome sounds of *Autumn* filled the apartment.

"Progress." Addison went over to put the fixings for peanut butter shortbread cookies in a shopping bag.

Right on cue, Kylie emerged with her school backpack after the end of the song.

Addison held out the shopping bag. "Threw in some sprinkles; don't overdo it. Tell Taryn we'll make tacos the next time she comes over for dinner. And tell her mom I'm halfway through the book she recommended and loving it." She then shoved a cold water bottle in the side mesh pocket of the backpack and a travel pack of Kleenex in the front compartment. "Stay hydrated, and be home by nine."

Lower lip quivering, Kylie abruptly threw her arms around Addison. "You were a better mom than that woman could've ever hoped to be. And I'm thankful for you every single day."

Aw, hell. Just when she thought she was all cried out.

Meanwhile, from the living room, Alec simply shot her a big 'told-you-so' look as Kylie made her way to the door.

Later, after another few sniffles following Kylie's departure, Addison went back down to her office to shut everything down for the day with Alec shadowing her silently the entire time.

"I'm sorry I kept it a secret all these years," he said finally when she was done and locking up. "The part about your folks hiring me."

Addison joined him in the reception area where he was staring at her worriedly. "Honestly, it's really okay. I got a best friend out of it. And truth be told, if you'd told me from the start, I don't know that I would've trusted you enough for that to have happened."

"Do you?" he asked quietly. "Still trust me?"

"Alec, of course I do. Always will."

"Good."

Studying his relieved expression, she asked curiously, "How much longer do I have before the guilt wears off and you're no longer obsessing over being a hundred percent honest with me?"

"Probably another few minutes. Five, tops."

Gotta respect the guy for telling it like it was. With the clock ticking, she laid it all out there. "I want to know your honest thoughts. Do you think it'll ever work out for me and Caine? Truthfully? I'm talking David behind bars, no more nightmares, possible future white picket fence, the whole nine yards."

"I think," he replied without a beat of hesitation, "that in all my years as a P.I., I've never met a man more determined to find his target, or more determined to protect his woman. I think if anyone can make it happen for you two, it'll be Caine."

He nodded over to the front entrance. "Plus, he apparently has that whole Casanova thing to keep you happy in the meantime, so there is that."

She spun around and gasped when she saw a delivery boy approach with the biggest bouquet of flowers she'd seen outside of a funeral.

"So my final answer to your question is yes babe, I do believe it'll eventually work out for you two." He plopped a smiling kiss on her cheek. "And I'm damn happy he makes you happy because I can't think of anyone who deserves it more."

After he went off to grab a bite at the dining hall, Addison waited all of two seconds before rushing the floral arrangement back up to her place so she could properly swoon over it in private. She barely made it past her front door before she carefully opened the attached card.

Only to have the vase slip through her fingers and shatter on the ground a moment later.

The flowers weren't from Caine.

CHAPTER 12

IT'D TAKEN a number of tries over the weeks, but Caine no longer jumped instantly to DEFCON 5 alert status whenever Addison called. At least not fully. Or outwardly.

That said, he still hadn't managed to master the whole civilized saying hello thing whenever he saw her number on his caller ID though.

"What's wrong?" Caine stopped mid-stride to answer his phone on the first ring, forcing oncoming officers to swerve around him in the busy hallway.

He heard her hesitate before asking quietly, "Is this a bad time?"

Telling himself to remain calm and not go all half-cocked until he knew why she was calling him at work, he drew in a breath and replied in as even a tone as possible, "My shift is almost over; it's been a pretty slow day. Now

I repeat. What's. Wrong?"

"I-I need to show you something. In person."

"I'll be right there."

"No, wait. I'm not at home. I'm actually at your precinct."

"I know. I'm heading down to the lobby right now to clear you in."

"How do you…" She sighed. "Did you *lo-jack* me again?"

"Honey, I think we both know you won't like my answer to that." He got downstairs a few heartbeats later to sign her in.

As they made their way across the main floor, he studied all the signs of distress she was displaying, watched her hands shake and repeatedly fumble with the clip on her visitor's badge.

On her third failed attempt, he officially snapped. "Come here."

Tugging her toward the privacy of the emergency stairwell, he pulled her into his arms and just held her as her body continued to tremble in silent terror.

A full minute passed before she could finally whisper, *"He's back."*

Even though Caine had been expecting it, the words still hit him like a grenade to his gut, detonating rage and fear of the most violent, helpless kind all through his system.

"Tell me everything that happened."

"H-he sent me f-flowers. And this." She dragged a crumpled envelope out from the front pocket of her jeans.

It was an envelope Caine recognized well. Had a matching set of seven of his own.

After he managed to pry the evidence out from her fingers, he was surprised to find a photo inside the envelope instead of a note. Even more unexpected was that the photo was of him, outside of the florist where he'd ordered the wrist corsage for Addison.

"H-he's been watching you." The moment the words left her lips, she began rubbing the cuffs of her sweatshirt sleeves over her arms as if trying to wipe away something oily, foul. Unwelcome. "And he wanted me to *know* he's been watching you."

That much was obvious.

Unlike his own yearly notes from David—with its serial-killer-lettering-on-white-paper simplicity—this picture had a lot more to say. Namely, via the big jagged X's over his eyes, done so violently that the photo paper was gouged out almost all the way through.

Even the message included on the photo was different. The straight-out-of-a-horror-movie colorful alphabet cutouts were the same, but the wording was less taunt, more demand.

STAY AWAY FROM HIM

Analyzing it quickly, his main takeaway was that David was starting to slip up. And he told Addison so.

"How can you possibly tell that from this awful picture?"

"I've seen a lot of threatening letters over the years, sweetheart. And this one has a ton of clues all over it."

That made her breathing steady a little. "Show me?"

He nodded and began going over the small details one by one. The photo was clearly taken through a vehicle's windshield, which gave them location, day, and time so—that was all Drew would need to hack into a surveillance footage to hopefully find the vehicle. The visible agitation displayed in the gouged-out parts of the photo was also an important clue. "The guys and I will study this more, but I can already tell you by the timing and nature of this photo, he's pissed as hell at me."

Addison frowned. "Isn't that a given? He hated you even back in Creek Hills."

"But this is different. He could've chosen any photo, specifically, a more recent one. But he didn't. He's been sitting on this one for a few weeks. Fuming about it. And on the photo, it's clearly me he wants to harm. He's not threatening to punish you; he's threatening to punish *me*. Which is good. That means he still doesn't want to hurt you."

"But he *does* want to hurt *you*." Her face paled

again, even as her eyes narrowed with the same fierce protectiveness she displayed over her siblings.

"Better me than you. I'll buy flowers at that shop every day and twice on Sunday if it'll keep his violence focused on me and not you."

He closed his hand over hers and walked her up to the break room by the lockers. "Sit for a bit while I finish up here. I've got to go see my captain." Waving over a fellow officer he'd known from police academy days. "Addison, this is my buddy Grayson. Good cop. Scorpio. Currently in love with a woman half the guys on the force think he has no chance with."

"Thanks, man," called back a not-at-all-upset Grayson as he joined them.

"Hey, I'm on the half that thinks you've got a shot."

Grayson turned to her. "Is he this invasive in your life?"

That brought on her first smile since she'd arrived. Caine shot Grayson a silent thanks.

"The fact that Caine hasn't let me meet you until now should answer that question."

Grayson shook his head at her appreciatively. "Can't say I blame him."

For once, Caine wasn't *too* bothered about leaving Addison with another guy, mostly because in Grayson's case, the man really was completely smitten over another woman.

That said, the part he wasn't all that thrilled about, however, was—

"So did Caine ever tell you about the time a buck naked guy fell out of a tree—high as a kite and covered in baby oil—and landed right on top of Caine like a spider monkey in heat?"

Caine grunted in annoyance. *Couldn't even wait until I left the room.*

Just so happened that Grayson had been on scene with him during the top three weirdest cases he'd ever responded to. All of which had required him to have his uniform dry cleaned...with extra special solvents to get out stains he never wanted to think about again.

Addison's eyes began dancing with amusement. She sat with him on the break couch and asked curiously, "By 'on top' did the man land on Caine's back?"

No. He hadn't.

Caine shuddered at the reminder of the man the guys at the station had dubbed the Viagra monkey. For reasons he'd blocked out of his memory.

"So wait," broke in Addison, interrupting Grayson's storytelling, "you're saying a *second guy* fell out of the tree onto Caine's back?"

Criminy, he could've done without that traumatic reminder.

He swiftly exited the room before Grayson could bring up why Caine had stopped eating bananas as well.

About a half hour later, Caine returned to the break room in his civvies to see Addison laughing so hard that tears were streaming down her cheeks.

Relieved, and grateful to say the least, Caine joined them and shot Grayson a silent nod of thanks.

Wiping her eyes, she went over to give Grayson a hug. "Thanks for keeping me company. I'm telling you, if your baker girl doesn't see what an amazing thing she has standing right in front of her, then it's her loss. You give me a call if she ends up being that foolish. It'll take half a day, tops, for me to get you the names of a few dozen women who'll happily give me a spare organ for a chance to go out with you. No joke."

Grayson tossed Caine a look on his way out. "If Sophie shoots me down, and you don't marry this one within a year, I may ask her myself. Just saying."

Jesus, was there *no one* loyal to him where Addison was concerned?

On that note, Caine handed her a giant, baggy department sweatshirt that engulfed her from neck to knees. Seeing as how Grayson was the *least* houndish guy in the building, it really was a necessary precaution. "Put that on. I want to give you a quick tour, and the AC's always cold downstairs," he reasoned half-truthfully.

"What's downstairs?"

He treaded carefully as he explained, "I know you're not a fan of guns, and if you hate it, we'll stop...but, given the situation, it'll give me some peace of mind to take you down to the shooting range so I can arm you with some basics. I'd take you to the Spencer Securities range, but it's more for larger firearms, and whatever crazy covert weapon Gabe is cooking up. The one here is way less intense." He paused to study her expression. "You up for this?"

She hated the idea, he could tell. But, she was giving it careful thought though, which was something.

"Can we practice with a pellet gun?"

That gentle heart of hers was going to be the death of him. "No, honey. We don't use pellet guns at this range."

Her face fell.

"You know what, forget I brought it up. We can skip the range and—"

"I'll try it," she interrupted softly.

Holy shit.

He couldn't believe she was actually agreeing to target practice. Just the other day, he'd watched the adorable woman squash a giant scorpion and then sadly scoop it up to go bury it outside by some pretty flowers.

As if hearing his amazement out loud, she added quickly, "I only want to learn enough so I don't shoot off my own foot by accident. I don't want to blow David's brains out or anything. Maybe just...one of his knees so he falls and stays down until you get there and beat the daylights out of him?"

Adorable, adorable woman.

"I'm fairly certain I'm going to be really bad at this," she warned.

"You'll do great, sweets. It's not really all that difficult."

A fairly quick half hour later, he had a well-prepped, kitten-fierce Addison staring down a bullseye.

Gently removing his hands from her shoulders, he murmured what soothing words he could, and stepped to the side. "Go for it, sweetheart. Remember everything I taught you."

Jaw set in determination, brows lowered at the target, she took a breath to steady her shaking hands. Then went completely trigger-happy, emptying out a full round in mere seconds.

Unbelievable.

...He stared at her in shock when her gun clicked empty.

"What?" She pulled off her earmuffs and protective glasses.

He was speechless.

Pushing a button to bring the target sheet closer, he peered at it to make sure he wasn't seeing things. "Addison, in all those shots, you didn't come remotely close to hitting the target once," he informed her in utter amazement. "Honey, you didn't even hit the paper."

He would've laughed if he weren't so perplexed. "Even by *accident*, you should've landed a shot somewhere." He checked the bullets to make sure they weren't blanks. "Did you square off like I told you to, aim the way I showed you?"

She gave him a disappointed nod, then scrunched her nose. "Told you I'd be bad at this."

There was bad, and there was *impossibly* bad. "Sweetie, can you *see* the target?" Maybe she needed distance glasses. Or complete Lasik eye surgery.

"Of course I can see the target."

That's when he caught her playing with her pinky nail. One of her many cute tells that made her a horrible liar. "Tell me the truth, babe, are you shutting your eyes before you pull the trigger?"

Her entire face turned bright red, and a defensive pout made an appearance. *"Possibly."*

He sighed. "You and your sunshine and goodness."

Kissing the tip of her nose while safely disarming her of the firearm that would be as useful as an indiscriminate rock in her hand, he came up with a Plan B. "C'mon, let's head to the workout gym. I think some basic self-defense moves might be more your speed."

As they made their way over to the gym, she finally asked the question he'd been waiting to hear since she arrived at the precinct, "You think he's coming for me soon, don't you?"

"Yes." Caine had to grit his teeth to keep from punching the wall when dread filled her expression. "But I won't let him near you, Addison." Voice hardening with conviction, he added gravely, "I'll stop him. And this time, I *won't* be aiming to arrest him."

"What do you mean?"

Surprisingly, it wasn't difficult to say the next part. "Earlier, when I went to go see my captain after you got here, I turned in my gun and badge."

Her eyes snapped up to his in horror. "Caine, *no.*"

"It's done. He told me he's not officially accepting my resignation until the morning, but I'm not changing my mind. Now, I don't need to pick between keeping my oath as an officer and keeping you in my life by whatever means necessary." He slid both of his hands through her hair. "Now, I can do what I need to do to keep you safe."

"I-I can't let you do that for me."

"Believe me, I'm doing this as much for me." His tone roughened as he did his best to find the right words. "My whole adult life, it was like there was something missing, but not truly lost until the day I came home and found you and the kids gone. Disappeared without a trace. I didn't know if you were alive. And it *gutted* me. Left a gaping wide cavity in my chest where my heart used to be."

Her face crumbled. Voice splintering with pain, she whispered hoarsely, "I'm so sorry, Caine. I will never, ever forgive myself for putting you through that—"

"There's nothing to forgive. You were being you. Thinking about me, about my career, my honor. But what you failed to consider back then is that you meant more to me than all of that combined. And honey, that's even more the case now. So let me return the favor this time around. Let *me* protect *you*. Let me be me."

"But being an officer *is* who you are. You love being a cop."

"I love you more."

Her breathing hitched.

His did too.

Heart rammed up somewhere by this throat, he watched her simply refuse to let any words fall from her lips while she studied his gaze. Intently. As if expecting him to take back his confession.

Never.

Tears came to her eyes.

"Happy tears or sad tears, baby?" The feeling of déjà vu hit him like a wrecking ball.

Thankfully, as was the case seven years ago, she didn't leave him wondering for long. Slipping her hands behind his neck, she gave him the answer he needed more than his next heartbeat, via one *hell* of a kiss.

…At the end of which, she also gave him the words he'd waited a long damn time to hear.

"I love you too, Caine."

His arms instantly locked around her. "You just

sealed your fate, sweetheart." Voice now a deep, throbbing mass of emotions, he told her plainly, "No more debates about me quitting the force. I may return after all this is over, or I may transition fully to Spencer Securities. I don't know yet. All I know is that no matter what I do, I can't, *won't* lose you again, Addison."

Face buried against her neck, lips *needing* to find and feel her beating pulse, he murmured raggedly, "Because if I did, I'd be a man not just lost, not just broken. But decimated beyond saving."

CHAPTER 13

ADDISON FELT her heart slam against her ribs and just plain stop working.

Until she felt his five o'clock shadow rub over her skin, that is. Then her heartrate went haywire. Bombarded feelings, sensory overload. It was almost too much.

But more so, *not enough*.

He pulled back, gaze unguarded, expression more possessive than ever. "No tempting me with those sex kitten noises." Gruff and hungry, his voice was pure sex in a growl. "First I need to see how well Alec has trained you to defend yourself."

This time, the sound that escaped her was one of mild distress.

"What'd I just say, woman?"

Why was all this barely restrained control of his so

intensely sexy?

"Caine, the thing is, I'm just not that good at martial arts eith—"

The words lodged itself in her windpipe when she saw Caine drag his t-shirt over his head as they stepped foot into the gym and headed straight for the sparring mats.

Just like that, she forgot everything she was about to say.

And possibly everything she'd ever said in all of existence.

Caine shirtless, barefoot, and casually walking around in an old pair of jeans...lordy, that was a good look on him. In uniform, he was fantasy-inspiring, no doubt, but this scruffy, laidback, ready-to-neck-on-the-couch look?

Wow.

"If you keep looking at me like that, I'll be sporting wood soon. Which will be dangerous when we grapple for a couple of different reasons." He took her phone and keys and stuffed it into a nearby locker with his own things. "You start stretching. I'll go grab us some gloves and pads for warm-up drills."

That served as a splash of lukewarm water in her face, and other parts of her that benefitted from the cooldown. "Um...could we maybe skip those drills and go straight to grappling?" Hand-to-hand combat just wasn't in her wheelhouse.

He frowned. "Ideally, I want you able to fight David

off *before* he has a chance to get you onto the ground. Didn't you work on boxing basics with Alec?"

"It's not his fault."   Addison had of course participated in a number of self-defense workshops over the years back at the women's shelter in Tucson. And God knows Alec and Hale had tried their best to work with her as well. But she'd been, at best, comic relief for everyone in attendance. "Caine, I just really suck at it." She shrugged helplessly. "You know those girls you see on TV who punch like their shoulders and elbows and brain have lost communication, who swing like they're drunk, and juke like they have absolutely no sense of rhythm? Yeah…even *those* girls would make fun of how awful I am."

Caine's eyes crinkled at the corners. "It can't be that bad."

"Ohhh, but it is."

"Honey, back at Joe's Diner when David first tried to attack you, you were ready to slice and dice him with meat cleavers from the kitchen."

"Totally different situation. That was pure instinct. But without fear and adrenaline suppressing all my natural *in*abilities, I'm afraid I lack the aggression, and more importantly, the *coordination*, to even land a decent punch." Following him out onto the padded floor, she added on the bright side, "But apparently, I'm very good at kicking. That's why I asked Alec and his brother Hale to teach me a little of that kicking-like-a-roach-on-its-back style of MMA defensive fighting. I actually got pretty good at it, too."

Caine stopped and gaped at her like she was shitting him.

"My point is that I'm not *totally* hopeless." She looked around for an open area she could lie down on to demonstrate her mad cockroach techniques. "You should probably be wearing a cup if we're going to do this though because one time—"

"Sweetheart." Caine looked like he was struggling not to laugh his ass off. "Why don't I just see what we're working with? Come here and show me a punch."

She sighed. "Okay."

Was it just her, or did it get really quiet in the gym all of a sudden?

Calling on all her past lessons, and doing some last-second visualizations of Wonder Woman in battle, she balled up her fist and let it rip.

Sort of.

To his credit, Caine didn't laugh when her rabbit punch barely tapped him. "Not bad. But you need to put your hips into it, plant your feet and pivot at your core. Take a full swing. Try again. Just go a hundred percent. You won't hurt me."

He asked for it.

Curling both her hands in front of her face like she had a clue what she was doing, she wound up, and unleashed an epic, wide-sweeping roundhouse punch with her right that—in her mind—was going in movie-slow-mo for a massive fist-to-jaw showdown.

But in reality, whiffled right past him.

Her momentum after the missed punch sent her spinning like a figure skater on ice. And if not for Caine catching her wrist when her body made an entire revolution around, she probably would've knocked herself out with her own forearm.

"Um." He had no words.

She hid in her comfortable heap on the ground for as long as she could.

When she eventually pulled up her big girl panties and peeked out from between her fingers, she saw him glaring down everyone in the room.

My hero.

"My fault for telling you to take a swing," he graciously took the blame as he helped her to her feet. "I think you should stick to short jabs for now."

My sweet, delusional hero.

That one, she apparently said out loud because he just smiled and gave her an atta-girl coach's butt pat. "C'mon. Let's keep trying."

His next pat was decidedly un-coach like. And all the more effective because of it.

They practiced for another half-hour or so, during which time, no one laughed, and she actually managed to clock him once in the chin at the end.

"Hey, that was pretty good." He grinned, loosening out his jaw. "How'd that feel?"

She frowned.

His eyes grew troubled. "Is all this upsetting you? Do you want to work on more defensive moves instead?"

"No, no. That's not it. The punch felt great. Kind of empowering, really."

A pleased and proud smile tipped his mouth up at one corner. "There's my kick-ass girl. So then why'd you look upset just now?"

Oy. She shifted her eyes up to the ceiling to avoid his. "When I punched you just now, I was aiming for your chest, not your face."

The laughter he'd been keeping impressively bottled-up this entire time finally broke free.

"Here I thought you couldn't get any cuter." He wrapped a brawny arm around her and put a gloved hand under her chin. "On that note, I think that's enough training for today."

"But..." She sighed in frustration. "I'm still really bad."

"We'll keep practicing every day. No worries, you'll get there. And in the meantime—" His eyes melted to a molten dark chocolate. "Guess that means I can't ever leave your side." Brows raised a wicked inch, he added huskily, "That definitely works for me."

"No."

He blinked in disbelief. "What?"

"I said no. You have other, *bigger* things to stress over. Like a madman gouging your eyes out in photos." Unstrapping her gloves, she gave him a determined look. "I'll keep working on my own day and night. And I'll look into other ways to protect myself. You said it yourself; David wants to hurt *you*. So don't go spending your time worrying about me. Let me worry about that."

A low, combative growl rumbled out of him.

"Growl all you want, but I don't want you to think that my safety is all on you. You need to stop looking at me all the time like a victimized woman who needs constant protection."

"And *you* need to stop thinking that's the only reason I never take my eyes off you," he grated out in a wholly riled rumble. One quick tug and she was strapped up in his vise-like arms, his gaze roaming her face like she was a work of art he was trying to understand. "Sweetheart, I don't look at you and see a victimized woman who needs saving. I look at you and see *my* woman, the one who needs to stay alive so I can spend the rest of my life with her."

Oh. Well, when he put it that way... "I'm sorry I'm not better at defending myself."

He pressed his lips to her temple. "Don't stress yourself out. Like you said, when the adrenaline is going, it'll be different. Your inner badass will come out. I guarantee it."

"Maybe with the fighting. But the gun thing…"

He waited patiently, just stroking her back.

"The reason I'm bad with guns is because it takes all my strength not to shake while holding it in my hands, all my concentration not to jump and drop it after hearing the shot."

Concerned, he tilted her face up to his. "I thought this was just because you were a pacifist. Sweetheart, are you afraid of guns?"

She took in a shuddery breath. "Deathly. At a few places my mom and I lived, there would be guys pulling guns on each other almost every other night, seemed like. My mom was always too high to care, or even remember. For me, I was always terrified." She squeezed her eyes shut to block out the visuals. "At one house we lived in—before Tanner was born—there was this little area under the stairs that was closed on three sides where I'd curl up and hide every night."

Her body started quaking from the memories.

The sound of Caine murmuring softly in her ear managed to keep her talking. "Since I was only in grade school, I was the only one in the house small enough to fit under there so I always thought I was safe. But then one night, when I was crawling in like usual, I heard a click, and then a gun getting shoved at my forehead. A tweaked-out high school kid started going off at me, stark-raving mad, accusing me of trying to take his stuff from his room."

Clenching her fists, Addison willed herself not to cry over something that hadn't even turned out badly. "I'd never seen anyone get shot or anything, but still, having that gun in my face, with the shooter on a bad trip... I just...I thought I was going to die. The gun was maybe an inch away from me, and it seemed *huge*. Cold, and metal, and so....real. Nothing like on TV."

When Caine's granite-like frame started vibrating with rage, she quickly skipped ahead to the end of her story, "Luckily, someone crashed into something against the stairwell and I was able to get the heck out of there. It wasn't until I was a little older when it really sunk in that the loud noise could've startled the kid and made him pull the trigger. That's why now, when I see a gun, I sort of freeze up and picture my face getting blown to bits." She dropped her gaze away. "Silly fear, I know, seeing as nothing even happened."

"Jesus Christ, Addison. Why the hell didn't you tell me? Why'd you let me put a gun in your hand?" His hands slid through her hair, cradling her head on either side as he tucked her in against his chest. "I am so sorry that happened to you, sweetheart. So sorry I made you re-live it." He cursed under his breath. "I'd never have brought you to the range had I known."

"It's fine. You didn't trigger a repressed memory or anything, Caine. Honest. A lot of it was just getting used to seeing a gun again that close. It's been awhile. The housing complex has a no-weapons policy—even the guards only have stun guns and tasers. Alec is the only one with a firearm on site, but he keeps it locked up, or concealed under a jacket whenever he's around me."

Caine exhaled harshly. "I know it's not rationale or fair, but it drives me crazy that he knows things about you that I don't."

She gazed into his sad eyes. "I promise, you know a lot of things about me that he doesn't."

"Somehow I doubt that. Hate to admit it, but the guy's a good P.I. He knows it all."

Shaking her head, she placed a hand against his rugged, sandpapery jaw. "He doesn't know where I'm ticklish, or how to hold me so everything around just disappears." Closing her eyes when she felt Caine's arms do just that, she added softly, "And he doesn't know how to kiss me in that way you do that makes me forget my own name."

When his eyes dropped down to her lips like a magnet, she smiled, unable to resist, "Then again, Alec hasn't kissed me, so I don't really have a basis for comparison."

And just like that, she got herself good and kissed. Until she forgot her name. And the name of the guy they were just talking about.

Caine kissed her so deeply, so *elementally*, it was like

the remaining air in her lungs had no choice but to morph into a wispy vapor with his name on it when she finally exhaled.

"Damn, I've missed hearing you purr my name." His entire body was now a solid rock wall...with a giant parking brake pushing up against her belly. "See what you do to me, woman?"

She really wanted to. See, that is. "Can I?"

"Can you what, honey?"

Fighting back a blush, she said as bold as can be, "Can I see? You? Back at my place?"

———◆———

CAINE RELEASED a rough, ragged groan.

Instead of attempt a reply—which would no doubt involve some sort of dangerous show and tell deal—he crashed his lips against hers again to drag a few more soft, sexy purrs out of her.

Of course, the mind-wrecking kiss just rattled the iron restraints he was holding back his hunger with. "I'll follow you back to your place. Is Kylie asleep already?"

In an instant, Addison's eyes went from hazy to amused. "It's only eight p.m. She's still over at her friend's house on site." Her brows furrowed then as if she'd just realized a doozy of a conundrum. "And she'll be back in an hour. Which means we can't actually do anyth—"

He grazed her thumb over her lush lips to stop her from finishing that sentence. "I'm coming over to your place," he repeated, in a low voice he hardly recognized. "But not to finish this." His free hand instantly flexed against her hip, in clear defiance of the rational decisions his brain was making.

But he held firm. "We're not finishing this until I'm the one and only man on your mind."

She gave him a startled frown. "You already are."

"Nope. David's in there too." His forehead fell to hers. "But not for long. We're getting him the hell out of our lives once and for all." He grabbed their stuff from the locker and led her back out to the main hallway. "C'mon. I'll text Gabe on the way to meet us at your apartment. Drew can loop in online."

"You're going to have one of your dude squad meetings at my house? *Tonight?*"

No sense sugar-coating it. "Now that we have confirmation David is on this side of the border again, there's no better time for us to start hunting."

Down by the guest stalls next to the main entrance, he stopped her before she could get into her car. Crowding her against her door, he felt a primal part of him howl with satisfaction when she all but melted against him on contact. "Thirty-minute drive ahead of us," he murmured as the perfectly rational reasoning for his actions. "Gonna need a proper kiss to tide me over."

His lips were on hers before she could blush. Lordy, he could get drunk off of her kisses. The breathy sounds she made. The shy, quickly retreating swipes of her tongue. The way she'd gasp every so often and open her eyes to stare into his for a beat before dropping her lids back closed on a sigh. All of it made him nuts.

It was a long, gratifyingly oxygen-deprived minute before he managed to yank his lips off of hers. And that was only because her curious hands had started getting in on the insanity-inspiring fun by skimming a slow, hesitant path from his chest to his abs...

He caught her hands before she made it any lower. "You're killing me here."

Full, kiss-swollen lower lip between her teeth, she unconsciously leaned into him more, pressing all her soft curves against every one of his hard inches. As if she couldn't stop herself.

He wrenched back like she'd stroked him with a live wire. At this rate, he'd be cited for public indecency. In front of a police station, no less.

"Put that thing away, Spencer, before you hurt someone with it," ribbed a voice from the top of the steps belonging to a cop from homicide with a pack-a-day rasp he'd recognize anywhere.

"Hey man, when'd you start packing a mini-revolver in your pocket?" called out another highly entertained voice from the gathering group. Definitely Grayson.

Caine flipped him off and hollered back, "A long time before you learned how to use that pez dispenser you play genie in the magic lamp with."

A riot of rowdy male hysterics echoed behind him.

"I'm getting you back for this, sweetheart."

She had the audacity to look offended. "*You* kissed *me*, remember. So don't go blaming that bazooka busting through your zipper on me, buddy."

Damn, he liked her feisty. "But *you're* the one who turned it into a dare again with that sexy body of yours." He helped her into her seat and buckled her in. "So I repeat, I'm getting you back for this."

Wide, openly intrigued eyes looked up at him. "Then I guess it's a good thing you didn't have to turn in your cuffs with your gun and badge. Could come in handy..."

"*Jesus Christ*, woman."

An utterly unapologetic, utterly female smile was her only reply.

CHAPTER 14

AS SOON AS they got back to her apartment, Addison went straight to the kitchen to get a pot of coffee going. Even though she hadn't brewed her special blend since Creek Hills, she did have all the fixings for it...on account of all the necessary ingredients—along with a coffee maker—having hopped into her grocery cart on her way home the day Caine had pulled her over.

"Why is your door unlocked?" demanded the ferocious, thundery storm cloud of male protectiveness she'd left outside sometime after his inspection of the elevator's security system, and before his muttering complaints about the fire escape access. Not waiting for a response, he dropped a big black SWAT team looking duffle on her floor with a thud before proceeding to head right back out the door with his trusty compact cop notepad

flipped open.

She hadn't realized how much she'd missed seeing Caine use an old school writing pad over that fancy tablet computer docked in his Phoenix patrol car. Idly, she wondered if he still had the one he used to use back in Creek Hills, with the notes he'd jotted down the time he'd wanted to find out more about Kylie and Tanner before taking them to the movies.

Still one of her favorite memories.

"Sweetheart, I know you trust everyone on the property, but it's still not safe," he broke into her thoughts, for once, not reading her mind. "And having a restricted elevator access code to this floor doesn't mean you can forego the deadbolt either."

He glared at the chain lock on her door next, flicking his pen at the ridiculously bulky, fully reinforced, cut-resistant steel chain on steroids like its mere presence offended him. "*What* was Alec thinking when he approved *this* flimsy-ass thing?"

Ten bucks says he'll have a new titanium door with a retinal and handprint scanner installed by tomorrow.

She waited until he was done doing a visual sweep of the hallway, before informing him, "Wasn't me that left the door unlocked."

Alec popped his head up like a gopher from the couch, where he'd been lazily lounging with a magazine. "Oh yeah, that was me."

Caine got downright grizzly. "Cripes, don't you *ever* go home?"

"And miss out on these delightful moments with you?" Alec flashed him a toothy grin.

Addison shook her head. "I swear, if not for the fact that I'm actually glad you two have each other to expend all your excessive alpha energy, I'd be a little jealous of this bromance you two have got starting."

Caine snorted incredulously. "He should be so lucky. Also, I'm pretty sure your boy there has a big ole dude crush on Gabe and all his gadgets."

Gabe walked in behind Caine. "Heard my name. What'd I do now?"

Alec didn't miss a beat. "Addison thinks Caine has been pulling my hair and kicking the back of my chair in class because he likes-me-likes-me. Caine, on the other hand, was just telling Addison that he thinks I'm man-lovin' on you." He shrugged and exchanged the magazine for the TV remote. "If those are my only two choices, guess I'm going with you, Gabe. At least you're not *quite* so ancient and curmudgeonly."

Gabe dropped a duffle bag similar to Caine's and gave Alec a big thumbs-up. "Wise choice. I've been trying to get Addison to see how ancient Caine is and trade him in for a newer, better model." He redirected his outstretched thumb to his own chest.

Caine looked ready to throttle them both.

These guys are all nuts. But highly entertaining.

Gabe looked over at what she was doing in the kitchen and gave her a grateful smile. "Oh good, coffee. I've been working till dawn the past few days. I'd kill for some caffeine right now."

"Addison doesn't drink coffee," called out Alec from the couch as he turned on the TV and began surfing the channels. "She only has tea."

Caine's brows shot up in surprise, as a very obvious, very pleased, very *possessive* grin spread across his face.

Addison pivoted without a word and began filling water in the coffee pot with all the super focused attention the difficult task required.

Totally unaware, Gabe planted himself on a barstool and tossed a quizzical look Alec's way. "What're you talking about? Caine used to sport some pretty serious caffeine wood over Addison's coffee back in Creek Hills. I've been dying to try it."

Alec shot up off the couch, shocked and wholly offended. "She's never made *me* coffee before."

Caine's eyes were positively dancing now. To his credit though, he didn't rub it in. He simply went over to set up his laptop on the dining table while Alec joined Gabe in the kitchen and watched her add her special ingredients to the coffee grounds as if she were milking a unicorn jumping over the moon.

Caine didn't come over to the kitchen until the

coffee was done, and she was through pouring out all the mugs. Even then, he waited until she was lifting her own mug up to her lips before he took his first sip...staring hotly at her the entire time.

How the man managed to make *that* flirty and dirty was beyond her.

A second later, their silently charged moment was shattered by the sound of Gabe and Alec groaning in bliss.

"I can't *believe* you kept this coffee from me all these years," complained Alec, truly and thoroughly indignant.

Meanwhile Gabe simply asked her again why she wouldn't even *consider* his multiple offers of marriage.

At least those were the snippets she caught them saying. Really, it was a feat that she managed to hear anything with her ears buzzing and every female cell in her body shouting at her to jump Caine this instant.

"Keep that water hot for me, sweets. I'm definitely going to want more of this throughout the night."

Evil, evil man with his double and triple entendres.

A beeping from the computer sounded then, and Caine's foster brother Drew came onto the screen. "Hey guys, sorry I'm late. Hey Addison."

She welcomed the reprieve. "Hey Drew." Avoiding Caine's panty-melting gaze, she escaped to the dining table to her conversational savior. "How goes everything at that fancy computer college of yours? You're not breaking too many hearts are you?"

Drew's ears reddened a bit—man, this was a hi-def video connection—but he just laughed off her compliment. "Been focused on school, mostly. You look great, by the way. And I've heard you're doing some amazing things with that housing complex. Let me know if I can help with anything."

Honestly, her brother Tanner was very much the epitome of a young gentleman and all, but Drew had to be without a doubt the most charming college boy on the planet. If she hadn't personally witnessed him break into a few dozen high-security websites back in Creek Hills, she would've called George Washington himself a liar if he'd said Drew was capable of such a thing.

"You be sure to come by and give me a hug the next time you're in town visiting your brothers and Lia, you hear?"

"Already planned on it. I'll bring some things from Texas back for Kylie and Tanner, too."

Seriously, the kid needed to run for president or something.

"Okay, Caine. Lay it on us." Gabe finally relinquished his empty mug to go zip open his duffle. "Now that David's made the first strike back in town, what's our next move?"

"I already turned in my badge and weapon to my captain today. I'll obviously still carry a sidearm, but just as private security detail for Spencer Securities. Without my police clearances, we'll be limited to Alec's P.I. contacts and privileges." He turned to the computer monitor. "So Drew, I'll need you to hack into every department and government database I pretended not to know about before. Max will have eyes on Tanner in California, and Lia will be in charge of Kylie here. Gabe, whatever extra tech you can arm us with, I'll welcome it. And Marco is on standby to jump in to provide muscle whenever we need him. Aside from a big court case I was subpoenaed to testify in the next few weeks, I'll be here 24-7."

The guys nodded solemnly. All the while, Addison couldn't help but get choked up. "You all shouldn't have to turn your whole lives upside down for this."

"Caine would do the same thing for us," reasoned Gabe.

"And so would you, and you know it," argued Alec.

Drew was clicking and clacking away. "I've been helping Caine chase this guy on and off for seven years. No way in hell am I sitting out now."

As the guys proceeded to communicate in security-speak for the next ten minutes, Addison discovered there was a whole, far more intense level of alpha-protectiveness to Caine. "You're not going to start staking out the complex every night or something are you?"

"*Start?*" Alec rolled his eyes. "What do you think he's been doing every spare night since the day he pulled you over? Seriously, the guy sleeps less than you do, babe."

Surprised, she shot her gaze over to Caine, who simply shrugged and nodded over at his duffle bag. "By the way, I'm moving in until all this is over."

Addison's surprise turned to supreme misgivings over his mental state when she realized he wasn't talking to her, but rather, to Alec.

"With *me*?!" Alec balked in horror. "Why do *I* have to suffer? More importantly, why the *hell* did Gabe hand you a giant dildo after hearing that?"

"You know," remarked Addison, now more amused than anything else, "these manly men meetings are way more interesting than I thought they'd be."

"It looks like the real thing, doesn't it?" broke in Gabe proudly, waving the dildo.

"Are you really wanting me to answer that?" replied Alec, avoiding eye contact with it completely.

"Not a real dick, you dick. A real dildo."

"It's not one?" Curiosity drew his gaze back.

"Nope. It's our newest security device." Gabe started pulling out a few more space-age looking gizmos and gadgets, along with some other standard household things. "Just like you taught Addison back in Tucson, hiding things in plain sight is half the battle."

She almost spewed out the sip of coffee she'd just taken when she saw him squeeze the base of the dildo to activate a crackling, electric blue spark at the tip.

Caine just sighed. "Are you serious with that thing?"

Gabe grinned. "Dude, I just introduced the stun gun dildo to our Spencer Security market site and it's already on track to becoming one of our best sellers. Unlike a gun or any other defensive weapon, no intruder would think anything otherwise seeing this on a nightstand. And the second the user squeezes the stun gun trigger, the dildo will alert our emergency response system. There's a two-way speaker at the base, which our operators can tie into to communicate with the user and gauge the situation to see if they need to ward off any additional intruders by emitting an alarm or a warning that the authorities are already on their way."

Caine had always said his little brother was a genius...

Gabe aimed the dildo at Addison like a big pointer finger and wagged it. "Just make sure you don't mix it up with one of your real ones. For obvious safety reasons."

Twin flags of heat burned her cheeks. "I don't *have* a real one of those."

Suddenly, the front door lock turned.

"Hey everyone," called out Kylie, tossing her keys and backpack on the dining table.

Wow. Addison had never seen three grown men turn beet red like that before.

In the blink of an eye, they became three giant boys attempting to conceal a dirty magazine, each trying to shove and toss the dildo at the other, in the most hysterical game of Hot Potato ever.

Meanwhile, Drew was hunched over on the screen with the audio feed now off, very likely to mute the hilarity shaking his shoulders.

Kylie eyed them all curiously. "What's going on?"

"Nothing!" they called out in unison.

"Yeah, that's not suspicious at all." She came closer, but instead of grilling them further, she simply pecked them each on the cheek.

Which prompted the three guys to work *together* now, in an impressively efficient choreography of hand-offs behind their backs.

So freaking funny.

Finally, it ended up shoved into Caine's bag and casually kicked a few feet away.

Kylie came over to hug Addison last. "Do I *want* to know?" she asked.

"Nope," confirmed Addison. "I sorta wish *I* didn't know."

"Okay, then. I'm going to bed so you guys can continue to be twitchy and weird without any more interruptions." She waved at Drew and made her way across the living room.

Halfway down the short hallway, however, she stopped and looked around, eyes darting up at the ceiling and floors. "Does anyone else hear that buzzing sound?"

Alec and Gabe made a run for it.

They scooped up Caine's bag and took off, sprinting toward Alec's apartment like they were holding a ticking time bomb.

Drew logged off without a word, leaving them with a snowy black screen.

Caine bravely held his post, but looked a lot like he was hoping the floor would open up and swallow him whole.

To put him out of his misery, Addison answered Kylie with a shrugging, "Oh that's nothing; it's just the guys' big ole vibrator. No big deal."

Addison knew she was bad enough at lying as it was—her siblings could always tell somehow—so for something like *this*, really, why make it more complicated?

Kylie blanched and sprinted toward her room. "Geez, you could've just said it was none of my business. No need to make up stuff that'll scar me for life."

When the coast was clear, Addison beamed at Caine. "Worked like a charm."

Caine looked visibly traumatized. And near catatonic.

He was so darn cute.

"Oh, relax, she doesn't know I was telling the truth."

Saucer-eyed like he'd just heard a ghost say *boo*, Alec slowly poked his head in the front door. "Did you just say what I think you just said?"

"She thinks I was making it up," defended Addison.

213

He didn't look at all comforted. "Can I make a motion for us to hold all future meetings at my place? Where there aren't impressionable teens just walking around."

"Seconded!" called out Gabe, still sounding a safe distance down the hall.

"Motion carried," agreed Caine haggardly. "Effective immediately."

Addison didn't think she'd had a more comical night in her life.

While she was busy trying not to let the guys see her twitching lips, Caine trudged over to the kitchen looking ready for a stiff drink.

He returned carrying the pot of coffee. Which he handed to Alec. "Do you mind, roomie? Thanks. I'll be there in a bit."

Alec shot him a wholly annoyed look. Which turned soft and buttery as the coffee pot was deposited in his hands. Gabe served as Alec's security detail back to his place, making sure the precious caffeine cargo was secure the entire way.

The sound of Alec shutting, dead-bolting, *and* chain-locking his door had Addison shaking her head with a sigh. "You do realize that if you two kill each other on site, my investors will probably frown on that a little?" She was legitimately worried. "Seriously, why don't you just crash here? I have a futon couch for Tanner when he comes to visit. Since he loved yours so much back in Creek Hills, I got one just like it."

He shook his head gravely. "Way more temptation than I can handle, sweetheart."

Aw. And...good point. "Okay, then. So what's happening tomorrow? *If* you survive tonight at Alec's that is."

"I'll come over here for a good morning kiss to start off the day."

Definitely on board for that plan. "And after that?" Feeling bolstered by the way he was now staring at her lips, she ventured shyly, "Earlier at the car, you promised something about getting me back..."

A rough male sound echoed out of his chest. "Behave, woman."

The man looked positively tortured. Which made her wonder... "Caine, just curious. Is my...'lack of experience' the reason you're holding back?" She felt her face catch fire. Honestly, talking about the buzzing dildo was way easier than bringing up her still active v-card membership.

Correction. *Now* Caine looked tortured. "I already told you my reason for wanting to wait. But thanks for making this—and *me*—ten times harder."

It took everything in her not to peek down and see for herself. "I'm sorry?" Saying it in the form of a question negated the fib, right?

215

"Yeah, you sound real torn up about it," he replied dryly.

"I am though. That's why I brought it up. Because we could do *other*—"

His eyes heated, then downright *scorched* her into silence. "Please don't finish that sentence. I'm on a hair trigger here."

"My point exactly. It's different for me because I've never experienced it before so I don't quite know what I'm missing. But you have. And you've now been celibate for *seven years*," she frowned, reasonably concerned for his *errr...anatomical* well-being.

Still didn't peek though.

"Honey, my current state has absolutely nothing to do with the absence of meaningless sex in my life, and absolutely everything to do with how badly I want to watch you come apart just for me again...preferably up against a wall again to start, and then a few more times in bed so I can see you sleeping and fully sated in my arms again."

So much to swoon over in that single sentence. But first... "I'm sorry I fell asleep on you our last night together in Creek Hills."

"Would've been a little insulted if you hadn't, to be honest."

Mental note: coarse male confidence=highly effective brain-scrambler. "N-no," she stammered, "I-I mean I'm sorry I fell asleep before I had a chance to make

216

you…come apart, too."

"*Hell.* You heard me mention that trigger, right?" he replied gruffly, jaw flexing.

"I'm serious, Caine. I didn't do anything remotely memorable to you that—"

"Baby, you did plenty." He held her eyes the entire time as he reached for his back pocket. "I even have proof."

The sight of a man pulling out a condom from his wallet shouldn't have stunned her nearly this much. Or made her misty-eyed. "You *kept* that?"

"Of course I did." He tucked it right back behind his driver's license like it belonged there. "I still can't believe you brought it out that night. *And* that you wanted to actually use it. It has a glow-in-the-dark happy face on it for crying out loud."

"That was the only condom I had," she defended with a pout. "It was a perfectly acceptable one. They passed it out to all the seniors in high school. Yes, it was a few years old, but still hadn't expired. And I checked, it was from a respectable condom company. The website said the glowing was supposed to help you find it at night, which I thought might come in handy."

He gave her a slow, incredulous headshake. "See, this is why I kept it. As evidence when they decide to make me a saint one day for leaving the world's most adorably sexy virgin untouched when it was all I could do not to take you ten ways to Sunday."

Her brain was only about halfway through imagining these ten ways he spoke of when he speared his fingers through her hair and rubbed a calloused thumb against her cheek. "Actually, while we're on the topic of you falling asleep on me, is there room in that bed of yours for two?"

Seriously, his zero-to-sixty-and-back subject changes were going to give her whiplash one day. "But I thought you didn't want to—"

"To sleep, sweetheart. Just sleep."

"What?"

He flattened both hands against the wall beside her head, effectively caging her in. "Just think of me as a full-service bodyguard. I come complete with a cuddling package to combat insomnia and nightmares."

No exaggeration, the idea of curling up against him again *to sleep* sounded just as decadent as sex. "You don't have to do that," she said softly.

"Yes, I do. Again, it's partly for me. Because if I have to spend one more night without you in my arms, I'm going to lose it." He seared her lips with a quick, but potent kiss. "So I'll see you at midnight on the dot. Do me a favor and wear something flannel that covers you from neck to toe. I'm going to go see if Gabe can create some sort of locking device for my belt out of spare things from Alec's apartment," he added, sounding half-serious.

He was already across the hall before she managed

218

to un-scatter her thoughts enough to realize she'd never actually told him she went to sleep at midnight every night.

"Wait, how'd you know wh—" She cut herself off at the last second. The man was heading into a room with a brilliant hacker, an ingenious lo-jacker, and an expert snooper.

Probably best not to ask.

CHAPTER 15

"THIS IS THE address." Though he'd been preparing himself for today for over a week, it still gutted Caine to see Addison's look of apprehension mirrored in Kylie's and Tanner's expressions from the backseat of his SUV. "You guys ready?"

None of them made a motion to open their doors.

Instead, they each simply surveyed the big glass law building he'd just pulled up to as if it were the headquarters for the grim reaper and his pitchfork wielding senior partner.

"If you're not ready, we can always call to reschedule."

He didn't push any harder than that.

They already knew his thoughts about this meeting as a whole. Just like they knew he hated the idea of them going in without him.

All week, he'd made it clear he wanted to be there for moral support during the will-reading of Tanner and Kylie's inheritance. And each time, Addison and Kylie had gently insisted that they wanted to go through it alone.

Caine hadn't understood it at first, and was honestly a little hurt by it. Thankfully, Tanner had driven in from California yesterday afternoon and deciphered the girls' reasoning for him.

"They're embarrassed," Tanner had explained matter-of-factly. "Frankly, I am, too."

"What on earth do any of you have to be embarrassed about?" demanded Caine, utterly dumbfounded.

"Think about it, Caine. Those magical maternal and paternal instincts that are supposed to hit parents the moment their baby is born? Or that overwhelming need parents have to protect their kids at all costs? If *your* parents didn't possess or exhibit any of that, not just for you, but your two siblings as well, wouldn't you be ashamed to have others meet them?"

That had stumped Caine good and proper. Growing up, he'd always known he had the best parents he could've ever hoped for. Still did, in fact. He'd never once been anything but proud to be the son of Grace and Jack Spencer.

"Addison, Kylie, and I may know on a logical level

that we didn't do anything to warrant our parents not wanting us, or loving us. Regardless. Can you see how it's hard for us not to be just a little mortified? A little humiliated? Put yourself in our shoes. Would *you* want anyone else in a meeting with these people, especially when there's money involved?"

After that, Caine backed off.

So though it was absolute, bloody torture to sit behind the wheel and not offer, yet again, to go up there and slay any visible and invisible demons that may be waiting for them, that's exactly what he did. Resigning himself to support them from afar. "I'll be right here waiting when you guys are done. We can go grab a bite to eat; my treat. There's this restaurant over in—"

Suddenly, Addison's hand closed over his. "Actually, we've been talking, and…it would mean a lot to all of us if you would come in the room and sit with us," she said quietly, while two nodding heads bobbed in the rear view mirror.

No exaggeration, he was pretty sure his chest just cracked open a little right then and there.

"Can I bring my gun?" he asked by way of acceptance.

That earned him three tiny smiles.

Progress.

A few far less tense minutes later, after the kids checked in at the reception area of the law firm before making a quick pit stop at the restroom to collect themselves a bit, Caine gathered Addison in his arms and asked curiously, "What changed your mind?"

She raised her eyes up to meet his. "Seven years ago, you offered us a home where we could be a family. You actually wanted *us*. To be a part of your life. I guess subconsciously, we didn't want you to see a part of us that we ourselves have a hard time facing, didn't want you feeling sorry for us, maybe. But after talking to you last night, Tanner reminded us that though we didn't accept your amazing offer to be a part of your life seven years ago, it absolutely *wasn't* because we hadn't wanted you to be a part of our lives in return. We wanted it so badly then, and we want it just as much now. Good, bad, crazy, and everything in between."

Ah, damn. And here he thought this was only going to be an emotional day for her and the kids.

He tried to think of something wise and fitting to say in response. Maybe even something a little inspirational as the kids had returned to hear the tail end of her declaration.

But when he looked at them all standing there in front of him, what came out was a super classy and profound, "You can't take that back; I'm holding you to it."

Apparently, he chose well because he got chuckling grins from Tanner and Kylie, along with a jellyfish hug from Addison, which he didn't untangle himself from until a polite woman at the reception desk came over.

"Kylie? Tanner? We're ready for you now."

They walked down to a glass conference room where Sonny and Lara were sitting with two lawyer-type folk.

Caine had seen his fair share of low-lifes over the years, and that gleam in Sonny's eyes had scumbag written all over it.

"It's so good to finally meet you both," said lawyer number one, a distinguished looking suit in his fifties or so. "I'm Jim one of the senior partners here, and this is my associate Simone. We're so glad to finally meet you both. Lawrence was looking for you two for quite some time."

After the kids and Addison handed over multiple forms of ID for the paralegal to take copies of, the next few minutes were filled with pretty standard legalese, which mainly consisted of Kylie and Tanner nodding and looking at a bunch of paperwork.

"Before we get to the reading of the will, now that we've verified your identities, we wanted to first give you each several letters your father wanted us to give you if we were able to find you." Jim held out a thick sealed manila envelope with Kylie's name, and one with Tanner's. "These letters are separate from today's will-reading, and they're yours to take and read whenever you're ready." A sad smile hit him then. "Years ago, when Lawrence was first diagnosed with cancer, he started writing these letters to give to you. I was actually Lawrence's grandfather's probate lawyer who handled that family inheritance."

Sonny's teeth practically *glinted* like a hungry wolf's.

Simone held her hand up and added, "That's when I came on board. Lawrence retained me as his estate attorney not long after your great-grandfather's matters were settled. In addition to that inheritance he received seven years ago, which he invested wisely over the years," she slid over another official-looking document, "your father also had a life insurance policy." More folders of paperwork were opened up for the kids. "He didn't have it for very long, but there's a healthy amount for you both. Just to let you know, he did get married again after your mother, and in the year since your father's passing, we've since settled her portions of the policy."

While she readied a few financial papers that Sonny's eyes remained glued to, Jim tapped gently on the sealed manila envelopes in front of the kids. "Lawrence had a very tough battle with cancer. And toward the end, he didn't want us to film his will; he said he didn't want you two to remember him that way. So instead, he provided you both with quite a few photos. Some from his time with you, and some from after he left your mother."

Caine couldn't help but smile when the kids focused their sole attention on those big envelopes, the monetary inheritance paperwork completely untouched, forgotten.

"Did he have other children we should try to find?" asked Kylie, just as Tanner inquired, "Was his widow's settlement enough to make sure she's well taken care of?"

Good lord, those were two good kids.

Both lawyers blinked in surprise at the two earnest young faces before them.

"No other kids, and yes, his widow actually got the larger bulk of the settlements since he'd been unsuccessful in locating you two earlier."

That drew a frown from Sonny. "Can we contest that now since we found the kids?"

"*No,*" called out Tanner and Kylie in unison.

"Why don't we just proceed to the will," suggested Lara, an indecipherable expression on her face.

Caine sort of tuned out the lawyers then. The terms of the inheritance mattered nothing to him. Instead, he surveyed each of the people in the room.

Out of the group, Lara was the most difficult to read. He'd done his homework on her. She'd started trying to get clean a few years ago now, with only a couple falls off the wagon, as far as he could see.

Sonny, on the other hand, was fairly transparent. The guy was a piece of work. Though he wasn't conning folks anymore, he hadn't exactly been earning an honest living, either. He'd stuck by Lara through her addiction though—no evidence of any affairs that Alec had been able to find. That was pretty much the only thing semi-decent about the man.

"What?!" shouted Sonny then, slamming his hand on the table in outrage.

Shit, what'd I miss?

"You're naming *Addison* the executor for Kylie's inheritance?"

That got him caught up real quick. And it took everything in him not to reach over and break the asshole's finger, currently wagging in Addison's face like she was trash.

"Lawrence was very clear in his stipulations," replied Simone calmly.

"But *Lara* is Kylie's mother. And Kylie is still a minor."

"A minor who's been living with and being raised by *Addison* for the last nine years at least." Simone had a mean poker face, but the derision in her eyes cut like glass.

"That doesn't matter," countered Sonny. "Kylie is still Lara's kid. She's only been living with Addison because Lara has been letting her."

Addison paled.

Caine bristled. The bastard was getting close to crossing a dangerous line.

"But Lara and I can *easily* change that arrangement."

That was definitely a threat—one that Caine going to make him sorry for issuing in about ten seconds…

Jim was all business when he flipped to the next page in the stapled stack of papers he was reading from. "According to this, Addison doesn't have to be Kylie's guardian to be the executor of her funds. Further,

Lawrence actually stipulated specifically that your wife Lara not be allowed access. So we will be following his requests exactly."

"You can't be serious." Sonny looked ready to pop a blood vessel in his eye. "She's their half-sister who lives at a homeless shelter for chrissakes! Have you seen her credit score? Her below-poverty-line salary? How can you possibly trust her with this inheritance and not the kids' own biological mother?!"

"It's not a shelter, it's a housing complex," snarled Tanner. "And my sister runs the whole damn thing. She takes the minimal salary so the foundation has more money for the residents. Don't you dare make her out to be a deadbeat with no job like you."

"Why you smart-mouthed—"

Caine snapped. Before anyone had time to blink, he had a hand wrapped around Sonny's scrawny throat. "You finish that sentence and you'll be breathing out of a tube till Christmas."

"Gentlemen!" hollered Jim. "Don't make us call security."

Caine reluctantly let him go.

Which prompted the dumb ass to prove he just didn't know how to shut up. "Addison basically kidnapped the kids from us. You should be throwing her in jail, not rewarding her."

Caine lunged forward again.

Sonny jumped back, but after seeing Addison, Kylie, and Caine rush forward to forcibly restrain him, the asshole puffed up his chest and started spewing more lies.

"That's right. We came home one day and found them gone. You can ask her other boyfriend, the P.I. we hired." Sonny nodded in triumph as he continued to twist history in his favor. "He couldn't find them because she'd hid them from us. Who knows what kind of lies she's filled their heads with. Did you know she made them live in a van for years while their mother and I kept looking for them in vain? That's abuse on top of kidnapping if you ask me."

"Sir, that's a very serious allegation." Simone started jotting things down in a notebook. "I'd advise you to take a minute to think about what you're saying before proceeding further."

The idiot didn't take a minute. Instead, he looked right at Addison and spat out, "You know what? I think Lara and I ought to press charges. Bet all your little donors and supporters will *love* that. You'll splash that homeless cesspool of yours all over the news. 'Local do-gooder actually a kidnapper and child abuser.' I can just see the editorial headlines now."

"Enough!" screamed Kylie. "I don't want the money! I refuse to accept it. Keep it, burn it, do whatever you want."

"Are you out of your mind?! That's over a half million dollars!"

She stared Sonny down. "So what? It's just money."

"Kylie, calm down," said Addison gently. "Don't make a rash decision like this."

"I. Don't. Want. It." Kylie turned to Addison. "You taught us that we don't need a lot to survive, to be happy. You raised us to do good and to work hard." She glanced at Caine for a meaningful beat before returning her gaze to Addison. "You raised us to be strong enough to walk away from something we might really want, if it would help or protect the people we love."

Sonny scoffed. "Then you raised two idiots."

Caine broke free and punched him across the jaw.

Sonny went flying out of his seat.

When Lara fell to the ground to help him up, Sonny shoved her away and spat the blood pooling in his mouth at Caine's feet. "Now I can add abusive police boyfriend to my statement to the reporters. *And* my lawyer."

"I'm not a cop anymore. So, good luck with that." Caine reached in his wallet and pulled out a business card. "As far as a lawsuit goes, here—" He flung it at him. "Have your lawyer contact mine."

Sonny blanched when he read the name on the card. "*Connor Sullivan?*"

That's right, asshole. "Figured a guy who used to grunt work for one of the shadiest investment bankers in Phoenix would recognize that name."

"You're bullshitting. He wouldn't take a case like

this. He's a bigshot corporate lawyer."

"Connor has his own practice now." Caine couldn't help but smile a little over how his now happily domesticated buddy was still a feared bad-ass in corporate Arizona. "He's still as ruthless as ever, only now, he gets to be picky about which opponents he annihilates in court."

Caine showed his full hand then. "Fun fact: do you know who babysits for Connor when he has date nights with his wife? That would be my sister Lia. And his beloved niece Skylar? She's an honorary Spencer who's been working for my brothers' security firm for years now."

With Sonny now officially squirming like the worm he was, Caine reeled it in. "Truthfully, even if Connor wasn't such a good friend of mine, I know for a fact that he'd still happily take the case. Because he loves nothing more than putting shitballs like you away for as many years as he can creatively get. So go ahead and sue me. We'll counter with so many criminal charges, you'll be lucky to find a half-decent lawyer to help you defend your ass."

Sonny's eyes darted desperately over to the lawyers in the room. "I-I have witnesses. They saw you assault me."

"Actually," replied Simone—her poker face really a thing of beauty—"I missed the whole thing. I was on my phone fact-checking Addison's quite impressive 'homeless cesspool' as you called it, when you fell out of your chair. Admittedly, I was a little distracted, seeing as how doing pro bono work for non-profit organizations is sort of my thing."

"And as my former colleague Connor always tells me when we go golfing," added Jim, "I don't have the best vision. Can't really be sure what these old eyes of mine are seeing these days."

"This isn't over," vowed Sonny as he pushed out of his seat and shot Caine another hateful scowl. "We're going to fight this executor thing. But first, I'm going to bury that stupid homeless camp and piss all over its ashes. Connor Sullivan won't be able to protect you from good ole social media shit talk." He grabbed Lara's arm and stormed out of the room.

Caine was shocked to see genuine regret flash in Lara's eyes as she turned to look back at her three children through the glass door. It was replaced by a placating expression a moment later, however, when Sonny began barking at her as they made their way to the elevators.

"Well, now that ridiculousness is taken care of," said Simone with a smile. "Let's sign some papers, shall we? Your father was very eager for you two to have this money, and frankly, so are we."

Tanner looked out at the empty hallway. "But what about Sonny's threat? You don't think he has a case?"

Jim snorted. "I think he'll be lucky if the judge doesn't fine him for wasting the court's time."

"And don't worry," reassured Simone, "if he tries to

slander Addison or the CoRe Housing Foundation, we'll hit him with cease and desist orders, and a mountain of legal paperwork."

Kylie and Tanner both looked at Addison questioningly.

She gave them a big, bolstering smile. "I'll support whatever decision you two make a thousand percent."

After a quick, quiet exchange with her brother, Kylie turned back to the lawyers and asked in a bold, cute-as-a-kitten voice, "If we hire you as our lawyers, can you help us put some of this money toward opening up more Cohabitate-Rehabitate housing complexes in other areas with high homeless populations?"

"Along with sustainable agriculture projects and research," added Tanner. "I have a few ideas I think could really help some communities in need."

The lawyers looked positively charmed by the pair.

"You did that," whispered Caine into Addison's ear. "You raised your siblings to become those two amazing human beings right there...and the world is all the better for it."

CHAPTER 16

"IF YOU ASK ME, I still don't get why David hasn't made another move yet." Gabe threw his thinking ball— an old blue tennis ball that was practically bald, but apparently very good luck—against Alec's living room wall, and caught it on the rebound. "It's been almost two weeks since he sent those flowers to her. What the hell is he waiting for?"

Caine was wondering the same thing.

It'd been nearly two weeks since he'd turned in his gun and badge, and like Gabe, he'd honestly thought David would've made his presence known by now. With no further threats or anything else to go on, all Caine and Alec had been able to do since was go back over things they might've missed over the past seven years.

From every close call he'd had nearly catching David

in Mexico, to all the impressively invasive P.I. details Alec had dug up on David—eating habits, product preferences, hell, even favorite colors. They'd analyzed every recorded surveillance photo of David over the years, which Drew had obtained via hacking the hell out of government systems and big-brother cameras that Caine just didn't ask questions about anymore.

From what Caine had found down in Mexico, David had been doing dirty dealings in designer drugs for years. Even before he'd jumped bail.

Far as they could tell, David hadn't just been in possession of date rape drugs for his own use, but he'd been working on creating and distributing new hybrid recreational narcotics as well. Not to the level of getting on the DEA's radar, however—according to Drew's don't-ask-how-I-know intel. David's was more a boutique signature cocktail service where he made customized concoctions for his individual clients' very specified requests. Like a person who wants to slowly coerce a boss for a raise or drive a spouse paranoid to the point of criminal aggression.

At one of David's abandoned residences, Caine had found a sick journal cataloging every detail he made his buyers tell him about the effects of the drug on its victim. It was like he was living vicariously, and getting his own high by slowly—always slowly—manipulating the victim to reach the buyer's goal.

It was twisted.

And it terrified the hell out of Caine.

Imagining David doing something like that to Addison...

He couldn't even bare to think about it.

The thing was, even with their working together, the only new thing that had developed since was Caine's grudging admiration over Alec's tracking abilities. The guy definitely did things different from a cop, but he got results.

On cue, Alec pulled up some photos on his laptop. "Last week, I went back over to Mexico to check a few leads and I was able to find more on that last American girl who went missing in Rocky Point you told me to check on. The one that didn't quite fit the profile of the other victims."

A few years back, Caine had discovered a string of rape victims—all American women, all drugged by narcotics unlike any they've seen in the States. And all spitting images of Addison when she was twenty. It'd been the real big break after David's trail had gone cold for nearly a year. Though all the girls were still alive, most of them were in heavy therapy, over half with memories all but wiped from the drugs.

The most recent victim, however, hadn't resembled Addison at all. But, everything else about her case pointed back to the same non-standard drugs.

"Your hunch was right about that last victim," Alec continued. "It wasn't a random on-site abduction, even though it was made to look like one. The girl had been getting harassed for some time by this rich dude who evidently, got tired of getting turned down. I did more digging, and it looks like David has developed a pretty high-end clientele, all by referral."

That part wasn't a surprise considering David's lavish lifestyle. Each of the places of residence he'd tracked David to had been more extravagant than the last. And being bankrolled by wealthy clients would also explain how he's been able to fund his access to the seemingly unlimited resources helping him avoid capture on both sides of the border.

"The thing is," reasoned Gabe. "Just because he hasn't made a move on Addison yet doesn't mean he's not working while he's here to get some funds for whatever he has planned. I say we should get Drew on a dark web marketplace to see if there are suddenly any new players in Arizona willing to 'help' in situations where buyers want a drug to control someone. Seems like as good a place as any to see if we get any nibbles."

Caine's look of shock matched Alec's. "That's actually a really good idea."

"Geez, you guys don't have to make it sound like some sort of *miracle*," groused Gabe. "I may not be part of the dynamic deputy dog duo, but I've got some skills." He traded his thinking ball for a fresh slice of pizza. "One of which is keeping your two sorry asses fed at these meetings. By the way, when are you guys going to start chipping in?"

Sidestepping the question—but not before stealing another slice for himself—Alec changed the subject entirely, "You know what's still bugging me? That photo he sent with the flowers of Caine's eyes gouged out. It just doesn't match his MO."

Caine grabbed Gabe's thinking ball and bounced it on the back of his hand a few times. That part had struck him as off as well. He was missing something, and it was killing him.

"What did you do that week? Did you set him off somehow?" asked Gabe. "Back in Creek Hills he flew off the handle and held Marco at knifepoint because you and Addison drew him out by making out in plain sight?"

"I don't see how. Other than the police fundraiser and the precinct, we've never even been together outside of the housing complex."

"Maybe he got to one of the residents," offered Alec quietly, sounding fairly disgusted at the possibility. "Some folks would do just about anything if the price tag is big enough."

"I don't know. I think these families respect Addison too much." But Alec was right, he couldn't completely rule out the possibility. "Before we go down that route, I think we should look for some sort of basecamp. David never had a reason to *stay* on this side of the border until now."

Caine put down the ball. "Back in Creek Hills, he'd moved to a building that had a bird's eye view of the diner so he could keep tabs on Addison. For a big housing complex like Addison's, that's probably what we should be looking for this time around, too."

Gabe frowned. "We're in the middle of an urban neighborhood, which, from a security standpoint, is actually worse than being in downtown because of all the staggered building heights. We're talking dozens of residential and commercial buildings, hotels, motels in all directions of the complex, even a few condo hi-rises further away, all of which would give a clean sightline to anyone with a telescope.

Caine grabbed his phone to dial in Drew. "Still. We have location parameters and we have a timeline. Drew should be able to pull info on all the rental units, motels, and hotels occupied within the search radius from the day I pulled Addison over to the day she got the flower and photos. Almost every rental management office and every craigslist renter nowadays asks for photo ID to make a copy for their records, which Drew can hack and run facial recognition on."

Alec looked dubious at best. "Dude, are you serious? The kid would have to backtrack through every possible rental and sublet listing site, not to mention airbnb, craigslist, and like fifty others. And that's not even counting newspapers, college websites, and military listings. That's *hundreds* of possible units *if* we're lucky. And from there, he still has to hack every hotel, and every building manager's office, and every offsite landlord's computer to check guest reservations and tenant applications. At the very least, it'll take him forever."

"I can have the results in a few days," called out Drew over Caine's speaker phone, matter-of-factly. "Maybe sooner if I can finish this term paper by tonight."

Alec blinked at Caine's phone in astonishment, while Gabe just tsked good-naturedly, "A few *days*? Man, this college thing is slowing you down, bro. You should just quit; we all know you're smarter than most of your professors anyway."

He was kidding, of course. Caine knew that next to Lia, Gabe was one of the biggest advocates of Drew going to college before hacking for Spencer Securities full time.

"I'll be sure to send Lia a copy of the audio clip of you saying that," promised Drew before raising his eyebrows in an evil half smile and hanging up.

Gabe scrambled to call him back. "*Oh shit.* Lia's totally going to kick my ass."

"What'd you do now?" asked Addison with a grin as she walked into Alec's apartment. "And where can I buy front row tickets to the show?"

Gabe mimicked getting a bullet to the chest and fell to the ground.

Unmoved, a laughing Addison stepped around his

body to head to the kitchen.

A few seconds later, Gabe groaned and left the room to answer his phone, which was now pealing with the *Kung-Fu Fighting* ringtone he'd assigned to Lia.

Caine followed Addison to the kitchen. "Are you going to bed already? Because we're almost done here; I can be there in a few."

Reaching for another pizza slice, Alec shook his head and put in his two cents, "Okay, I know I'm not exactly an expert on this whole relationship thing, but this whole you going over there every night to be her sleeping teddy bear and then coming back here and waking my ass up in the process before dawn, seems a little bit messed up. Just saying."

Before Caine could promptly refund Alec's two pennies, Addison shocked the hell out of him by saying, "Actually, that's what I came over to talk about." She looked up at Caine and explained gently, "I want to try and sleep solo tonight, if that's okay."

"Gotta go, Lia," stage whispered Gabe from the hallway, *"the Addison and Caine saga just had a major plot twist. I'll keep you on the line."* He hurdle-jumped over the back of the couch to get comfy on the ottoman, cell phone shamelessly held up in front of him.

Smirking, Alec put his feet up and settled in as well. Bunch of nosy bastards.

Lucky for them, he had more pressing things to deal

with. "Do you agree with him?"

She shook her head quickly. "No, of course not. I love sleeping with you. But I just…I think I need a little alone time tonight."

Frickin' A, Caine hated that. But he didn't argue. Hell, he understood needing time to yourself. That's why he went for runs every morning and either went a few rounds in the ring or shot a few rounds in the range every afternoon. If that's really what she wanted… "Call me if you get lonely?"

Her gaze softened. "Of course."

"Boo, false alarm," said Gabe. "Those two are being level-headed and boringly rational like usual."

"I dunno," countered Alec. "Did you see that tell just now? It was little, but it was there. I say this isn't about her just wanting some time alone."

At Addison's startled look, he gave her an unapologetic half-shrug. "Sorry, babe. I can always tell when you're fibbing."

She narrowed her eyes at him in annoyance. "Not always."

"Uh, yes always."

Crossing her arms, she volleyed back, "Tell that to the background check you ran on the guy who bought me drinks at your cousin Jo's wedding. What did I tell you his name was again?"

Whoa. Caine went over to plop down on the couch,

just as Alec shot up to his feet. "You *lied* to me about that? What the hell, Addison? What if that guy had been working for David? Or what if he'd been an even bigger psycho than David?"

"He was a harmless flirt that I didn't want you terrorizing."

Pure and utter disbelief marred his features. "I can't believe you actually lied to me."

"Why not? You lie to me all the time."

"No, I embellish and conveniently reword or omit. All to keep you safe."

"Well, I was keeping this poor guy safe. Alec, you *picked the pocket* of the last man who'd made the mistake of asking me out, and then when you found out he had debt up to his ears, you went and got him *audited by the IRS*."

As Addison began listing a few more of the awesome things his new best bud Alec had done to the guys who'd hit on Addison in the past, Gabe leaned over and commented, "I think we should make him an honorary Spencer. He's got the right stuff."

"I was just going to say."

A now mouth agape Addison cut him a look that said, *traitor.*

"Honey," he reasoned placatingly. "Let's face it, the guy bugs me about as much as Max and Gabe do so he really would be a logical fit."

When Alec gave them a big thumbs-up sign from

across the room, Addison looked ready to throw something at all of their heads.

That's when Caine realized something belatedly. "Hey, wait a minute. What tell?" He frowned at Alec. "I didn't see any tell just now."

"I missed it too," said Gabe. "Was it the lip thing?"

Alec rejoined them on the couch. "Naw, she only does that one for little fibs."

"Was it the scratching her left elbow thing? Oh! Or did she fiddle with her pinky nail?" Gabe shook his head. "I played poker with her the other week and seriously, the poor girl can't bluff even a little. I swear, she has like ten tells."

Caine shook his head. "It's a lot more than ten."

"Yeah," agreed Alec. "A few of them, she only does when she's—"

"Enough!" Addison stomped her foot on the ground. "You both," she pointed at Gabe and Alec, "have just lost your coffee privileges for the next week—maybe that'll teach you to keep your nosy little butts out of my business sometimes."

The pair whimpered in perfect harmony.

"And you." She lasered her sharpest glare on Caine. "Alec was right. I *was* holding something back on my reason for wanting to sleep solo tonight. The other week when I was dropping Kylie off at Lia's place in Cactus Creek, I met the owner of that adult toy store over by the brewpub.

We got to talking and she ran back to her store to go get a...vibrator thingamajig for me when I told her that I'd never had one—or had sex—before. And since taking an ice cold shower every morning after cuddling with you and your massive hard-on every night hasn't been helping one bit, tonight, I was thinking of actually taking the thing out of its box and trying it out. Alone." She put her hands on her hips. "How was that? Did you see any tells?"

No. No he hadn't.

She then promptly spun on her heel and zipped back to her apartment.

It took all of five seconds for Caine to pick his jaw up off the floor and unfog his brain enough to shove past the two applauding yahoos next to him, and go storming after her.

———————◆———————

CAINE HIT the hallway just as Addison slammed her door shut.

And triple-dead-bolted it.

Growling, he stomped back to grab his keys off Alec's dining table. One by one, he unlocked all the new locks he'd added to Addison's door, cursing now over his decision to go with the 6-digit key-coded entry on the knob itself as well.

The longest two minutes of his life later, he finally

burst through and went right over to her bedroom. Only to come skidding to a halt at the sight of Addison carrying something in a hand towel calmly over to her bed.

In nothing but her bra and panties.

She got under the covers. "You can just see yourself back over to Alec's. I'm not in danger, and I'm not planning on sleeping anytime soon. You have no obligations here." Seemingly in defense of that statement, she opened up the small towel to reveal a compact metal vibrator. And open on her nightstand? The *instructions* for said vibrator.

God, this woman.

"So yes, I've got everything I need for this solo mission."

Really, she was just throwing kerosene on top of a raging bonfire now.

"Who says this mission needs to be a solo one?" He took off his boots first, and his t-shirt soon after, nearly busting through his zipper as he watched her heated gaze track his progress. His belt and jeans hit the floor next. "You sure you want me to leave, baby?"

Lord have mercy, that thin, lacy bra she was wearing hid nothing from him. "Sexy new tell to add to the list," he rasped his approval, voice a deep, feral octave lower. "I think that one—or two, more like—may be my favorite yet."

He gently caught her hands before she could cover

herself up, and tried like hell not to lose it when his mention of her tells caused an indignant flare of defiance in her eyes.

...Followed by her staring him down, and clicking the vibrator *on*.

With his sanity—and her virginity—hanging on by a thread, he pulled back the covers.

Knowing full well he was in critical danger of coming right then and there if she actually followed through, he let go of her wrists.

And called her bluff.

For several mind-numbing beats, she simply laid there like his wildest fantasy on a silver platter, vibrator buzzing away. All but forgotten. Lids at half-mast, breathing scattered out of control, her undivided focus was now exactly where his was, between her legs as he slowly rocked against her.

Judging by the fluttering of her core muscles against him, she was close...maybe seconds from going off like a bottle rocket.

So he stopped.

Her thighs trembled. His name fell from her lips in a reverent curse.

But he stayed the course.

He had a virgin vixen nearly naked under him who had seriously thought he'd let her go off on a *solo mission* without him. *Not freaking likely.* And she best be disabusing herself of any more insane notions like that here

247

and now.

Easing the humming vibrator out of the death grip she had on it, he slowly began tracing the lines of the artwork that disappeared behind her bra. He'd been dying to see the rest of that tattoo since he first laid eyes on it. Fake or not, it was the sexiest ink he'd ever seen.

He flicked open the front clasp of her bra and watched, mesmerized, as it parted. Her berry-ripe nipples still partially hidden from his view, the soft swells of her cleavage—and the rest of that tattoo—played a dangerous game of peekaboo with his self-control.

Damn.

Dropping his lips to her neck as he let the vibrator keep trailing lower, he murmured roughly against her skin, "Let me hear that fib again. The one where you don't want me here helping you…because sweetheart, I can't *wait* to trigger all the rest of your tells."

CHAPTER 17

JUST AS ADDISON was trying her best to get her runaway nerves under control, suddenly, Caine stopped and shut the vibrator off, cursing under his breath.

"Dammit, I don't have a condom on me. Well, other than the happy face glowing one, which I'm sure is expired by now—not that I'd ever use it. And not that a single condom would last us tonight, with the way I'm feeling right now." He grimaced. "I'm going to have to make a run to the store."

Pure female pleasure swamped her. She couldn't help it, there was an irrepressible satisfaction that came with knowing Caine wasn't walking around packing condoms on him 24-7.

That said, this *was* a problem. A quick store run sounded like an eternity at this point.

"Oh wait!" She lit up. "*I* have some condoms. A lot, actually."

"Why do you have condoms?" he growled, eyes narrowed.

Good lord, that growl was a thousand times sexier when the man was nearly naked.

"They're not *my* condoms. We had this teen talk thing here last month and had some extra pamphlets and condoms and things leftover." Since she obviously couldn't just leave the condoms in a fishbowl on her desk like candy, she'd just tucked it under her bed for safekeeping until their next teen talk. "Hang on a sec." Dangling over the edge of the mattress, she rummaged under her bed for the box.

"Found it!" she called out triumphantly before gasping. "*Oh.*" At the feel of Caine's hand slowly sliding her panties down to her knees, her brain blitzed out and the box went shooting out of her hands, sending condoms and safe sex pamphlets scattering all across her bedroom floor.

"Sweetheart, you really shouldn't be tempting a hungry man like this."

Peering back at him over her shoulder, she saw his gaze riveted to her bare behind with open appreciation, the look in his eyes more…*unbridled* than she'd ever seen it.

With gravity sending way too much blood to her head, admittedly, she didn't think her next step through fully. Scooting back away from the edge of the mattress, she pulled herself up and flipped over.

With her panties at her knees and her bra hanging off her shoulders.

Face blazing, she immediately tried to cover up.

Which caused Caine to growl again. And catch her hands at the last second.

Threading his fingers through hers, he pinned her arms above her head. "Open your eyes."

She hadn't even realized she'd shut them.

Slowly peeking through her lids, she found his eyes locked on hers.

"I won't look unless you tell me it's okay, baby."

Did the man have any idea how unbelievably hot his being such a gentleman was?

Far too shy to actually speak the words aloud, she simply nodded.

And then spent the next minute feeling his molten hot gaze run over like a live wire, tingling every inch of her until she was a trembling mass of arousal.

"You are so beautiful." He speared one hand through her hair and touched her cheek with the other. Then he dipped his head down and kissed her. A deep, penetrating kiss that stalled the air in her lungs and stole every last thought from her brain.

By the time she was floating back to reality, he'd somehow divested her of the rest of her clothing. Throat bobbing, steely body corded tight with tension, he held himself over her as if he didn't trust himself to touch her.

So *she* touched *him.*

Smoothing her hands across his broad chest, she watched in fascination as his eyes darkened and his breathing roughened while he slowly lowered himself to settle between her thighs. Only to pull back up again sharply.

Logically, she knew he wasn't teasing her, but it tormented her all the same. Became a whole-body craving she couldn't ignore. Timidly, she raised her hips up to his, wanting, *needing* to feel him nudge against her core again.

He snapped.

His hips rocked between her legs with unerring accuracy, against the throbbing pulse point at her core that set off exploding colored lights behind her eyelids.

"Open your eyes," he repeated gruffly.

As soon as she did, his mouth latched down over her nipple while a large, calloused hand encompassed her other breast, both working in tandem to deliver the most exquisite torture.

His hips flexed against hers with more dominant force, and that's when her lust-fogged brain cleared enough to fully feel how hot, hard…and *huge* he was.

Um. "C-Caine?"

He stilled. "Do you want to stop?" His words were a labored, sandpapery groan that made butterflies flutter and faint in her stomach over its intensity.

God no she didn't want to stop. She swiftly shook her head. "I-just wondering if we should maybe, um, look in that box for something to...ease you into me a bit easier?"

She wasn't a complete sexual moron. She knew how lube and things worked. And she'd read romance novels describing what sounded like supernaturally monstrous erections managing to work their way into the tiniest of holes.

His lips twitched in adoring amusement, causing his five o'clock shadow to abrade her nipple...in the *best* possible way.

A sound she'd never heard come out of her before seeped past her lips.

And a rushing river of arousal drenched her core.

Ohhh.

She hadn't realized the books weren't exaggerating about how...*avid* the response would be to...*errr* 'greet' its first male caller at the...um, entrance.

Okay, so maybe she was a bit of a sexual moron.

His mouth now curved up into a knowing male smile, he pumped his hips once more, fitting his hard, thick length against her wet center with perfect precision.

Again.

His eyes flared.

Had she really said that out loud?

By the way he was now rocking against her and

gripping the backs of her thighs, evidently, he liked her quiet little demand.

She did too.

"Don't move, sweetheart."

And apparently the liking of the sexual demands worked both ways.

More liquid heat flooded out of her.

With a harsh curse and a truly pained expression, he lifted himself off of her so he could reach over to grab a condom from the cornucopia of prophylactics on the ground.

Before she could properly admire how erotic it was to have a man lock his eyes on you while ripping open a condom and sliding it on, Caine was back, his broad, hard tip easing into her with heart-melting care.

"I don't want to hurt you." He sounded tortured, nearly at the end of his tether.

"You could never hurt me," she whispered, hitching her legs around his waist. "I want to feel you inside me, Caine."

He groaned and pushed in part way.

"So tight," he rasped, his voice gravelly with a whole different kind of torture.

Rigid, muscular forearms tensed against the bed as he pulled back and gradually slid the rest of the way inside her in one slow, careful plunge.

He was being so gentle with her, despite how much

it was clearly taking out of him.

"You okay, sweetheart?" he gritted through his teeth.

Unable to answer with words over the shockwaves of pleasure quickly eclipsing the pain, she tilted her hips, and gasped when the new, deeper angle caused her to flex against him.

"Christ, Addison. I have to move." It was a strained, husky warning. The only one she got before his lips landed on hers and his hips began thrusting into her. First in firm, measured strokes that eventually turned into a hard, relentless pace.

He watched her intently as he edged her closer and closer to the edge, scanning her face the entire time to make sure she was alright.

Soon, she was better than alright.

Her teeth sank into her lower lip to keep from crying out, and she watched the fire in his gaze *smolder*. He fit his mouth to hers and delivered a mind-scorching kiss, scoring his teeth against her lip the way she had. Only better. "Mine," he murmured before taking her lips again.

With each passing second, he seemed less capable of holding back the dominant force he always tried to keep under control around her.

She wanted him to lose control.

"Caine, I'm going to come."

That did it.

His hands slid under her knees and he buried himself to the hilt. He held himself deep. Unmoving. Until her knees shook, and her heart began spinning out of control.

He held her hostage with a long, hot stare before sliding one hand up to cup her breast, and another one between them, where she was slick, sensitized. And ready.

"Come for me, Addison."

She shattered, flew over the edge into oblivion.

Through the pulsing, mind-altering sensations crashing over her, she heard him expel a final, deep, guttural groan, and then he was coming with her—hot, hard, seemingly neverending.

Long minutes later, fierce pleasure colored his features as he caged her with his body and gave her a slow, bottomless kiss that was humbled, reverent, and all-consuming, at the same time. Arms now rigid steel bands around her, he looked deep into her eyes. "Tell me the truth, sweetheart. Did I hurt you? Was I too rough?"

She melted. "No, not at all."

When he continued to gaze at her worriedly, she said simply, "Read my mind. What am I thinking right now?"

Again.

———◆———

HE GROWLED.

The swift relief rushing through him was quickly

overtaken by lust, pure and simple.

"Ready for me again, baby?"

Her inner muscles fluttered against him in response, sending destructive bolts of pleasure surging down his spine, hardening him in an instant.

As she began experimenting with her newfound hidden power, stealing his sanity one shy squeeze at a time, he tried like hell to slow the hammering of his heart in his chest.

She owned him. Of that, he had no doubt. And it was messing with his head in a big way. His heart, just as badly.

Even now, as he slid out to quickly put on a new condom, he was having a hard time accepting that there had to be even that single layer separating them as he took her again.

It was damn primitive of him, but he simply didn't see himself evolving when it came to Addison.

As he sank back into her damp heat and slowly brought her to the brink again, he took his time to appreciate all her soft, sweet curves, sliding his hands over every inch of her, not wanting to leave any part of her untouched, un*claimed.*

Panting, she whispered his name, drew her teeth over his shoulder, likely without even knowing it, and locked her legs around his waist when he drove in even *deeper* at the feel of her teeth testing the cord of muscles along his neck next.

Just like that, hard and fast was the only option he could manage. He needed to see her, *feel* her come apart again. Like he needed air to breathe.

Grasping her chin gently, he told her gruffly, "I can't get enough of you, sweetheart. Can't ever, won't ever get enough of you."

Her orgasm crashed over her a moment later, swiftly taking him over the edge with her, making him come so hard he blacked out for a beat or two.

Eventually, his muscles gave out and he collapsed onto his back beside her. Seeing the sleepy, satiated look on her face, he felt a rush of piercing satisfaction speed through his system. He wanted to see her like that every night, every morning. And a half dozen times throughout the day if he could manage it. Gathering her up against his chest, he felt another sharp hit of pleasure when she automatically snuggled in against him.

Holding her flushed cheek in the palm of his hand, he asked her curiously, "Were you really going to use that vibrator earlier?"

She looked up at him from beneath her lashes and smiled. "Absolutely."

No tell. Damn.

Never did he think he'd be jealous of an electronic device.

"Check the instructions on the nightstand," she

murmured, giving him another one of her secret smiles.

He really didn't want to. But she was insistent.

Flipping the offensive little booklet open, he started reading. Under extreme protest.

Addison pulled the booklet from his hands and closed it so he could read the cover.

Handheld shoulder massager.

She simpered at him, mirth twinkling her gaze. "I was going to use it on this wicked knot in my shoulder that the shower massager just wasn't helping with."

"Why you little—"

CHAPTER 18

ADDISON OPENED her eyes the next morning and found herself encased in a cocoon of heat. And a large parking brake at the small of her back that she remembered well.

"Caine."

Her sleepy murmur triggered his arms to tighten around her.

He laid soft kisses over her shoulder blade. "Go back to sleep. You still have an hour before you have to wake up."

That sobered her immediately and she turned to face him, frowning disappointedly, "You didn't sleep?"

"I did for a little while." He smiled. "Not nearly as deeply as you did though."

She became fully awake then. "Is that code for

saying I was snoring?" Kylie had mentioned once that she snored sometimes when she was super exhausted.

"Just a little bit a few hours ago. It's actually why I woke up. I thought there was a kitten in our bed."

She bolted upright and studied his expression to see if he was kidding.

He didn't look like he was kidding. "It's cute," he insisted.

"Snoring *isn't* cute."

"It is when kittens do it."

"When have you even seen a kitten snore?"

"Sometimes the department has us do these cop outreach programs at the zoo. And the last time I was there, a momma lion had just given birth to a cute little lion cub that was snoring away. Seriously adorable."

She reached for her pillow under her head and whacked him.

Then gasped and grabbed the pillow back to cover herself.

"Why am I laying here buck naked?"

"You fell asleep like that," he replied innocently.

Had she?

The crinkle at the corners of his eyes told her she hadn't.

Scanning the area in search of her missing PJs and panties, she discovered that not only had Caine slingshot her clothes clear across the room, but he'd neatly balled up and launched her comforter over there as well.

"*How* did you get my clothes off without me noticing?"

"We went over the sleeping so deep you were snoring thing already right? And the part about me being awake in bed for the past few hours?"

She looked around for something soft but substantial to sock him in the gut with.

And that's when she noticed *he* still had on his boxer briefs.

At her pointed look, he glanced down. "It got a little chilly this morning."

He shot a placating hand up when she began sputtering in disbelief. "I promise, I made sure you were warm the entire time, sweetheart. Admittedly, I may have warmed up some parts of you a little more than others…"

Her jaw dropped. "*That's it,* I'm cutting you off for the rest of the week."

"Coffee or sex?" he asked, sounding appropriately alarmed either way.

Honestly, she wasn't sure which one would be a bigger punishment for the man.

"Okay, okay. No need to make any rash punishments." He reached over to grab something off the nightstand. "What if I give you a peace offering?" He handed her a thick folder of documents.

She peered at it curiously. "What is it?"

"That's a full background check of my life, basically from the day you left."

Gazing down at the folder, she said softly, "You didn't have to do this."

"It's only fair," he reasoned.

Her head snapped back up so hard, she got a kink in her neck. Digging her fingers into the muscle to stop the pain, she demanded, "Meaning you did a background check on me?"

"About two minutes after I pulled you over," he confirmed, looking wholly unapologetic.

Before she could rip into him for invading her privacy, he added quietly, "The reason I did a background check wasn't to be nosy...okay, not entirely. But it was more because I'd missed so much of your life. A lifetime, felt like. I just...wanted to know what your life had been like. Make sure you were happy."

Suddenly, she couldn't feel the crick in her neck. The blooming ball of emotion in her chest was eclipsing it all. She hugged the folder to her chest. "*Were* you happy? All these years?"

"Tried my best. But I missed the hell out of you. Every day. Every night."

Her chest tightened with pain. "Caine, I want you to know, leaving you was *the* hardest thing I've ever done."

He pulled her into his arms. "Truthfully? I don't know that I would've been able to do what you did.

Fighting for you to the death? Easy. Walking away from you? Try impossible."

A sharp knock on the door interrupted their talk.

Caine checked the time. "That's probably Gabe. He said he was stopping by to install some sort of new gadget."

She got up and grabbed her robe off the hook on her door. "I'll go let him in."

"Hold it." He confiscated her robe and went over to her closet. "Do you still have that big winter coat I saw you wear once back in Creek Hills? The one that covers you from neck to knees?"

Oy, him and his jealousy. It was so darned cute.

"*How* can you still be jealous of Gabe, after all this." She pointed at the tornado-like damage to her bed after their marathon sex.

"I can and I will. Until he gets it through his thick skull that you're mine."

Addison knew full well that Gabe thought of her as 'Caine's.' He'd told her more than enough times.

Just as he told her he wasn't going to quit messing with his big brother anytime soon.

While he was digging around her closet, earnestly looking for that winter coat, she quickly threw on the t-shirt he'd been wearing last night. It was thin and worn, but it fell well past her thighs. Gabe would never know she wasn't wearing any underwear.

She headed out to the living room to let Gabe in.

Only to get all but tackled halfway there.

"You are *not* answering the door wearing that."

"*Fine,*" she relented magnanimously.

When he let her loose and gruffly swiveled her away from the door, she chose to take his growling dictate literally.

…By giving him back his shirt right on the spot.

"Gabe, come back in a couple hours," hollered out Caine as he proceeded to practically *stalk* a now sprinting Addison back to the bedroom.

It ended up being way more than a couple of hours.

———◆———

BRIGHT AND EARLY Friday morning, Addison just shook her head at the sound of Caine knocking on the front door—just an hour after he'd slipped out of her apartment to go for a run, and then back to Alec's place to shower, before returning as if he hadn't spent the night here.

"You've slept in my bed every night for almost a week now." *And making sure I was exhausted enough after sex to sleep soundly through to morning.* "Don't you think Kylie has figured out that you're sneak in every night and sneak out every morning?"

He looked appalled at the possibility. "Do you really think she knows?"

Honestly, the man was just too adorable for words.

"I'm pretty sure she does. Just as I'm pretty sure she's pretending with all her might and imagination that we're playing board games in here all night before bed."

Sounding a tad traumatized, he asked solemnly, "You think it's time we had the talk with her?"

"Oh god! *No.* And that's a no for all eternity. If you start talking about the birds and the bees with her, you'll see a Kylie-shaped hole in that door and cartoon whoosh marks lingering in the air behind her."

Caine almost staggered back a step, looking like she'd just swung a baseball bat at his gut. "I meant the talk about you and I being back in a relationship. *Not* any sort of talk like the one you're suggesting—that I assure you, would result in a matching *Caine*-shaped hole in the door next to Kylie's."

She couldn't help it, she had to let out a tiny chuckle. The man looked positively green around the gills over the idea of having *that* 'talk' with Kylie. "Oh don't worry, I told her about us a while ago. And as far as the *other* talk goes, that safe sex presentation with the pamphlets and condoms I told you about actually had a section where parents and kids could dialog a bit. It was a pretty big hit."

"Move over, I think I need to lie down," he rumbled. "I feel like a scuba diver with the bends. Instead of having seven years to slowly—albeit super reluctantly—come up to the water's surface, you just torpedoed me from pink two-wheel bicycles with streamers to teen sex talks."

With a smiling headshake, Addison tossed her work clothes onto her dresser and made room for Caine on the bed. He collapsed onto it, arm flung over his head as if bracing for the roof to collapse.

"While we're on the topic, Kylie actually wanted to know—"

He shot his hand in the air and shook his head rigorously, eyes shut tight.

"While we're on the topic of *your early run every morning*," Addison clarified, lips twitching, "she wanted to know if you'd mind if she tagged along some days."

He peeked one eye open at her. "Really? That's it?"

"She wakes up as early as you and I do. Sometimes, she just takes it easy, but most of the times, she comes to survey the gardens in the mornings before everyone starts getting up for breakfast. But in the winters, we usually finish the garden pretty quick, so she's got tons of time left over."

Exhaling in relief, he replied, "Of course she can run with me. It'll be fun."

"Good. I'll let her know."

He studied her. "So you really told her about us being an us, huh?"

"Yup. Well, it was more I confirmed her suspicions when she wouldn't stop badgering me about it."

"And did she sound happy about it?"

Addison smiled softly. "Yes."

"What about you? Are you happy about this? About us?"

She wrapped her arms around his neck. "Absolutely."

"No more reservations?"

"Oh I have a ton of those."

"Yeah? Me too."

Her brows shot up in surprise. "Mr. Believe-In-The-System actually has reservations?"

"It's true. Before you, I believed simply in right and wrong, good and evil. Then you waltzed into my life. With all your hardships and heartaches and sheer determination to help your siblings get past all that, and in turn overcoming it all yourself."

He smiled and rubbed his thumb against her lower lip. "You didn't 'teach' that to me or anything cliché like that. You were just you, and before I realized or even fully understood it, you became the thing in my life that I had hope, belief, and trust would remain in my life...even without a single piece of evidence supporting the belief, even with stuff like a whacked-out stalker trying to extinguish that hope, and absolutely no precedence to garner any trust. Hope amidst worries, reservations, fears, and everything in between."

He leaned forward to nibble on the lip he'd successfully made tingle like crazy. "That's how I got through the last seven years of nights without you, and how you and I will get through every year from now no matter what gets thrown at us. It's going to be hard as hell…but without a doubt, worth it."

Practically floating on a mindless bubble now, she shivered, both over the maddening patterns he was tracing along her neck with his tongue, and the rigid proof he was nudging against her core as to how hard and worthwhile the foreseeable future was indeed going to be.

"Is that your way of saying you want a quickie before I have to head downstairs to work?"

"A *quickie*?" he repeated in an affronted tone. "Now that's lacking both faith *and* vision." He pinned both of her hands above her head and slipped first one nipple and then the other into his evil, evil mouth.

"Vision and faith, I have," she managed to gasp out. "It's *time* that I don't."

He scored his teeth gently over every sensitive part of her he discovered last night. The ones above her waist at least. His smoldering hot eyes promised all the ones below her waist was on deck very shortly. "I bet I could change your mind…convince you to head in late for the first time ever."

He'd totally win that bet. And her eleven poker tells were probably all admitting that unabashedly. Didn't mean she couldn't keep on raising the stakes though. "You're good, but I don't know if you're good enough to make me want to try being bad."

That was a bald-faced lie and they both knew it.

He grinned, and held her gaze for a long, distracting beat, until—

Click.

Every nerve ending in her body flared to life, in response to the cool metal now circling one of her wrists.

"Did you think I forgot all your mind-messing curiosity about my handcuffs?"

She looked up at her flat headboard. "There's nothing for you to cuff me too." *Why was she helping him find ways to restrain her?*

His brows dropped and his gaze darkened dangerously. "I could handcuff you to *me.*"

Click.

He secured the other end of his handcuffs to his own wrist.

Then dragged his hand down past his abdomen, taking her hand down with his when he started to—

Wow.

He groaned when she showed what a quick study she was and began mirroring his actions. Fingers gripped around him, just above his own, she matched him stroke for stroke.

Double wow.

"Christ, I'm going to come if we keep doing this."

She halted.

...And then slowly, shyly dragged her manacled

hand down *her* abdomen instead.

This time his curse was harsher, his groan deeper.

That settled it. She was *definitely* starting to like this being a little bad thing.

CHAPTER 19

THE NEXT NIGHT, Caine knocked on Addison's door promptly at midnight, more eager than usual to see her since she'd been busy with errands all day.

When she answered, he felt his jaw go slack, and his boots turn to cement blocks.

"What do you think?" she asked softly.

She'd changed back. All of it. Make-up, hair, clothes. Instead of her black leather and lace, she had on a pale yellow cotton tank top, with matching sleep shorts. Her skin was smooth, silky and completely bare of cosmetics, and her hair was back to its shiny brown tresses.

She was so damn adorable, he couldn't help but smile, and so damn sexy, he couldn't help but growl. "You're gorgeous," he belatedly answered. "It's literally all I can do to *not* take you right here in the hallway."

Her cheeks stained bright with pleasure. "Figured no point in hiding now since David already knows I'm here. So I may as well be myself."

"Best idea ever."

Studying him as intently as he was studying her, she frowned. "What's wrong?"

"What do you mean?"

"You look...I don't know, concerned?"

She knew him well. "Truth is, I've been having a hard enough time controlling myself without all this." He rubbed a lock of her hair between his thumb and forefinger, and ran his eyes over the rest of her. "But now..." He exhaled roughly, and gave her a grave, dubious headshake. "Now I'll never be able to keep my hands off of you."

She bit her lip. Likely to hold back the smile he could see twinkling in her eyes. "Well...you're keeping your hands off of me pretty easily right now." She took a step back. Then another.

The woman and her dares. The sight of her retreating from him was all he needed to regain the use of his legs again.

Catching her before she took a single step more, he gripped her hips and crashed his lips down on hers before steadily walking her backward right to her bedroom. He didn't stop until she fell back against the bed.

Then he took his time. Undressed her slowly. Unwrapping her like the ultimate birthday and Christmas present rolled into one.

But the moment her panties slid off the tip of her toe, he broke.

"You're so wet." Eyes locked on the liquid heat between her thighs, he brushed a thumb over her slick, sensitive flesh. "Is this all for me, baby?" He wanted to hear her say it.

"Always."

Damn. Lust hit him like a wrecking ball.

Leave it to Addison to turn a simple yes or no question into so much more. Didn't help one bit that she answered him in that tone she reserved just for him—equal parts innocence, mischief, and sass. Never failed to drive him out of his mind.

The need to touch her, taste her, possess her in every way he could, began coursing through his veins like a drug until he had no other recourse but to fall to his knees and latch his mouth onto her honeyed center.

With just one swipe of his tongue, tasting her became a compulsion, those soft, sexy noises she was making, a new addiction.

He slid his palms up her torso, skimmed his fingers over her hardened nipples, nearly coming in his pants when more of her sugary heat coated his tongue.

She was close, but for some reason, she was holding back, edging back away from him, smothering back her soft, sexy cries.

He gripped her thighs in his hands and spread her legs wide open, baring her fully to his gaze. "No hiding from me," he growled against her skin. "I want to watch you come apart just like this. Your pleasure is mine baby, let me see it. Taste it."

———————•———————

ADDISON SHOOK her head, sank her teeth into her lip to keep from tumbling over the edge.

At least when he was inside her, he was every bit as far gone as she was. But this...with his mouth destroying her with every molten hot lick, his dark, dominant gaze scorching over every inch of her like he *owned* her...

It was too intense, too intimate.

Too out of her control.

So she valiantly fought off the climax she could feel starting to white out her vision.

He tsked. "So stubborn."

Undeterred, he brushed his lips across the dip of her stomach and then slowly traced the outline of the tattoo on her hip with his tongue. Her other real tattoo. The one he'd been obsessed with since first laying eyes on it.

It didn't take long for the evil man and his talented tongue to make the tiny Easter egg tattoo on the blade of her hip, with the laurel leaf design she'd drawn specifically for him seven years ago, feel like a red hot brand, directly hardwired to her sex.

Her hips bucked up involuntarily. Which prompted Caine to smile wickedly and shift back over to his original mission of sliding his tongue along her slick center, swirling over the bundle of nerves now absolutely *throbbing* with pleasure.

His teeth followed next, raking over the same path. Once, *twice...*

She gasped out his name before he could do it a third time.

He growled in triumph. "Again." Tongue and teeth. Teeth and tongue. He was relentless. "My name, Addison. *Again.*"

Oh God. She wasn't going to make it. Though a part of her wanted to do exactly as he ordered, she couldn't speak, could barely even think.

Not with the sharp, intense satisfaction burning in the depths of his gaze the more she unraveled.

By the time he pumped two thick fingers deep inside her, she was freefalling, his name a hoarse cry clawing out of her throat as he held her legs open and sealed his mouth over her to wring out every last bit of her orgasm.

She was boneless, mindless when he stood, hands gently caressing her legs as if he simply couldn't stop touching her.

"Hell, I'm not going to last, babe." His heated, *tortured* tone sent pleasure curling through her, need wrapping around her. "Where's your box of condoms?"

Slowly, she slid over to the edge of the bed, and attempted to stand on the wobbly ground under her feet. She took comfort in knowing she wouldn't be standing for much longer.

"I hid the box," she informed him, her voice husky even to her own ears.

"Why?"

She put a hand on his clenched abs and pushed gently. "Because…it's my turn."

Running her hands over the solid wall of muscle that he called a chest, and the spectacularly ripped work of anatomical art that made up his abs, she managed to pull a low, slow groan of pleasure from him.

When she began undressing him, inch by impressive inch, his darkening gaze threatened to swallow her whole.

By the time he was as naked as she was, he looked two seconds away from doing something absolutely *carnal* to her.

Maybe next round.

Locking her gaze on his, slowly, so slowly, she slid her hands, one over the other, down his now fully engorged length.

With his rough voice warning her that he was already starting to lose control, she quickly started pumping his granite hard shaft with one hand, while sliding her other hand lower.

He cursed, every muscle in his body corded and clenched.

"Addison."

Before she could talk herself out of it, she dropped her mouth down to shadow her hand's movements, showing him just how good of a teacher he was.

Lips, teeth, and tongue... Lips, teeth, and tongue...

She finally understood what his fascination was with her saying his name. Hearing Caine utter her name in deep, gritty, *reverent* growls while he came had her quickly following him over the edge, by the force of his voice alone.

"Holy hell, woman," he exhaled on a rough rasp, eyes hot and turbulent as he watched her eventually return back to earth. Looking about ready to ravage her right then and there, he picked her up and deposited her back on the bed with his token gentle gruffness. "I think you better tell me where you hid that box. Because we're going to need it in about two minutes. Maybe less."

Now who was the one throwing down dares?

Instead of give him the answer he was looking for, she just gave him a soft smile and gamely accepted this less-than-two-minutes dare of his.

———◆———

"JUST OUT OF CURIOSITY, why do you do that?"

Seconds away from falling into a deep post-sex

slumber, Addison looked up from Caine's chest sleepily. "Do what?"

He gave her hand a gentle squeeze, smiling. "Whenever I hold your hand, you always stare at our hands. Sometimes for minutes at a time."

"I do?" She'd never noticed she did that.

"You don't have to tell me. I was just wondering."

She reflected on it for a bit as she looked at their twined hands resting next to her cheek. "I think...I think it's because you *like* to hold my hand. When we're together, you reach for my hand all the time." And she loved how often he did it. Whenever they were together, really. Wholly instinctual, almost unaware, they could be walking and talking after separating for a bit to tie a loose shoelace, and he'd twine their fingers mid-speaking.

He nodded, waiting for her to shuffle through the rest of her thoughts on the matter.

"Also...you were the first guy to ever hold my hand. Back in Creek Hills. You slid your hand into mine and just...stole a big chunk of my heart right then and there." She'd always felt comforted, cherished with his big, warm, calloused hand engulfing hers.

He lifted her hand and pressed his lips against her knuckles, making it tingle.

"And yeah...that. I love it when you do that." Whenever he kissed her hand like that, it was a cross between the most natural curling-up-in-your-favorite-chair feeling…and foreplay.

Every time.

"Honestly, aside from Kylie and Tanner, you're the *only* person who's ever held my hand." Addison had no working memory of her mother ever having held her hand as a kid. Not out of affection or comfort, at least. To tug her in annoyance, sure.

"I'm sorry your mom never held your hand, sweetheart." His tone was gentle, but his expression was anything but. She knew he wasn't a fan of her mom, and this little tidbit probably sent the woman skyrocketing up his shitlist.

She shrugged. "It's okay. I mean, it wasn't, of course. I'd never ever bring a kid into this world without wanting to hold his or hand through the good and bad parts, you know?"

"Do you think about that? Having kids?"

"Sometimes."

He began stroking her hair with his free hand. "Me too. Sometimes. I've always wanted a big family. Did I mention that? Whether by blood or not. Permanent or not. I've always just wanted to fill a home with lots of kids to love."

She rolled partially on top of him and perched her chin on her free hand. "You want to foster children like your folks did?"

He raised a brow at her question. "I told you back

in Creek Hills that I wanted to foster Kylie and Tanner."

She drew in a wobbly breath at that amazing memory. "I-I know. I wasn't sure if that was just because of the situation."

"It was, but I also do want to be a foster dad in the future as well." His eyes locked on hers. "Later. When you and I are married. By the way, are you okay with us having lots of kids?"

Her heart snagged in her throat. That was a masterful segue into a relationship talk. Instead of answering right away, she sidestepped it to buy herself some time, "You think about that? You and I having kids? I thought only women did that sort of thing—I actually think that was on a movie once as a rule of what not to do when you're first dating a guy."

He gave her an affronted look. "Of course guys think about that kind of stuff. I used to know a guy in the NFL that only dated athletic women since he'd read somewhere that kids inherit a lot of their athletic prowess from their moms."

She laughed. "You're making that up."

"Totally true story."

"So that's what you do, too? Think about your future kids with every woman you date?"

He kissed her knuckles. "Not until you."

Butterflies started fluttering around in her insides.

Alright, she was ready to answer his question now.

"I think I'd want a big family, too."

Okay, maybe not *totally* ready. Baby steps. "Full disclosure, though," she added, to give him an escape hatch out of this conversation if he wanted one. "I'm terrible at sports. Every single sport. It's a miracle I passed P.E. in school."

He chuckled. "Duly noted. But it's okay if they don't play sports. As long as they're all happy."

With a dad like Caine? That was an absolute certainty. "So when you say 'big family' how big are we talking?"

He didn't even stop to think. "Three to start."

"Don't tell me, three boys like you, Max, and Gabe."

"Nope. Three girls. Hopefully all like you. Beautiful and smart with big hearts."

Oh lord, the man knew exactly how to reduce her to a melted puddle of goo.

She bussed her lips over his knuckles. "Well then we better plan on fostering and adopting a bunch of sons who'll be as overprotective as you are. With a mom like me, our daughters are *probably* going to be a handful."

Suddenly, Caine's arms became steel bands around her as he scooped her up and dragged her across his chest. "Say that again. Just like that. All of it."

She studied his primal, alpha intense gaze for a beat. "If I do, are you going to want to start making these babies right now?"

Completely serious question.

He rolled them both over on the bed until he was on top of her. "Probably." Framing her face with one hand, he added, "But I'd settle for just practicing a whole lot."

"Deal."

CHAPTER 20

ADDISON CLOSED up her office and took a slight detour down the hall to swing by the day care center before starting her daily site rounds.

It was her third visit of the day.

For the past few days—ever since Caine had brought up the baby thing—she'd been finding herself there more and more.

That whole thing about the ticking biological clock?

Might have merit.

"Oh, Addison, there you are." Maggie, one of the moms that had been with CORE from the very start intercepted her on the way to the day care center to give her a warm hug. "I wanted to tell you, the new tutor you hired is great. A real hoot. I thought he was a little odd at first, but he's great with the kids; especially the girls.

Apparently, he could pass for the way older brother of one of their favorite teen— Hey, you okay?"

Every muscle in her body locked up as her blood ran ice cold.

She hadn't hired any new tutors.

"Maggie, I need you to go inside and tell the kids that it's time for the self-defense workshops with the police officers outside. And that they should just leave everything here and head on out. Don't make it a question. And don't make it sound optional. Then just get those kids out. Go straight to the room we hold Georgia's sewing classes in and lock the door."

Maggie's expression changed from confusion to alarm. "What's going on, Addison? Who is that man?"

"I'll explain later. Right now, please, just do exactly as I just said. But stay calm in there." Addison knew Maggie was tough, but when kids were involved, even the toughest could panic.

But Maggie just nodded and hustled into the study room, her voice clear and strong, her expression giving nothing away.

Addison tried to see his face. David. After all these years. But his back was to her the entire time. As soon as she saw Maggie start leading the kids out of the room, Addison quickly headed to the daycare center, hands shaking all the while as she group-texted her security guards and Alec, praying that at least one of them was nearby.

Frank, her main security guard texted he was on the phone with 9-1-1 to report the intruder.

She stepped into the daycare center and said the two words she'd never had to utter before to her staff. "Emergency lockdown."

Terrified panic hit the young volunteer who'd just started a few weeks prior. She looked rooted to the spot, silent questions posed on her startled, mouth agape lips. But before Addison could tell her to follow protocol, her main daycare center manager ran up.

They didn't have to exchange a word. The seasoned woman knew this wasn't a drill. She gave Addison a quick nod. "We're on it."

Addison watched the two women quietly get the attention of the parents in the room.

Fear descended on the room like an invisible cloud. Horrified glances were shot Addison's way, but everyone remained calm as they gathered up the children.

Addison swiftly flipped the blinds for the windows facing the hallway closed, giving herself just a tiny sliver to peek out through to watch the last of the evacuation of the study hall.

David was nowhere in sight.

Another minute—that felt like the longest and shortest of her life—passed before she finally got the text from Frank that the police were on their way.

The halls were deserted. Everyone was ready,

286

prepared for the worst.

And so was Addison.

She walked calmly over to the door.

"Addison! What're you doing?" hissed one of the mothers. "Don't go out there."

But she had to. "He's looking for me. You'll all be safe. Just stay here and protect the kids until help arrives."

Knowing she'd never be able to hide the fear in her eyes from them, she left the daycare center without looking back at the scared parents and workers, the unknowing children.

Slowly, she made her way down the deathly silent hallway.

Until a hand swiped over her mouth from behind.

She rammed her heel down on his foot with everything she had.

Alec grunted. "Calm down, it's just me." He let her go, cursing quietly, "*Shit,* those boots of yours are lethal."

"*I'm so sorry,* I thought you were David."

"Of all the things you had to keep from your bad-ass wardrobe," he muttered, the approving praise clearly evident in his voice. "Next time, toss an elbow to the throat in there too."

It was like having a Caine back-up on hand.

"Have you seen him? Is he still in the building?"

Alec pulled her into the main office and had her crouch down behind the reception desk. "No. We've had conflicting reports come in so Drew's doing a digital sweep, building by building. Frickin' dude is a genius; he's hacked everything hackable. When the cops are done mobilizing their units to send in, they'll do a physical sweep to confirm."

"But what if he has hostages? Maybe if he sees me, I can stop him from—"

"*Sit your butt down.* I don't need Caine castrating me, thank you very much. If David is still on the property, we just need a confirmation on his location so we can take him out. Snipers should be getting into positions soon." He checked the ammo in both of his guns.

Just as a gasp burst out from the other side of the room.

Addison shot her gaze over to the source, and saw a horrified pair of eyes peeking out from behind her desk in the back. "*Jaimie?*" She ran over and found two terrified fifth graders huddled together, crying. She immediately wrapped her arms around them and tried to calm them down.

"Jaimie and I thought this was a drill like they have at school," sobbed Molly. "We didn't know it was real."

"Shhh, it's okay. It's almost over. You heard Mr. Alec," Addison reassured them quietly, trying to sound as composed as possible. "We don't know anything for certain right now. There are security teams and officers out there checking things out, keeping us safe."

Meanwhile, Alec got on his Bluetooth and finished strapping on a few different weapon holsters on various parts of his body. When he was done, he looked up to signal that he had to leave. She knew the lockdown protocol backward and forward. There would be no covert evacuating like on TV. They all just had to sit tight until told otherwise.

"Be careful," she mouthed.

He saluted her with his gun and quickly made his exit.

The snick of the door locking behind him was almost deafening in the silence. Hearing the housing complex without all the normal sounds of families bustling around was a sobering blow that would've had her in tears if the girls weren't there with her, counting on her to hold it together.

She gave them each a squeeze. "It'll be fine. Just a little while longer."

An hour passed with no change.

She did, however, receive a text from Drew—angel that he was—about twenty minutes ago letting her know that all the apartments had been swept with no sightings of David, and so far, no injuries reported.

It was nearly dusk when the lights finally came on without warning.

A weary Alec came in to give them the official all-clear.

The girls cried with relief and ran out to join their friends across the hall, past a half dozen full-tactical SWAT guys filing through the halls, and uniformed officers going into each room to check on everyone.

There was terror reflected on every single face she saw out there.

And it gutted her.

"Addison." Alec came over, his expression grim. "There's something you need to know…"

———◆———

THE NOISE in the dining hall was deafening.

All the parents who weren't comforting their kids— or packing—were crammed into the big room, all standing, most shouting at the top of their lungs.

Sixty-four families.

Two hundred seventy-one parents and children.

All panicked and horrified over the day's events, even now, hours later.

"So what are you saying, Addison?" bellowed a voice from the crowd.

She couldn't distinguish them from each other anymore; the distress in their voices all sounded identical, the sounds of anger and betrayal piercing.

"You've known for *weeks* now that this sicko stalker was after you and you didn't tell any of us? You didn't think to have the *decency* to let us decide if it was worth the risk to stay here?"

Addison tried, but failed to swallow back her shame. They were right. She should've notified all the families right after David had sent her the floral bouquet. They had every right to know. And she'd done them a severe injustice by not saying anything.

"Just give her a chance to explain," hollered another voice.

That managed to calm some of them down. At least enough for their attention to be focused collectively on her.

So explain she did.

She started at the beginning. Talked about how she'd raised Kylie and Tanner. Divulged everything about David's priors, his stalking, and his intention to drug, rape, and likely kill her seven years ago. And the suspicions of his ties to the Mexican drug trades now.

The room once again broke out into a symphony of outraged chatter. *"A known rapist was in here with our daughters?!"* That voice she did recognize. It was the single mother of three girls who'd taken to the streets to get away from her husband, who'd been abusing her for years.

Addison had no words. No defense. Instead of providing these families with a better alternative to living on the streets, she'd placed them all in danger. Put them at the mercy of a madman. "I understand your concern and wouldn't blame you at all for wanting to vacate the premises."

The outcry started up again.

"Where are we supposed to go?"

"Can't you just increase security?"

"Isn't your boyfriend a cop?"

The questions just kept coming.

"We've already hired one of the best security firms in the state, and beyond that, we'll continue to bring in additional safety measures. That said, I can't in good conscience provide you with any sort of guarantees that it's safe here for your families. So I've already talked to several shelters," she raised her voice to be heard over the chaos.

The mention of shelters had a few families walking out on the spot.

"What is it going to be?" called out one of the newest dads on site incredulously, "first come first serve? Then the rest of us have to decide between staying here with a psycho rapist stalking the joint, or going back on the streets again?"

"Hold on," argued his neighbor, "I don't know where the rest of you used to pitch your tents, but I'd rather take my chances here where there's security rather than have my kids worry about stepping on broken needles or running into a tweaked-out druggie."

Maggie, the mother she'd relied on to evacuate the children from the study hall walked straight up to her and looked her dead in the eye, voice cold and wholly betrayed as she spat out, *"You brought us here, and promised us a better life, a better shot at getting out of the homeless cycle, and now you're saying our BEST option is to go back?"*

That one hung in the air like a dark, dense fog that cloaked everything around them. A brutal summary of the reality they were all facing at the moment.

Just like that, most of the families were done listening. Many lined up to reserve shelter space, while others began grouping up to discuss their next move, the best areas they could set up tent again. And still others broke away from the pack without a word, leaving behind the community she'd tried to build for them, looking more alone than when they'd first come here.

In all the nightmares of David she'd suffered through over the past seven years, not one of them were half as devastating as the scene unfolding before her.

One of the few single fathers on site, who was doing a remarkable job raising twin boys came up to her. "You tried, Addison. That's more than most people can say. Keep your head up. Don't let this one day undo all the good you've done for us for the past months."

So saying, he left as well.

The head of her afterschool activities, who lived on site, stepped forward, tears in her eyes. "Addison...my girls and I, we owe you everything. But...a rapist. A criminal that's unstable at best..." Equal parts regret and motherly resolve reflected across her features. "I'm so so sorry, but we're going to go."

"Don't apologize," whispered Addison, returning the fierce hug. "Your girls and your safety come first. Always. You let me know if I can help you once you get settled, you hear?"

It didn't end there.

One by one, her staff members that were also residents each came forward to let her know they were leaving.

By midnight, the building was a ghost town.

When finally, there was no one else she needed to be strong or brave or calm for, she crumbled.

Caine caught her before she hit the floor.

Gathering her up in his arms, he pulled her into his lap, and just held her.

"This was all my fault," she whispered.

"Don't say that. Don't even *think* it. You are not accountable for David's actions."

"But I'm accountable for my own." After talking for so many hours straight, her throat was raw, and she welcome the pain. "I endangered the lives of all these families, Caine. All because I was arrogant enough to think that I could outrun my past, that it wouldn't continue to haunt me. I've spent the last few years telling hundreds of families in shelters that they could rebuild their lives, do one better than simply restoring it. I stood before *these* parents and children and promised them they could overcome their pasts...all the while being the fraud that's been hiding from hers."

Bitterness bled through her words. "I thought I was helping them, saving them. It never once occurred to me that I could in fact make things so much *worse* for them."

"You can't let what happened here today negate all the good you've done, everything you've given back to these families."

Slowly, she unclenched her fists for the first time in hours. To look down at the blackened soot on her hands. "What I've *given* them is more to be afraid of than they'd ever had before, more to be devastated over."

She shot back up to her feet and pointed out the window. "Look what he did, Caine. Not only did he have them fearing for their lives today, but he *torched* the gardens they've all worked on. He showed them cruelty that for once, wasn't the universe's doing. He deliberately took something they grew with their own two hands and *burned it to the ground.*"

The charred gardens—the only parts of the complex that had been set on fire—was a pointed, destructive message for her, that all the residents had had to feel the wrath of as well.

Anguish tore her to shreds on the inside. "These families don't come by trust easily, and today, I *decimated* that trust. All for..."

Us. "Guess I'm the apple that didn't fall that far from the tree."

Swift fury and frustration swept across Caine's face. "Don't let him do this to you. To what you and I just got back. Addison, you know you're nothing like your mother."

"Maybe not. But it sure does look like our destinies are aligned, doesn't it?" she replied brokenly, halfway to defeat, with a fresh helping of disappointment *in herself.* "It's ironic, really. My mom chose to be with a whole lot of men and ended up failing her family. I chose to be with one man and ended up failing a whole lot of families." She hated irony.

"You didn't fail us, Addison."

Addison spun around to see one of the bigger pilot families that had moved into the complex during their soft launch a month before they officially opened their doors.

Hell, what right did she have to hold a pity party for herself when her families were losing everything? *Pull yourself together, woman.*

"Tim, Nancy. Is everything okay? I thought you left a while ago."

"We were getting ready to," replied Tim candidly. "We had most of our stuff packed up and everything."

Nancy came forward. "But just when we were about done, the Jorgensons from next door came over and gave us a Ziploc bags of energy bars Jill had made, because she knew it was our favorite." Her voice wobbled, but she trudged on. "Then Al and Sue from across the hall said they would watch the kids for a few hours so we could go find a place to set up our tent."

"A tent that Bill from the next building had patched up for us," continued Tim, "right before he went to his shop to put some hinges on some pieces of plywood that we'd be able to fold up and take with us, with some little ottoman feet we could screw in when it was opened up so we could make a bed off the ground for my momma, on account of her bad back."

When he, Nancy, the kids, and their nana stepped off to the side, Addison saw a dozen more families starting to fill the hallways.

"*This* right here is what you did, Addison. You didn't fail us. You showed us that we could be more than the product of our misfortunes. That we could be in charge of our own destinies again. That we could be a part of a *community* again, in a world that literally spit us out onto the street like social outcasts." He drew in a deep, impassioned breath. "You gave us good homes we could have pride in, safe playgrounds for our children to play in. You turned our neighbors into our equals—into colleagues we worked alongside, into our teachers as well as our students...into trusted friends. You gave us the seeds to grow our new lives as families, the tools to build the futures a lot of us stopped dreaming was possible."

"...And most important of all, you gave us *hope*

again."

Nancy turned to look out into the hall. "None of us here are willing to give all that up. None of us here are willing to give up, period."

Addison quickly discovered that there was nothing in her entire lexicon sufficiently strong enough to express what she was feeling, to translate how much their staying meant to her own formerly dwindling supply of hope.

As she stood there, struggling to speak, Caine swooped in to give her a minute to use her words again by sharing a story with the crowd. "Earlier tonight, I'd called up my captain over at my precinct to see if we could organize some sort of community service event out here to help with the clean-up. Turns out, they'd already beaten me to it. A steady stream of officers have been signing up all night to take shifts here. And that had nothing to do with me. Or Addison, even. The officers said they want to help *you all* rebuild what you lost. From restoring your gardens to restoring your feeling of safety here, they want to do what they can to help."

Alec materialized in the doorway. "The community beyond these walls feel the same. Our phones have been ringing off the hook all evening with calls from fellow urban farmers all across the state, neighborhood shop managers, some of your bosses and colleagues as well—they all want to help out too."

Oh sweet lord, at this rate, she'd never be able to

speak again. She was pretty much just a crying ball of emotions right now.

Luckily, none of the families required her to talk. They all just wanted to hug the news out with her and then head on back to their apartments to sleep so they could start the clean-up first thing in the morning.

By her estimation, over half the families were heading off to sleep in their beds tonight.

"Tomorrow, I'm going to go out and find the rest," she told Caine firmly when her voice eventually returned. "I'm going to bring them all home."

Caine came up behind her to wrap one strong, supportive arm around her waist. "Thought you might say that." Using his free hand, he swiped the screen of his phone to life, and after four quick passcode entries, he showed her a map of the city with a whole bunch of red blinking dots.

Then he just held her and waited.

It took her a second, but when she finally figured out what exactly she was looking at, her heart just about burst wide open. She turned and gazed up at the crazy wonderful man she just flat-out loved the heck out of. "You *low-jacked* them?"

He grinned. "Every single family on their way out."

CHAPTER 21

"ARE YOU SURE I can't change your mind?"

Addison shook her head, reaching up to smooth her hand up Caine's suit-clad chest. "Nope. You need to go to the courthouse to testify—you worked on this case for nearly a year; they need your testimony far more than I need a babysitter."

Caine frowned. "I still can't believe Alec just up and left like a thief in the night without telling me anything. Did he give you any more info on where he went?"

"He just said that he'd be back as soon as he can, but that there was something he really needed to do today."

"I hate having to leave you to start the fire clean-up on your own."

"I'm not alone. Close to thirty families and five more of my staff members stayed last night. Most of them are already out there with the clean-up crew and groundskeeper."

He pulled her into his arms. "Guess I should go take the tracking devices off the ones who came back. As far as the others go, I've been keeping tabs on them through the night—had some buddies do drive-bys to check up on the ones I was worried about. Built a pretty efficient route we can take to track them all down as soon as I get out of court today."

She just shook her head and drank in every intense inch of him, immediately getting herself sucked into the orbit of his dark, stormy gaze—freshly charged today with relief, hope, and a hundred other emotions she'd been feeling alongside him since David nearly broke her yesterday.

"Tell me the truth, if the families hadn't returned, and I'd chosen flight over fight yesterday, would you have cuffed me to the bed to keep me from leaving this time?" She distinctly remembered him making a threat similar to that seven years ago.

…She'd be lying if she said she wasn't still more than a little intrigued over the idea.

"Not cool getting me worked up before I have to go be a witness in a trial, woman."

She buried her lips against the now corded column of his neck. "Is that a yes?"

"No."

Oh. Bummer.

"Would've cuffed you to *me*. Indefinitely, this time."

Oh. Even better.

A loud, amused *'ahem'* from the living room kept her from asking how then this morning's shower activities would've gone in that particular scenario.

Caine shot his eyes over to her previously closed front door. If looks could neuter.

"Don't go glaring at the cavalry." Marco walked right up between them and scooped her into a big bear hug. "You two can continue your dirty bondage talk later."

Addison's felt her whole face turn tomato red.

Caine pulled her out of Marco's arms. "Your timing sucks as usual, man." He cupped her face with both hands and grazed his thumbs across her red hot cheeks. "Cereal's on the counter. And there's a quart of that chocolate almond milk you like so much on the fridge door."

"I knew you loved me," announced Marco as he headed off to the kitchen. "Sorry you had to find out this way, Addison."

Caine rolled his eyes with what could only be called affectionate male annoyance. Tugging her toward the door to see him out, he gave her a proper goodbye kiss to leave her with a nice little buzz clear till lunch, and then handed her a Phoenix PD business card. "I'll be back hopefully by this afternoon. If you need me and my phone is off, call the station. Just tell them who you are and someone will make sure to get a message to the courtroom I'll be in."

"Stop worrying. We'll be fine. Now go, before you're late."

"Wait. Did I give you Lia's number? Do you know what their scheduled ETA is to meet up with Max and Tanner in California?"

"Kylie called early this morning when she woke up. Lia and Hudson were getting the car ready for the drive over about an hour ago."

When he still didn't look anywhere near ready to leave, she tilted her head in question, but didn't prod, didn't push.

He stared at her for a silent beat before finally asking gruffly, "You're going to be here when I get back, right?"

Her heart tore open a few humbling inches at the seams. "*Yes.* I promise, I'm not going anywhere this time."

The tension in his shoulders eased just the tiniest bit. He dragged her in for one final kiss before turning to Marco. "Keep my girl safe until I get home."

Marco gave him an extra-long thumbs-up with his spoon, while answering Caine with extra-deadly seriousness. "I'll guard her with my life, man."

———◆———

A LITTLE AFTER ELEVEN, following an exhausting morning of fire clean-up with nearly a hundred volunteers,

Addison got a call on her cell from a number she didn't recognize.

Marco—who hadn't left her side all day—immediately shifted into alpha bodyguard mode.

She waited for him to finish tapping something out on his own phone and give her the go-ahead before picking up. "Hello?"

"Addison? It's Sonny. Don't hang up."

She shot Marco a 'false-alarm' look. "Sonny, now's not a good time. And as you well remember, you're only supposed to be communicating with me via our lawyers."

"That's what I'm calling to talk about. At least partially, anyway. You and I both know Lara doesn't have a chance in hell at getting named executor of Kylie's trust. Even without your bigshot attorney."

Honesty. How so very unlike the man. "Then why are you calling? If you're thinking of trying to borrow money or something—"

"It's about your mom."

That made her stop and clutch the phone a little tighter. The woman may not be mother of the year, but she was the only mother she had.

"She's using again, Addison. I swear, she tried real hard this time, I want you to know that." He sighed. "Your mom, she's not perfect, but I love her. And I'm real worried this time."

"That bad?" She knew Sonny had seen her mom

reach some pretty bad lows. But before he came along, Addison had seen worse.

"She's spiraling out of control. Haven't seen her like this since I first met her. I finally checked her phone log yesterday and saw she's been contacting her old dealer, the one that got her hooked on all that crazy shit before she went into the rehab when you were in high school."

It was strange how no matter how many years passed, or how bad things got, she still couldn't bear the thought of her mom struggling, suffering like this. "Have you called her sponsor?"

"Hasn't helped. Lara won't talk to anyone right now. That's why I'm calling." He sighed again, this time sounding less resigned, and more optimistic. "Honestly, I think the only person who can pull her out of this one is you, Addie."

"*Me?* Why on earth would you think that?"

"Because, after everything that went down at the lawyer's office, she started getting real depressed. Started talking a lot about you hating her. She kept saying over and over again how she did wrong by you and the kids. The next few nights, she drank so hard I had to watch her to make sure she didn't suffocate on her own vomit while she was passed out. A few days ago, I started seeing the needle marks again."

Addison slammed her eyes shut to try and stop the far too familiar images from flooding her memories. It'd always been painful to watch her mom fall off the wagon. The first few days were always the worst. She remembered how her mom would take the biggest risks, care the least about consequences, whenever she'd start using again. Almost like in punishment. From standing on the railing of a balcony or daring one of her equally high friends to throw a knife at an apple on her head, Lara found new and increasingly reckless and terrifying ways to self-destruct.

"Last night, I thought I'd really lost her this time, Addie." Anguish vibrated through his voice. "She told me she doesn't want to feel anything anymore. She went right past the high, and went straight to blacking out. On purpose. I don't even know what she took."

"Sonny, it sounds like you need to give her sponsor another call, and get her to a hospital or rehab clinic right away."

"None of that is going to cut it this time. Please, Addie just talk to her. You'll see. It's different. Something's really different and all I know is that for once, even I can't help her. *Please*, Addie. I'm afraid I'm going to lose her for good this time."

The man sounded downright desperate. She remembered the feeling. How alone it felt, how helpless. "What makes you so sure she'll even talk to me—"

He sucked in a hopeful breath. "Are you saying you'll meet with her?"

In the entire time she'd known Sonny, she'd never

once heard him like this. "Of course I will. Just tell me where she'll be detoxing and I'll stop by."

"No, no. I'll help her get cleaned up and we'll come to you—"

"Oh. You want to meet *today?*"

Marco gaped at her, looking all but ready to yank the phone out of her hands.

"Sonny, hang on for a second."

She muted the phone and tried to calm Marco down before his head exploded. "I know you think I'm crazy, but she's my mom. I've been taking care of her for even longer than I looked after Tanner and Kylie. Sonny may be a con man always looking for an easy score, and a grade-A ass to boot, but he's stuck by her through even her worst times. And if he's this worried that she's not going to be able to come back from this, frankly, I am too."

"Addison—"

"No, hear me out. If there's a chance that I can help her get back into rehab, I want to try. I'm not absolving her or even forgiving her. This isn't about second chances. I believe in helping people who I'm in a position to help."

"But she doesn't *deserve* your help. She deserves to go to jail for abandoning her kids, and for being a shitty excuse for a parent your entire lives before that."

"I'm not arguing any of that, but holding her accountable for being a neglectful parent, and looking the other way when she's at the mercy of an addiction she can't control are two completely different things. If you saw a defenseless criminal dying at the hands of an even more dangerous and ruthless criminal he had no chance of protecting himself against, would you just turn a blind eye and walk away?"

"Dammit," he cursed. "Caine was right, you are like Jiminy Frickin' Cricket."

She chose to take that as more compliment than complaint. "Marco, I'm just going to try and talk to her, that's all. Get her to listen to her sponsor, hopefully even check into a full treatment center this time. Over the last few years, I've made a lot of good contacts who I know can help her. If I'd found these folks a decade ago, I truly think things would be better for her now."

He paced back and forth for at least a full minute before finally coming to a decision. "Put the phone on speaker."

She did.

He got straight to the point. "Look asshole, I'm not Caine, but I'm under direct orders from him to watch the love of his life and make sure she doesn't so much as get a papercut. So if this is some ploy to get money or guilt her into—"

"It's not," came the rushed reply. "I just want her to talk to her mom, that's all, I swear. I'll keep a hundred yards away from them the entire time if you want." Even Addison could hear how genuinely on edge Sonny sounded.

She glanced at Marco, who reluctantly nodded.

"I'll let the guard at the front know you'll be coming today. We've got a lot going on right now. Do you know when you'll be by?"

"She's awake, but I'm going to need another hour or so to help her sober up more—I know she won't want you to see her like this. I'll call if it takes me longer than that." A gusty sigh of relief hit the phone waves. "Thank you, Addie. This means more than you'll ever know."

After she hung up the phone, Marco gave her a stressed-out, albeit loving glare...*whilst* checking the firearm in its shoulder holster. "I'm warning you now, if this guy so much as raises his voice at you, I'm going to shoot first, ask him to quiet down second, are we clear?"

She gave the violently sweet man a hug. "Caine is rubbing off on you."

"No trying to flatter me. If your mom upsets you and Caine finds out..."

"She won't." Honestly, after everything that happened yesterday—both tragically bad and amazingly good—Addison would be shocked if anything her mom had to say fazed her at all.

———◆———

AN HOUR LATER, almost on the dot, Sonny arrived at the main office. Without Lara.

"Where's my mother?"

"I can't get her out of the car. She was fine when we left the motel. Nervous, but in a good way. But in the car ride over, she started zoning out. Now she's just sitting in there staring out the window, not saying a word."

Marco abruptly stepped in between them, proving exactly why he's earned himself the reputation as one of Spencer Securities' most imposing personal bodyguards. "Then it's pointless for Addison to try and talk to her. We'll reschedule this after she detoxes."

Sonny looked beside himself. "She really wanted to talk to you, Addie. But when we got here, it was sort of like someone let all the air out of her. Remember how she was that time we got kicked out of our second place? The one that had the pool she liked?"

How could she forget? She and Sonny had taken turns taking care of her for nearly a week. While Sonny hadn't been able to get Lara to eat, she did eat some oatmeal when Addison had tried feeding her.

Addison gently eased her elbow out of Marco's grip. "I'll go to her. Where'd you park?"

"Right out back."

They followed him out to his car—Marco under protest—and found Lara in the front, glassy-eyed and staring unfocused out the window.

Even Marco looked struck by sympathy at that point. It was painful to see *anyone* like this. Strung out, lost eyes, seemingly unresponsive to life as a whole. She climbed into the driver's seat quietly so as not to startle her.

"Hi mom. It's me, Addison. Can you hear me?" she asked softly.

She watched as her mother's cloudy eyes slowly widened, and filled with tears.

Her own eyes filling with tears, Addison grabbed a fast food napkin from the cupholder and wiped the drool from her mom's face, murmuring in a soothing tone, as she had for more years than she wanted to remember.

A broken gurgle was the best Lara could manage in reply as her body began to twitch.

"You'll be okay mom," she said firmly, using her best pull-yourself-up-by-your-bootstraps tone. "I know everything seems really hard and really bad right now, and the drugs are making you feel like you can't get through this, but you can. You *will*. This is the worst of it. It'll get better from here."

"Now why would you go and lie to her like that?"

The oily, twistedly excited voice coming from just behind her headrest froze the blood in her veins, terrifying her every bit as much as the barrel of a gun now butting against her temple.

But even with absolute fear holding her hostage, she couldn't help but scream at the windshield and try to warn Marco when she saw Sonny come up from behind him on the sidewalk and stick a heavy syringe into his neck.

Marco went limp instantly.

At a good fifty pounds of muscle lighter, Sonny struggled but somehow managed to drag him backward to the bushes near the dumpster. And all the while, Addison just watched helplessly. He'd sworn to Caine earlier that he'd protect her with his life; she prayed for that not to be the case.

Normally, there'd be at least a few workers around here at this time of day, but today, every available body was over on the other side of the property at the fire clean-up. No one would find him for a while.

They planned this well.

Knowing her chance of survival was quickly reaching zero, Addison did the only thing she could think to do.

She slipped her phone out of her pocket and into her mother's.

No response.

"Sonny drugged my mom didn't he?" She wasn't even sure why she was asking, but she wanted to know. "She never started using again did she?"

"It's the same injection you should've gotten seven years ago, but just a little more sophisticated."

"Is she going to remember that Sonny did this to her?"

"Nope. Isn't ketamine a beautiful thing?" Sick, sick glee echoed throughout the car. "You'll see soon enough."

Bile erupted in her throat just as the driver's side door opened.

What timing.

She spat in Sonny's face. "My mother was always too good for you." It was the truth.

Dark, ugly rage overtook his expression, but one nervous glance over at the backseat was all it took to temper his wrath.

Contempt burning in his eyes, Sonny wiped his face off with his sleeve, before giving her a sneering shrug. "With everything *he's* no doubt going to do to you, I actually feel a little sorry for you."

Yanking her out of the car, he was all business again as he patted her down and promptly reported, "No phone."

"Dump her watch, and that Fitbit on her ankle. If it's electronic, those Spencer boys probably lo-jacked it."

Sonny jerking her around like a ragdoll to follow orders, tossing her watch and Fitbit—both of which were in fact lo-jacked—while telling her callously, "You know this is all your fault right, Addie?"

God, she hated that nickname.

"If you hadn't raised those stupid siblings of yours to be so hippy dippy, I would've had my payday already. Wouldn't have had to resort to all this." He grabbed her by the scalp and pivoted her face toward her mother's unfocused one. "That's your fault too." He gave Lara a pitying look that morphed into disgust. "You ruined her for me with all your damn do-gooding."

His anger was short lived, however, when the rear door was thrust open. As he dragged her over to the back by her hair and shoved her into the car, he looked *almost* sympathetic...

Almost.

"It was nice knowing you, Addie."

Then the world went dark.

CHAPTER 22

OUTSIDE OF THE courtroom, Caine checked in once more on a few witnesses he'd interviewed during the investigation, and then signaled to the DA that he was heading out. He'd finished his testimony a few hours ago, but decided to stick around to make sure there weren't any surprises in the case. So far, his gut was telling him this trial was going to go their way.

Just like it was telling him to get over to Addison's *right now.*

He'd texted both Addison and Marco after he'd testified to see how the clean-up was going, but had yet to get a response from either of them. And a few minutes ago, just before the judge had called an afternoon recess, he'd felt his phone buzz once in his pocket, only to find his screen blank when he went to answer.

Neither occurrence was too far out of the ordinary, but something in the back of his mind was making him uneasy.

Then it happened.

On his way out of the lowest level of the parking lot, he felt his phone buzz again.

And he nearly crashed into the wall on a turn.

Son of a bitch. Caine had testified in this courthouse enough times to know there was no cell reception in the underground garage.

Which meant one thing—

"*Addison?* Where are you?"

For the last seven years, he'd prepared himself to get this call on his satellite phone. But not once in all that time did he expect to answer and hear nothing but fading, labored breathing on the other end.

His heart stopped, and his entire world came crashing down around him.

"Addison, stay with me. I'm coming, baby, I promise."

Grabbing his other phone, he speed-dialed Drew's number.

"Hello?"

"Get me the GPS location of Addison's cell phone."

Per usual, Drew didn't bother with unnecessary questions. "Got it. Loading the coordinates to your SUV now. It's a motel ten minutes from Addison's housing complex."

"Call in some back-up and then trace Marco's phone." If they were together, her chances of safety were infinitely better.

Drew's reply came back a minute later. "Marco's phone is still back at CoRe. Several uniforms from your precinct are on their way to both locations. Gabe's close. He'll be at the complex soon." He paused, then relayed grimly, "According to the vitals tracker on Marco's watch, he's alive, but the numbers are low for a guy his size. Been that way for a few hours."

Caine slammed his palm against the steering wheel, but otherwise, forced himself to keep his shit together.

"Addison, sweetheart, can you still hear me?"

A faint groan was the best she could manage.

"Did David hurt you? Is he there with you right now? Push a button on your phone if you can. One button if he is, two if he isn't."

No response.

Fear slid through his gut, and ran ice cold through his veins when her groans soon tapered off into silence.

Caine had never driven so fast in his entire life. "Drew, I'm almost at the address. Have an ambulance meet me there." When the motel was in sight, he nearly lost it. "Dammit, Drew. This place is big. Four different buildings. Can you narrow it down for me?"

"Give me one sec. I can triangulate to ping her exact

location over a satellite map using Gabe's phone as a third, but I need him to get within range."

Meanwhile, Caine just kept listening to Addison's frail breathing on the sat-phone like a lifeline.

"Got a lock on her." The sound of typing through the speaker went up to hyper speed. "Building with the water fountain out front, third unit from the right facing the back of the property. Can't tell which floor though."

Good enough. Gun drawn, Caine broke down the door of the unit on the ground floor first and came to a screaming halt when he saw the small, crumpled body next to the bed.

"Lara."

After checking the room to confirm she was alone, he ran over to Lara's side to check her pulse. Her eyelids opened a fraction, revealing pupils nearly entirely dilated. "Lara, look at me."

She couldn't. Her lids slid closed again, and her pulse started to slow. Other than Addison's phone clutched tightly in her hand, the rest of her body was limp, nearly lifeless. Whatever she'd been drugged with was starting to shut her system down.

Glancing at the phone screen, he saw Lara had managed to punch in the first speed dial number, most likely by accident. Thank God Addison had programmed his number in. As far gone as Lara was, he wasn't sure she'd even have been able to dial 9-1-1.

"Drew, it wasn't Addison that called me. It was her mother. She's been drugged. And her husband Sonny's nowhere in sight."

"I'm on it. According to Addison's cell log, she got a call from a burner phone a few hours ago so I'll run that one down, too. Give me a few minutes to get more intel." More lightning fast clicking and clacking echoed before he reported back, "Just got an update from Gabe. He just found Marco drugged and dumped in some bushes behind Addison's office. Alive, but unresponsive."

Lara wasn't much better off. "ETA on the ambulance here?"

"A few minutes out."

As Drew continued to work on his end, Caine dragged the comforter off the motel bed to keep Lara's shaking body warm. "Stay with me, Lara. Remember who I am? I'm the guy that's in love with your daughter."

Caine had no idea if the woman could even hear him in her state, but he kept talking anyway. "You did good calling me, Lara. As soon as the ambulance comes for you, I'm going to find Addison and bring her home. So you have to stay alive. If not, you won't be able to see the big day when I finally get a ring on your daughter's finger. You hear me? I want to see you at the wedding in the front row next to my mom, so just…keep fighting off those drugs and just stay with me."

A stream of tears leaked out of Lara's closed lids.

He rocked her and kept talking to her until the paramedics arrived to take over.

Caine had no idea what Drew had called in to dispatch, but when he stepped outside, he saw a dozen of his precinct's best officers already coordinating a man hunt.

Grayson came over and tossed him a set of keys. "Captain's orders."

Though it was breaking ten different kinds of police protocol, Caine didn't argue. He took the keys to the police cruiser gratefully.

"Drew already sent us the info on the vehicle Sonny was driving," continued Grayson. "An APB went out. Units all over the city are looking for him. We've got everyone on this, buddy."

Caine followed him over to the group of officers that had gathered to get instructions. Half weren't even in uniform.

He couldn't find the words.

Grayson was his saving grace. "Thank us all later. You do what you need to do; we'll assist in any way we can. Go save your girl."

That last dictate propelled him to action. Caine gave them all one final, emotional nod of thanks and then headed to the full tactical squad car Grayson had brought him, switching to his Bluetooth earpiece. "Drew, any updates?"

"The burner cell was ditched nearby so that was a dead end, but I was able to hack the traffic cams around the housing complex to track a car matching the one Sonny left in. Followed him to an abandoned lot twenty minutes east. He didn't stay for long, and I couldn't get a clear visual from the security cams there, but I did see a second sedan leave seconds after he did in the opposite direction. I couldn't see the driver or confirm if Addison was in the car though."

"Can you track both cars by traffic cam footage?"

"Already on it. Sonny looked like he went straight to that motel you found Lara at. The other black sedan headed north on the 101. I'd say they have roughly a three-hour lead on you."

"My gut's telling me to follow the sedan. Have Grayson keep on Sonny. Can you stay on the black sedan and get me as close as possible to its current location?"

Drew grunted like it was an insult he'd even asked. "Already hacked your phone and synced it up with my satellite app so your Bluetooth will now work as a com link. I'm going to focus on tracking the sedan, but you'll get updated coordinates guiding you. Just be sure to keep your phone charged."

An hour later, sirens blazing him through every traffic slowdown, Caine had managed to cover the distance between him and the sedan in half the time thanks to his police sirens. But it still wasn't fast enough. Sunset had come and gone. Soon, it'd be pitch black in the direction they were headed; if he didn't catch up to the sedan's real time location before then, there was a good chance he'd lose them completely.

As if responding to Caine's worse fears, the sound of Drew cursing up a storm broke through the silence. "Shit, Caine, I can't find David anywhere. The last street cam sighting was in Pinnacle Peak, but then he vanished off the main roads after that. I've been looking for the last ten minutes, but haven't found a single vehicle matching his. The only logical reason is that he headed toward the mountains, meaning I can't track him anymore. And worst of all, there are at least a hundred different routes out he could take." The sound of a fist connecting with some expensive equipment split across the air waves. "This is all my fault. I took too damn long to find him."

"Cut that out right now." Caine almost never needed to big-brother Drew—hell, growing up, the kid had been easily twice as mature as Max and Gabe combined. But every once in a while, even Drew had his mortal moments. "Listen to me. You're the *only* reason I'm this close to finding her. Without you, I'd have nothing to go on. Without you, I wouldn't have any hope at all right now. You got that?"

Drew made a non-committal sound, which Caine fully expected. The guy just put too much of the world's weight on his shoulders, always beating himself up for things well beyond his control. "Drew, I'm serious, this isn't your fault."

After a long, tortured pause, Drew finally replied, "It's not your fault either, you know."

Geez, what the hell were they teaching the kid in college? Invasive psychic tactics 101?

"You've been muttering to yourself for the last hour while you were driving."

Huh, no kidding? "What was I saying?"

"A lot of crap that just isn't true," chimed in Gabe, breaking into their conversation over the com line. "You know as well as we all do that David would've eventually found Addison, whether you stayed away from her or not."

No, he didn't know that. "But if I hadn't pulled her over that day, if I'd just left well enough alone afterward, maybe she'd still be—"

"Miserable," finished Gabe matter-of-factly. "She'd be as miserable without you as you've been without her. You and Addison belong in each other's lives. Don't let this asshole take that away from you."

"If he hurts her in any way—"

"He won't."

"If I lose her again—"

"You won't."

While he knew Gabe's assurances had absolutely no foundation, they still managed to calm him down.

"By the way," added Gabe, "If you look in your rearview mirror, you should see me right on your tail. When—not if, but *when*—you find Addison, no worries bro, I've got your back."

Caine peered into the mirror and found one of Gabe's drones hovering behind him.

He had no clue how the drone related to the rest of Gabe's cryptic statement. But before he got a chance to ask him about it, Drew's weary voice broke in again over the coms.

"Caine, I think I found them."

———◆———

Caine felt like he was taking his first breath of oxygen in hours. *"How?"*

"I just hacked all the rental info in the area like you had me do in Phoenix. Luckily, there aren't all that many cabins and homes out there so it wasn't hard to find one that'd been booked as a vacation rental a week ago. The alias is a fake and the payment was wired from a temp account. Won't have full verification for a little bit, but all the evidence so far adds up."

"You're a freaking genius. Send me the coordinates?"

"Already uploaded."

Caine quickly re-routed and turned his sirens off.

Fifteen miles. He wasn't going to risk spooking David.

When he finally got within a hundred yards of the

coordinates, he surveyed the area surrounding the cabin. It was a friggin' tactical nightmare. His best bet was to go the rest of the way by foot. "I'm close, guys. I'll keep my com transmitting, but I'm going dark on my end."

"Wait." Drew clacked away on his keyboard as he quickly exchanged a few words with someone on his other line. "Alec needs to talk to you first. Sounds important. Hang on a sec; I'm patching him through."

A loud crackle echoed through his Bluetooth. The connection was fuzzy at best, and noisy as hell. "Caine, can you hear me, man?"

"Barely. You okay? Where are you? Addison said you left in a hurry."

Static sputtered over the phone line, but Caine was pretty sure he heard Alec say Mexico.

"*Mexico?* What the hell are you doing in Mexico?"

Alec's voice came through stronger for a bit, but continued to cut in and out. "Had a hunch...the fire...turned out I was right."

"Alec, look, can we talk later? Drew can fill you in, but he thinks he found the cabin David's holding Addison in." Caine hid his car at fifty yards out and started gearing up.

More static.

Not that it mattered. Caine was nearly checked out of the conversation completely at that point. Positioning himself behind a large boulder behind the cabin's blindside, he used his tactical scope to survey the interior. There was definite movement.

Alec crackled in again sounding like he was all but shouting something.

"What? Say again. Your connection is really bad, man. I can't hear you."

"*It's not David,*" barked Alec, his voice finally coming through again. "David's still here in Rocky Point. I got him before he could cross the border and head for the cabin. Addison's out there with—"

"*Georgia.*" Dumbfounded, Caine stared into his scope and saw her clear as day inside the cabin, keeping a gun trained on someone out of his line of sight.

Caine felt the betrayal deep in his bones.

All this time.

"Georgia's the one who's been helping David stay a step ahead of you," confirmed Alec, now crystal clear over the line. "He's been paying her a shit ton in exchange. *She's* the one who delivered those notes to you every year. *She's* the one who arranged for the decoy tutor that distracted everyone while she set fire to the gardens. And *she's* the one who's holding Addison for David right now."

CHAPTER 23

ADDISON EYED the gun-toting woman she'd never
once suspected as being in cahoots with David, and tried
to get a better measure of her current situation.

So far, things weren't looking so good.

For one, the blow to the back of her head—courtesy
of Georgia's gun—had knocked her out for the entire ride
over here so she had no clue where she was.

And more importantly, if Georgia's irate phone
messages to David were any indication, the woman was
certifiable.

Who screamed and left threatening voicemails on a
psycho's answering machine?

A bigger psycho.

Maybe if she got her talking…

"How could you do it, Georgia? Caine treats you

like a sister. He's been there for you and your kids since your husband died. How could you throw all that away for some quick cash?"

A twisted scowl freeze-dried across Georgia's lips for a long moment as she stood there, fists squeezed, limbs shaking in fury.

Oookay, so maybe this wasn't the best idea...

"I would've done it for *free!*" Georgia snarled, a violent sneer slashing across her face. "Did that backstabbing boyfriend of yours ever tell you *why* Internal Affairs started investigating my husband to begin with?"

Uh oh.

"That's right, it was *Caine*. Instead of talking to Rick first and giving him a chance to explain or make it right, he just threw him under the bus without a second thought."

"But Caine was just doing his job, Georgia. He had an obligation to—"

"Don't talk to me about obligations!" she screeched. "He had an *obligation* to be a decent friend to Rick, who was only doing what he needed to do. Rick had his reasons; I know he did. But Caine didn't care. He just hung him out to dry. Even helped the department dig up more dirt on him. Enough to make Rick a liability to bad folks who would've hurt me or the kids as punishment. That's why Rick killed himself. To protect us. That's all on Caine. He stole the love of my life from me, stole my kids' father from them. *And he deserves to suffer for that.*"

Addison couldn't begin to imagine what Georgia had gone through. A part of her even sympathized with the woman. "I'm sorry you lost your husband."

That seemed to throw Georgia for a loop.

But only for a second.

The ugly rage returned an instant later. "You're not nearly as sorry as you're going to be. I realize you're just an innocent bystander, but so was I, so were my kids. When David finally gets his ass over here to cart you back off to Mexico to do whatever sicko fantasies he's been planning all this time, Caine is *finally* going to know what I went through, what I continue to go through every day. And your siblings are going to feel the pain my kids went through when they lost their father."

Okay, not feeling so sympathetic anymore.

Back to the original plan. "So were the annual notes to Caine your idea or David's?"

A frighteningly pleased, wholly *cracked* smile skewed Georgia's lips. "Those notes were all me. I mean the money David was paying me was good and all, but it didn't make up for my having to put up with Caine all these years. Like I said, the man deserved to suffer."

She grinned as if remembering a fond memory. "Actually, the notes had originally been the extant of my plans. The day David skipped town, I'd planted the first note just to torture Caine, not thinking it'd bloom into all this." Waving her gun in a lasso motion in the air, Georgia let loose a disturbingly gleeful, helium-filled giggle. "He just made it so darned *easy*, too. Having me and the kids hang out in his apartment while my house was being 'fumigated,' thinking that silly lock on his bedroom door was enough to keep me out of his files. From there, I just had to find David first and strike a deal. You coming back into town was just gravy. A half-million delivery payment for me, and a lifetime of pain for Caine. Win-win."

"Caine's going to figure it out." Addison had absolute faith in that.

"Haven't you been paying attention? The man's an idiot. Who the hell trusts the widow of a guy he all but murdered?"

Clearly, there was no reasoning with the delusional woman. "Who the hell trusts an insane stalker who likes to drug and rape women?" Addison shot right back.

Georgia's glare filled with hate. And then turned mean. Slowly, her scowl warped into a sadistic smile. "Do you know why you aren't pumped full of drugs yet? It's because David wants you to be totally coherent when he's raping you for the first time. He's been making all these fancy drugs to use on you to punish you. He doesn't just want to wipe Caine from your mind, he wants to *torture* every good thought you have of Caine out of your memories."

She shrugged then. "So yeah, maybe it's a little risky to trust David, but what's a little risk when the reward is *that* good? I've been waiting seven long years for this. I'm going to get to watch Caine agonize over what David could be doing to you, and torment himself over it being all his fault." Another ugly, oily, twisted little smile. "And the best part? None of this is ever going to get traced back to me."

"*Think again.*" growled a rough, menacing voice from across the room.

———◆———

"*IT'S OVER, Georgia.* Let her go." Caine stepped into the room with them and watched for some opening, however minuscule, to take a shot while Georgia was caught off guard.

It never came.

Georgia kept her gun on Addison without once flinching, without once even bothering to turn in his direction. She sighed, long and loud. "Gee, Caine, way to take all the fun out of this." Her tone was shocked, yes, but in an unhinged, not-working-in-his-favor way.

Sure enough, her focus on Addison turned calculating. "You know... David just said I couldn't kill her. So long as I deliver her in *mostly* one piece, I'm sure I'll still get paid."

She cocked her gun. "Now that you've crashed the party, I think David would understand if I told him I was forced to put a bullet or two in her." Smiling, she became disgustingly cheerful as she pondered out loud, "What do you think? One in the arm? Or should I go for a matching set in each of her pretty legs?" Her voice turned eerily calm, almost clinical then. "Or maybe I don't shoot her at all. What if I just take a bat to her womb instead?"

He raised his gun up higher, now targeting the sick woman's head.

She chuckled. "You like that, huh? Well, I aim to please. How many hits do you think it'll take for me to make her sterile—"

"Caine, just shoot her!" shouted Addison, cutting her off. "She's a total psycho. You're never going to reason with her. So just—"

Suddenly, Addison screamed and dropped to the floor.

Caine felt his heart seize when he saw her clawing at her neck, muscles jolted tight like she was being tasered.

Georgia's voice was seething, but still somehow saccharinely buoyant. "Oh, did I forget to mention that the electric shock dog collar around your neck doesn't just activate when you breach the perimeter of the cabin, but also when I push this little remote as well?" Her smile faded. "I can practically fry your vocal chords if I feel so inclined. True, David might shave a lot off my pay for doing that, but I think it might be worth it just to get you to *shut up.*"

Caine was sorely tempted to tell her right then and there that David wouldn't be paying her a dime. But right now, her thinking that David was still coming was the only thing keeping Addison alive.

He knew Addison was right, that there was no reasoning with the insane woman. But he tried anyway. "Georgia, you said you want revenge. Well, I'm right here. Just let Addison go. You can torture me all you want before you kill me. I'll hand over my weapon—"

"No!" cried out Addison, getting back up on her feet. "Caine, just take your shot." Hands still gripping her throat in pain, she took a measured step toward Georgia.

Georgia faltered and looked at Addison like *she* was the crazy one. "What the hell are you doing? You think I won't shoot you?!"

"Oh, I know you'll shoot me; you're a complete whack job. But at least I'll have the satisfaction of knowing Caine will shoot you too. If you shoot me, you're dead. So what are you waiting for? You miss your husband so much, this is your way to go join him."

Addison, stop it.

She, of course, didn't heed his silent demand.

As Addison took another distracting step toward her, Georgia swung her eyes over at Caine. But her gun never wavered. Dammit.

He kept his expression neutral, his voice cold. "Addison's right. If you shoot her, I'll kill you. So choose your bullet wisely."

Choose. Me. If he thought it'd sway her, he would've said that plea out loud.

"Nice try, you two." Georgia flicked the button on her remote again and sent Addison to her knees once more before walking calmly over to her. "See, Addison. Didn't I tell you he was an idiot? Even more so where you're concerned. He won't risk a single hair on your little head."

Georgia yanked her back up to her feet and turned her into a human shield, repositioning her gun at Addison's temple while turning to fully face him for the first time.

Caine hardly recognized her. *How had she masked all that hatred all these years?*

"Now I get to shoot her point blank and watch you watch her die—"

Suddenly, the loud, unmistakable sound of a nearby chopper and dozens of armed men mobilizing outside cut her off.

Panic shrieked across Georgia's face.

Looking her dead in the eye, he said evenly, "That would be the cavalry. You know the drill, Georgia. They'll shoot to kill. If you want to make it out of this alive, just drop your weapon and let Addison go."

She didn't.

Now looking desperate as well as demented, she raised her gun to him and played her final trump card. "You won't shoot me. You wouldn't leave Kevin and Millie without a mother."

Even though he knew what she was doing, he still couldn't stop their innocent faces from flashing before his eyes.

Georgia pulled the trigger.

Addison screamed. Just as a bullet went blasting through his thigh, the explosion of pain nearly slaughtering him.

Shifting all his weight to his other leg, he stood his ground. He just needed *one* opening to fire without hitting Addison. He'd stand there all day bleeding out to get it.

Hate-filled eyes boring into his, Georgia raised her gun back up to Addison's temple for a kill shot.

But it never came.

Because somehow, his sweet, can't-fight-for-squat girl managed to wriggle out enough to get her arm loose, and send an elbow slamming back into Georgia's throat.

When Georgia doubled over in pain, Addison broke free.

Before he could finally take his shot, however, he watched in shocked disbelief as Addison spun right around and threw a half-cocked, horrendously executed, awkwardly-arced punch that somehow *miraculously* landed square in Georgia's chin, knocking her head back like a flip-top toothpaste cap.

Georgia went down.

Addison kicked her gun away, and then proceeded

to smash the remote for the collar around her neck to smithereens with her shoe.

With his gun trained on Georgia's fallen body, knocked out cold, he stormed over to them, the bullet lodged in his leg shredding his muscles with every stomping step he took. "What the hell were you thinking, woman?"

He yanked her into his arms. "You actually *told her to shoot you*." And took years off his life as a result.

"So did you," she replied calmly as she dropped to the ground and began to apply pressure to his leg wound.

At her sharp wince on contact, he immediately reached for her hand. "Let me see your wrist. You might've broken it with that Rocky Balboa punch."

"I'm fine." She ignored his fussing and continued to press her hands—cringing pain and all—against his bleeding while she hollered out, *"We need an ambulance in here!"*

A small smile slid over his lips. "Honey, no one's out there."

When she shot her gaze toward the window overlooking the dark, *empty* field outside the cabin, her jaw dropped. "But…I heard them."

Caine shook his head and pointed to the other window toward the back of the cabin where Gabe's drone was hovering just beyond the glass. "That was just Gabe playing a sound clip through his drone's speakers. I recognized it from a video game Max developed a few years

336

ago."

"Ambulance is almost here," called out Gabe, in a reverberating Oz-like voice from the drone's speakers. "Addison, that upper cut to the chin was a thing of beauty. Seriously, I wish I'd caught it on film."

A perturbed, almost dismayed frown furrowed Addison's brow in response.

Caine tipped her chin up. "Hey, you're not feeling remorse or something are you? For hitting her?"

Her eyes widened to the size of saucers. "Are you crazy? I'm happy as hell I punched out that insane woman. She totally got what she deserved."

He grinned at her proudly. "Then what's with the frown, baby?"

Her lips pulled down again and screwed over to the right. When he continued to wait her out, finally, she gave a resigned sigh. "It was all an accident." Her shoulders slumped a bit, and her ears reddened a lot. "I was actually aiming for her stomach. But, I sort of… *missed.* Luckily, her chin got in the way and stopped my fist—"

Caine's burst of laughter quickly turned to a groan of pain as he clutched his leg.

"Come here, sweetheart." He drew her into his arms. "Now that all this is finally over, I have something I've been waiting a long time to give you…"

CHAPTER 24

THAT NIGHT -- SEVEN YEARS AGO

"I HAVE SOMETHING to show you," he said, reaching over to his nightstand before propping himself up against his headboard and gathering her against his chest. "Before you see it, let me remind you that cops don't exactly bring home the big bucks. So three-months of my salary isn't all that much."

Addison had no clue where this was going, but she just smiled reassuringly at him, not remembering a time she'd ever seen Caine this nervous before.

He continued gruffly, "I wasn't sure if the courts look at things like how much money is in my savings account before they grant foster parent status so I didn't want to clean it out just in case. But I did want you to have something—like a down payment. I know you may think it's premature since I'm doing everything backward by asking you to move in with me before we officially start dating, but I also know how much the kids mean to you, how hard it can be to trust *anyone* given everything you've been through. So I wanted you to *know* how serious I am about this. About you…us."

He let out a deep breath and upended a little jeweler's pouch.

The most beautiful tiny loose diamond came tumbling out, triggering a sound from her throat that sounded like a cross between a gasp and a coo.

"This isn't going to be the actual diamond I want to give you one day. Like I said, I'll save up and make sure the one I give you when I do ask you to marry me is bigger. Big enough that guys a half mile away will see it and know you're mine."

Oh god, if he kept up with all this possessive sweet talk, she'd be a melted puddle of goo.

"The jeweler didn't have a setting for something this small on hand, but I didn't want to come home without it. It fit my budget exactly, and I don't know, when I saw it, I knew this was the diamond I wanted to give you tonight."

He picked up the tiny stone and held it between his thumb and index finger, dwarfing the shiny gem with his big, calloused hands, and making it all the more daintily beautiful. "Say something, sweetheart."

339

"I love it," she whispered, emotions overflowing in her voice. "It's the most perfect diamond I've ever seen."

"It's just a down payment," he reiterated, sounding almost embarrassed. "I promise, I'll get you a bigger one."

"No." She gave him a fierce frown. "No down payment. No bigger diamond."

"Honey, you're making me crazy. I know I haven't actually asked you a question to go along with this tiny-ass diamond—" he grinned a little when she glared, "but hearing you say 'no' in *any* context right now is messing with me. You don't have to make any decisions or 'accept' the diamond or anything. Just keep it safe for now. Until I'm able to give you a bigger one, along with that big question to match."

She was just about to insist, yet again, that she didn't want him replacing this perfect stone with anything, ever when he cut her off with a kiss. "Baby, you give me another one of your cute grumbling growls and tell me you don't need a bigger diamond, and this weak, simple male mind of mine will be taking that as a 'yes'...and just plain taking you, period."

That effectively shut down her ability to speak.

But not her ability to fantasize.

He groaned. "Don't ever play poker for money, sweetheart. I can read every one of your innocently wicked thoughts in your eyes."

That so? Her tongue peeked out at the corner as

she revved her dirty thoughts up to high gear. Which wasn't hard seeing as how he was now rolling the tiny diamond across her torso in sexy little patterns. Through her thin tank-top, she could feel each facet of the diamond, along with the brain-rattling contrast between the jewel and the stark heat of his fingers.

He stopped his ministrations near her belly, however, and simply stared. "Maybe I will turn this diamond into a ring after all," he uttered in a hushed, reverent tone.

She peered down to see what he was fixated on.

The bottom edge of her tank had climbed up a bit, but just a few inches—nothing to inspire his lust-filled gaze.

"You have a belly button ring."

Oh. That.

She clapped a hand over the silly birthday present she'd bought herself the year prior, when she'd turned nineteen. It had been a couple of months after she and the kids had been living in the van and she'd been feeling…emotional, maybe? Proud, in a way.

That she hadn't failed them. That despite not having a parent or four walls not on wheels, the kids had been thriving. *Happy.*

So she gifted herself with that particular navel piercing, designed with a tiny rhinestone at the top, with another smaller rhinestone dangling below it, and an even tinier third stone below that, all in a straight line. She got the three-stone navel ring partly to represent her and the kids, but also partly because it was her own feminine, pretty, magnificently frivolous secret that no one would be able to see.

It was a small secret in comparison to her life living in the van with the kids. But like the frugal home she'd built for her siblings, it was still beautiful and precious.

She barely felt Caine lift her fingers off her belly. But she did feel his lips.

Then his tongue.

Then his voice rumbling against her skin when he graveled, "This is the sexiest damn thing I've ever seen in my life."

Peeking down at her stomach again when his attention once again became fixed there, she saw the diamond he'd bought, lined up with the other three.

A tidal wave of emotions quickly overtook all the oxygen in her lungs.

Yes. That's where that diamond belonged.

A low, intense growl vibrated out of his chest.

Startled, she glanced up to find his eyes now staring deep into hers.

"You just said yes," he rasped.

Had she said that aloud?

Gently, he put the tiny diamond back in the little velvet pouch it had come in.

...Then he all but ravaged her mouth in a kiss that appeared to be on a mission to eclipse the earlier tidal wave of emotions, and steal every last bit of oxygen from her lungs.

By the time he lifted his lips from hers, with what few working brain cells she still had left, she determined his mission an outstanding success.

"I'm taking that 'yes' as a down payment, sweetheart."

———— ♦ ————

PRESENT DAY

GAZING AT THE STUNNING four-stone belly button ring Caine slipped out of a slim steel canister hanging from his keychain, which she'd always assumed held pills of some sort, Addison whispered softly, "It's beautiful, Caine."

Addison couldn't bring herself to take her eyes off of the gift, not even when Gabe's drone chose that moment to hover close and click open a bottom hatch to drop something down into Caine's waiting hands.

"Told you I had your back, man," said Gabe cryptically in his Oz-like drone voice before zipping back outside.

Addison hardly noticed the exchange. All she could focus on was the dainty, sparkling navel ring between her fingers, and all the memories of that one perfect night.

"Put it on."

Would these gruff non-requests ever stop being sexy?

Probably not.

Smiling, she lifted the edge of her shirt up and slid the piercing into place.

It looked exactly like it had in all her memories of that night when Caine had lined up his single loose diamond, which had been slightly bigger than the three rhinestones in her navel ring setting, below the littlest one.

The unique design couldn't have been all that easy to find. "Where did you—"

"I had it custom made."

Of course he did.

"I started with that first diamond I showed you that night." He traced a calloused finger over the four stones slowly. "Then I added another diamond each year for the next three years."

She gasped. "You mean these are— And this is actually the—"

Emotions swamped her brain and her heart, preventing her from completing a single coherent thought that wasn't overflooded with feelings.

"While you're processing and finding the words that come at the end of those sentences, let me see your hand."

Still staring at the beautiful gift, she automatically

put her injured hand in his, belatedly remembering to shake her wrist for his benefit so he could see that the pain was tolerable, and very likely just a sprain.

He bussed his lips over her slightly swelling wrist, and then proceeded to take her *other* hand in his. Without a word, he slipped a ring onto her finger.

Already running short on air from his other gift, she couldn't even manage another gasp.

"After I made the navel ring, I moved on to building you your engagement ring next. Another new diamond for each year. I'd say those two side stones match that center stone I bought this year pretty perfectly, don't you?"

Did the man honestly expect her to be able to formulate a response right now?

"The ring has been burning a hole in his pocket for weeks," announced Gabe. "He looks at it about a hundred times a day."

Caine shrugged. "I liked imagining it on your finger—seemed to be the only thing that could ground me the crazier things got."

God, this man.

"Do you like it?" he asked, sounding a shade vulnerable.

Her voice went soft, her eyes liquid. "Of course I do. It's absolutely gorgeous."

His eyes flared with fierce pleasure. "I know you didn't want a bigger diamond, but, as I'd mentioned that night, I want to make damn sure every man with functioning eyes *know* without a doubt that you're spoken for. By *me*."

Despite swooning at the intensity of his words and his possessive gaze, at the reminder of *that night*, Addison felt a sharp arrow of pain shoot right through her chest.

"Caine, I need you to know that when I'd left the beautiful diamond you'd given me on your pillow the next morning, I swear, that wasn't me returning your down payment." Even saying the words stabbed her in the heart. "I-I just didn't want to hold you to it if—"

"I know, baby." He slid his thumbs over her cheeks to wipe away her tears. "Like I already told you, what you decided to do after that night, and what you put yourself through for the next seven years as a result, all to protect my oath, my future... That was the single most romantic thing any woman has ever done for me. And I promise you, as far as my bleeding heart was concerned after that night, it was you or no one else. Still is."

Suddenly, his bloodied leg gave out and he hit the ground hard.

"Caine!"

When he looked up at her, he was grinning.

Down on one knee.

Crazy romantic man.

"We could get married this weekend," he said gruffly, by way of proposal.

"Caine Harrison Spencer!" cried out an outraged

346

maternal voice from the drone's speakers. "Don't you dare run off and elope this weekend. I will hunt you down myself if you do."

Addison immediately bit her lip to hold back the laugh threatening to get out.

Leave it to the Spencer matriarch to make big, bad alpha *Caine* look just a wee bit terrified.

"You're the first of my boys to get engaged," the voice continued sternly. "And very likely my best chance for a mother-son wedding waltz this decade."

"HEY!" called out Gabe and Max in unified offense.

Now Caine was joining in on the smothered amusement.

As was Drew, from the sounds of it.

Gabe and Max proceeded to *insist* that they were just as ready as Caine was to man up and get married. Probably. *Maybe.*

To which, their mother simply gave them a delicate little snort.

"Lordy, I love your family," Addison sighed. "Especially your mom."

"I'm actually pretty fond of *your* mom, too—despite all her faults, of course," Caine admitted, shocking the absolute heck out of her. "Sonny left Lara in a motel and skipped town, probably thinking folks would think she was a druggie who'd overdosed. He didn't get far, by the by. He's sitting in a county lock-up awaiting trial as we speak.

With the amount of drugs he'd pumped into your mother, along with all the other assault and kidnapping charges from today, Sonny isn't going to see the light of day for the rest of his natural life. Just like David."

Addison exhaled a ragged breath. "I-is my mother okay?"

He slid an arm around her and gently stroked her back. "Drew hacked into the E.R. records and found she's doing fine. Slated to make a full recovery. As soon as the anesthesia wears off after my surgery tonight, I'll go check on her. Bring her some flowers."

The man was just ridiculously sweet sometimes.

"Just thought you'd want to know," he finished gently. "Your mom came through for you when it counted. Your wanting to help her, and your faith in her, *wasn't* ill-placed. Even barely conscious, she still managed to call me. To save you. And I'll forever be grateful to her for that."

How was it that he always knew just what she needed to hear?

Crouching down to help him up off his knee, she was caught off guard when the stubborn man stayed put. "Not without an answer to my proposal, honey."

She blinked in surprise. "You mean you're actually *asking* me to marry you?"

He gave her a look that said he thought she was out of her mind. "Of course I'm not *asking*. I told you seven years ago, your yes is already mine. *This* one is just for the video Gabe's drone is recording."

She turned her head and sure enough, found the drone hovering just a few yards from them.

"Speak up clearly now. I plan on playing the video at least a thousand times on loop while I'm recovering in the hospital," he informed her. "So smile for the camera, baby. Give me something beautiful to watch post-surgery."

He was incorrigible. And she absolutely didn't want to encourage this kind of behavior for the rest of their lives.

So instead of doing as he requested, she brought her face down to his again and whispered yes between a dozen different kisses…the last few of which, had him growling.

"And…*cut*," called out Gabe from the drone. "Beautiful scene up until the slightly porny part at the end. But I can edit that out to keep it PG-rated. So that's a wrap, folks. Paramedics, thanks for waiting."

Caine was immediately strapped into the awaiting stretcher by the fully entertained emergency response team who had in fact been waiting patiently through all this.

As they loaded him up into the ambulance, Gabe hollered out, "No worries, buddy. I'll see if Drew can hack this audio clip into the speakers in your room before your anesthesia takes."

"No prob," confirmed Drew, clacking away on his computer like usual.

Addison just shook her head at the drone. "Why do

I have the feeling that you've all been lulling me into a false sense of security by holding back on the *really* crazy behavior up until now? I mean I've heard stories from Lia on what it's like having you all as brothers. If even *half* of them are true, maybe I should think this whole thing through a bit…" she teased.

"You already said yes," called out four male voices in stereo. Three just a tiny bit worried, one not at all.

Caine slid her hand in his as his brothers each began demanding that the others stop scaring her off. "I'm going to close my eyes for a bit, sweetheart," he murmured drowsily as he brought her hand up to his lips to brush a kiss over her ring-clad finger. "Just so you know, I approve of you messing with my brothers. They—"

And then he was out.

The alarmed medics quickly started checking his stats on the monitor they'd just hooked him up to…only to simultaneously gape in surprise when they heard Caine quietly snoring away.

"I-I can't believe this," said the stupefied main paramedic after running a few more frantic tests to confirm. "He's fine. Strong vitals. He just…fell asleep."

Finally.

Smiling, Addison hopped into the ambulance and curled up against his chest to join him.

EPILOGUE

THREE YEARS LATER

Caine took a swig of coffee and jotted a few surveillance notes in his notebook.

It'd been a while since he'd been on a stakeout. After leaving the force and joining his brothers at Spencer Securities, he never got to do them anymore. He kind of missed it, actually.

"Any updates?" crackled in Alec over the com line.

"Nothing to warrant us going in," Caine admitted, disgruntledly.

"Guys, I'm telling you, he's clean," repeated Drew for the third time.

He was quickly shushed in stereo when Gabe called out, "I got some movement on the secondary tracker. He ditched the one we put on his jacket, but according to the one on his shoe, he's headed around the building away from the crowd. Oh shit, they *both* are."

Oh *hell* no. Not on his watch. "Which way are they headed? Who's in a better position? Me or Alec?"

"Actually," Gabe sounded perplexed. "According to this, they're headed straight for *you*, Caine."

What? He turned around to check out the window.

Oh, crap.

"You all lo-jacked Kylie and her date?"

"Abort, abort!" hollered Gabe.

Dead silence echoed back over the com lines not a second later.

Traitors.

He offered Addison a big, placating grin. But no apologies.

"Caine, what in the world were you thinking? We're setting up for a kid's first birthday party *on the property*. Did you really think Kylie was going to run off with some guy in the middle of it?"

"Of course not." He frowned. "I trust her completely. It's her *date* I don't trust."

"Yes, because straight-A students with perfect manners who treat your sister-in-law with nothing but respect are classic public enemy number one suspects." Addison plopped the two rogue tracking devices onto his dashboard.

"In all fairness, if you and Kylie had told us about the kid *before* we had to see them holding hands at her graduation party last week, we wouldn't have had to go full surveillance."

"Funny, I didn't see you giving Tanner any grief when you met his new girlfriend at the graduation ceremony the day before that."

"That's because Alec already did a background check on her," he argued, not wanting her to think they had any double standards. Not *really*.

Addison rolled her eyes. "Don't get me started on that one. He's so much worse now that he's working with Spencer Securities full time."

"I know," agreed Caine approvingly. "He's fitting in great."

Her lips twitched. "You guys are all nuts. We'll talk about this more later. Evie just woke up from her nap."

Caine shot out of the car. "Why didn't you say so earlier. Where is she?"

Delighted tinkling giggles greeted him from the stroller.

"There's my beautiful girl. Are you all ready for your party?" He blew raspberries on her tummy until she was laughing hysterically. Best sound in the world.

"Honestly, Caine. What are you going to do when Evie grows up and starts dating?"

He balked and immediately shoved the thought out

of his mind. "Luckily, I won't have to worry about that for another twenty-four years."

Addison burst out laughing.

What on earth was so funny?

She brushed a still-chuckling kiss against his lips. "Party's about to start. What's this big birthday present you wanted Evie to open in private?"

"You're going to have to help her unwrap it." He handed her a small box with a big pink bow and picked Evie up so she could see what was inside as well.

Addison stared at the contents in the box for an emotional few seconds before gently pulling out the two pregnancy tests he'd placed in there—one with the name 'Gina' and the other with the name 'Sue' written in the windows where the two pink lines would normally display. "Really?" She turned her hopeful eyes up to meet his. "Does this mean we're finally fully approved to adopt them?"

"Yep." He smiled dotingly at his beautiful wife. "Evie's officially going to have two new big sisters before the end of the summer."

Gina and Sue, the two incredible little fourth graders they'd been fostering for almost a year now, had stolen Caine and Addison's hearts right from the start—practically from the moment they'd introduced themselves, arms linked, announcing boldly that they were best friends and a package deal. Take it or leave it.

The very idea of splitting up the precocious pair had been unthinkable back then, and even more so with each passing day since. Adopting the girls together had thus been the *only* acceptable next step as far as the Spencer clan was concerned.

"Just heard from the adoption agent this morning while you were getting everything ready for the party. I wanted to tell you before—"

Right on cue, their entire family descended on them in a loud, rowdy mass, all offering their excited congrats on the big news.

"Let me guess?" Addison turned to Drew. "You hacked the adoption system?"

He shook his head firmly. "Nope, wasn't me."

Addison shot her gaze over to Gabe and Max, who were now playing peekaboo with Evie on the grass. "Don't look at us," said Max. "We found out from Alec."

All eyes flew over to Alec.

"I'm completely innocent," he insisted. "Totally just the messenger."

"Then how'd you find out? *When* did you find out?" Now Caine was curious as well.

"I'm not revealing my sources."

"Source*s*, as in plural?" Addison gave a smiling headshake and turned to the two pairs of angelic eyes actively avoiding hers. "Gina, Sue...have you been playing with your uncles' surveillance equipment again?"

"No," they sang out in unison.

Gabe rolled over on the grass and reached into the undercarriage of Evie's stroller, grinning as he pulled out the baby monitor that had been neatly tucked out of sight. "Nicely done, ladies."

"We weren't snooping on you guys. *Promise,*" maintained Sue.

Gina nodded emphatically with an innocent shrug. "We *always* keep an extra baby monitor on Evie. So we can get to her really quick if she cries."

As everyone awww'd over that, Caine proudly wrapped an arm around each of his amazing daughters-to-be. "Welcome to the family, girls."

THE END

———•———

-- Up Next --

DREW & SKYLAR

BEFORE THAT PROMISE
(Book 1 of 2)

———•———

-- Turn the Page for an Excerpt --

BEFORE THAT PROMISE
(Drew & Skylar, Book 1 of 2)

For Drew Lawson, there isn't anyone else as undeniably *off-limits* as the addictively sweet, mind-wreckingly beautiful Skylar Sullivan. Hell, she's the very definition of the girl-next-door do-gooder. And while he *is* officially classified as a white hat hacker by the suit-wearing folks who keep track of that sort of thing, no one would ever say that hat of his is exactly pristine.

So when Skylar's arrival at his doorstep--on *the* roughest night of the year for him every year--leads to a downright memorable hotel mishap, an impromptu winter road trip, and the discovery of a secret that could change how she sees him forever, Drew is convinced the universe is on some kind of convoluted mission to thaw his cold, jaded heart.

...Because, lordy, they've certainly sent in a ringer to get the job done right.

———•———

AUTHOR NOTE: BEFORE THAT PROMISE is a quick & emotional, short & sweet crossover novella starring two of my favorite secondary characters -- Skylar Sullivan from my Can't Resist series, all grown up, and Drew Lawson from my Cactus Creek series, as swoon-worthy as ever (no worries, you don't need to have read either of those series to read this book). There's a HFN (happily-for-now) ending, with the second book in this duet (EVERY PROMISE UNSPOKEN) picking up a few years down the line for this utterly meant to be couple.

EXCERPT

His arms became full-body shackles around her when the thought of her being hurt slammed into him.

Skylar released a surprised mini-yelp, and then quickly tried to reassure him, "Drew, I'm fine. Nothing happened to me."

Where once he'd thought the neverending possessiveness he felt about her was his most primal fate, Drew now discovered his protectiveness over her far eclipsed it. "Don't ever do anything so recklessly romantic like that again. Not for me or anyone. I'd never forgive myself if anything had happened to you. And I sure as hell would've made certain no living soul would ever be able to forgive the man who harmed you."

Eyes glued to his, her breathing faltered at whatever she saw in its depths. "Wh-what happened to your due north?"

Drew slid his hands up to cup both sides of her face. "I'm looking at it. Don't ever doubt that where my moral compass is concerned, you're my due north. More than I realized. More and more every day, it seems."

Strange how this was the first time he was admitting out loud that he often pictured Skylar in his future, and yet it didn't sound at all foreign coming out of his mouth.

Her gaze fell to his lips as he uttered that declaration and it took every last bit of restraint in his body to keep himself from kissing her.

Because he knew that once he did, he'd never be able to let her go again

-- Available Now --

OTHER BOOKS BY VIOLET DUKE

The CAN'T RESIST Series
The acclaimed New York Times bestselling series, an emotional, heartfelt Top 10 Bestseller both in the U.S. and internationally.

RESISTING THE BAD BOY
FALLING FOR THE GOOD GUY
CHOOSING THE RIGHT MAN
FINDING THE RIGHT GIRL

The CACTUS CREEK Series
The laugh and cry USA Today bestselling small town series with strong heroines, romantic heroes, a quirky cast, and inter-series cameos galore.

LOVE, CHOCOLATE, AND BEER
LOVE, DIAMONDS, AND SPADES
LOVE, TUSSLES, AND TAKEDOWNS
LOVE, EXES, AND OHS

The FOURTH DOWN Series
The fun and sexy USA Today bestselling sports romance series starring three sweet and incorrigibly alpha heroes, from Random House Books.

JACKSON'S TRUST
BENNETT'S CHANCE
DONOVAN'S HEART

The UNFINISHED LOVE Series
Four brothers fighting for their second first chance at love. Years be damned.

5

BEFORE THAT NIGHT *(Caine & Addison, Bk 1)*
EVERY NIGHT WITHOUT YOU *(Caine & Addison, Bk 2)*
BEFORE THAT KISS *(Gabe & Hannah, Bk 1)*
EVERY KISS GOODBYE *(Gabe & Hannah, Bk 2)*
BEFORE THAT PROMISE *(Drew & Skylar, Bk 1)*
EVERY PROMISE UNSPOKEN *(Drew & Skylar, Bk 2)*
BEFORE THAT CHANCE *(Max & Kennedy, Bk 1)*
EVERY CHANCE WE LOST *(Max & Kennedy, Bk 2)*

The JUNIPER HILLS Series
An emotional new series from Montlake Romance

ALL THERE IS
WHERE YOU'LL BE

ABOUT THE AUTHOR

http://www.violetduke.com

New York Times & USA Today bestselling author Violet Duke is a former professor of English Education ecstatic to be on the other side of the page now writing emotion-rich stories with fun, everyday characters and sweet, sexy match-ups. Since her debut series in 2013, over a million readers have put all four of Violet's laugh & cry contemporary romance series on bestseller lists and Top 10 charts across the major eretailers, both in the U.S. and internationally.

When she isn't feeding her book-a-day addiction, Violet enjoys doing far too many things without checking the directions first (often with outrageous power tools she has no business operating), and cooking impossible-to-replicate 'special edition' dishes that laugh in the face of recipes. She lives in Hawai'i with her kids (Violet & Duke) and Mr. Violet Duke (their ringleader), with a PJs-and-rubber-slippers work dress code she takes very seriously.

———————•———————

Get alerts on new releases and sales by email at:
http://eepurl.com/bTG2pH

To enter epic giveaways and join in other fan fun:
http://www.facebook.com/VioletDukeBooks